All
My
Colors

Also by David Quantick and available from Titan Books

NIGHT TRAIN
(April 2020)

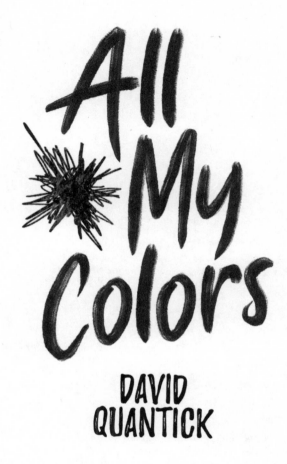

All My Colors

DAVID QUANTICK

TITAN BOOKS

All My Colors
Print edition ISBN: 9781785658570
E-book edition ISBN: 9781785658587

Published by Titan Books
A division of Titan Publishing Group Ltd
144 Southwark Street, London SE1 0UP
www.titanbooks.com

First edition: April 2019
10 9 8 7 6 5 4 3 2 1

A CIP catalogue record for this title is available from the British Library.

Printed and bound in the United States.

To Fub

PART
ONE

ONE

It was a Saturday night in March of 1979 in DeKalb, Illinois, and Todd Milstead was being an asshole. Not that Todd Milstead wasn't being an asshole every night of the week, but this particular night he was giving free rein to his inner dickhead. All the pointers had been in place from the off: there was booze, there were other writers present (although "writers" was pushing it), and Todd's wife Janis had made the dinner and taken the coats, so Todd reckoned everyone there was on his turf as well as his dime (although Janis' money from her late dad—who also gave them the house—had paid for the dinner).

So, Saturday night at the Milsteads'. Janis, in her best dress and her hair done nicely because even when there was no point, Janis made the effort. And Todd, looking like a youngish Peter Fonda, with a strong manly chin and twinkling masculine eyes and hair just the daring side of long, smoking a lot of cigarettes—he'd wanted a pipe, but

Janis kept laughing whenever Todd affected a stout briar and if there was one thing Todd couldn't abide, it was being laughed at—and holding a big tumbler of Scotch, because he liked the feel of the heavy square glass and because Scotch was a real drink.

And that was Saturday night at the Milsteads'; Janis bringing in the bowls and the plates and Todd holding forth. On Kissinger, on Farrah Fawcett-Majors, on Superman, on Carter, and on books. Always on books. The men who called themselves writers and met at Todd's on a Saturday night were a mixed bunch in the way the people crammed into an elevator that is plunging ten floors into a basement are a mixed bunch. They had one thing ostensibly in common— the writing, the being trapped in a falling elevator—but what they really had in common was that they were a totally disparate bunch of losers all screaming, "Get me out of this elevator!" And nobody was listening. Especially not Todd. Todd never listened. Somebody—Joe Hines, one of the people trapped in Todd's elevator—once said that the only way you could get Todd to listen would be if you taught a mirror to talk, and even then, Todd's reflection wouldn't be able to get a word in because Todd would be lecturing it on the best way to be a reflection.

Not that Joe ever said this to Todd. Nobody ever said anything to Todd. As another one of the gang, Mike Firenti, said, you went to Todd's for the booze and food and not the monologue, but the monologue was the price of admission. None of Todd's friends, if friends was the word, had enough money to indulge in blowouts of their own.

Joe's normal experience of a Saturday night was two beers

in front of the TV and a desultory jack-off, while Mike's was slightly better in that he could go to his sister's and drink his brother-in-law's beer while his brother-in-law talked about ice hockey, a game Mike didn't even know existed until his sister got engaged. Billy Cairns was worse off. Billy had nearly been something in the 1960s: he'd had some stories printed in a science-fiction magazine, and he'd started a novel, but then the mag went bust and the novel got lost somehow and Billy started drinking. Billy spent his nights in front of the TV staring at reruns of *Star Trek* and sometimes his breath smelled of cat food. Saturday night at Todd's was better than Saturday night not at Todd's. There was food, and booze, and Janis, who looked great in a mail order catalogue dress, and sometimes there was even, when Todd was feeling indulgent or had just passed out from booze, conversation.

And sometimes there was Sara Hotchkiss. Sara Hotchkiss was married to Terry Hotchkiss. Terry managed a supermarket outside town, and the times he attended Todd's parties his contributions were minimal. This was because Terry liked to talk about the supermarket to the exclusion of all else, and on occasion had been known to get heated about marrows. For this reason and others, Sara generally arranged for Terry to drop her off outside the Milsteads' house and collect her later, an arrangement which suited nearly everyone. (Sara didn't come to Todd's gatherings every week, because Terry liked her to entertain his suppliers when they came over for dinner and because she had a feeling that Janis didn't like her. She'd be at the Milsteads', and Janis would pass her the dip, and she'd look at Janis and know that Janis knew, and feel contempt for Janis for not smashing her face into the dip, and contempt for herself for not smashing her own face into the dip. But Janis never said anything and Sara never said anything and it was pretty good dip.)

So, it was a Saturday night in March of 1979 in DeKalb, Illinois, and 'Heart Of Glass' by Blondie was number one in America, and Terry Hotchkiss was entertaining clients, so it was just Joe, Mike, and Billy Cairns, and Janis. And Todd Milstead, who was being an asshole.

"Bullshit!" Todd shouted. "Bullshit!"

Janis moved his glass to a side table. Todd reached down and picked it up again. "That is *such* bullshit!" he said before swigging the whiskey down in one sloppy gulp. He put the glass down, making a visible dent in the table.

"All I said," protested Joe Hines, "was that Mailer's day is over."

"Over?" mocked Todd, whose knowledge of Norman Mailer was overshadowed by his fondness for any aggressive writer who liked boxing and his own penis. "Mailer's never had his day. His day hasn't even *begun!*"

"It's been years since Mailer wrote anything decent," said Mike. "That piece in *America* magazine…"

Todd Milstead actually sneered. It was a real Victorian sneer, the kind that went best with a pair of carelessly twisted mustachios. Todd's sneer said, I am going to demolish you for that opinion. It also said, because for once I know what I'm talking about.

"*Norman Mailer has been an American institution for so long that he's starting to come over like another kind of American institution,*" said Todd with his head tilted back and his eyes half shut.

"Oh shit, he's quoting. I love it when he does this," said

12

Joe, omitting the second part of his thought, which was: "to someone else."

"*Said institution being the electric chair*," intoned Todd, "*into which some of us would rather be strapped than endure another line of Mailer's unfortunately deathless prose...*"

He stopped. "Is that the piece you mean?"

"I guess so," said Mike. "But that's not the part I mean. I was referring to the quote from Mailer himself where he says—"

"*Writing books is the nearest men come to childbirth*—that quote?" said Todd. "*I am the embodiment of the American novel*—that quote? Tell me which one you mean. Because," and Todd tapped his forehead, "I got 'em all in here."

Janis, returning to collect some cigarette-butt-filled plates, made a mental note. If Todd was starting to boast about his powers of memory, that meant the evening was either going to wind down or get nasty. Not that the two were connected— although Todd Milstead's tendency to use his eidetic memory as a weapon could be a fight starter—but when Todd started boasting, he also started getting personal. She removed the more fragile glasses from the room.

"I can't remember 'em all like you can," said Mike.

"Yeah, Todd," said Joe. "You have to give us mere mortals some leeway here."

Todd, like all egoists, was incapable of extracting irony from anything that resembled praise. He got up and nodded.

"Time for a piss," he said. "Mailer!" he added scornfully, and left the room.

There was some silence. The three men drank their decent whiskey.

"You know," said Billy. "This morning I saw the strangest thing."

The others waited. It was a bad idea to interrupt Billy's stories, because it only made them longer and because he was so good at doing it himself.

"Or was it Tuesday?" said Billy.

"Jesus, Billy," muttered Mike. "What are they putting in cat food these days?"

"Anyway," said Billy, "I was in the store when this woman comes in. About thirty, thirty-five, kind of attractive though, blonde hair, and she says to Jimmy, he owns the store, nice man, sometimes lets me use the bathroom…"

"Billy," said Joe, a warning note in his voice as Todd returned, his pants spotted with piss.

"Okay," Billy said. "She says to Jimmy, I'd like to buy a hacksaw. How big, says Jimmy, and the woman says, I don't know, just big enough to get this off. And she holds up her finger. Third finger, left hand, the wedding ring finger."

"What?" said Joe. "She wanted to cut off her wedding ring?"

Todd came back in and sat down with a thud.

"No," said Billy. "That's what Jimmy said. But there's no ring there. She says, I want to cut off the *finger*. In case I'm ever stupid enough to get married again. No ring finger, she says, no ring. No ring, no wedding."

"I don't believe it," said Mike.

"I was there," said Billy. "Jimmy told her he couldn't be of assistance, but it happened. I was there."

"Billy," Todd suddenly said. "Billy, tell the truth."

"I was *there*," Billy protested. He cast an involuntary

glance at his whiskey. "I was there," he repeated.

Joe and Mike looked uncomfortable. It wasn't nice to be baited, but baiting Billy... there were unspoken rules about that. *Nothing personal* was one rule. And it looked like Todd was about to break it.

"'Fess up now, Billy," said Todd. He said it gently and that was worse.

"I was there," Billy repeated. "Jimmy was behind the counter and the woman came in and I was at the counter too and it happened." He was close to tears now. "You can ask Jimmy if you like."

He stopped. For a moment, there was doubt on his face, the look of a man who fears that nothing he says can be corroborated.

"I don't need to ask Jimmy," said Todd. "I just need to open a book."

He sat back and looked at Joe and Mike. They didn't respond.

"Oh, come on!" he said. "The woman who goes into a store and asks for a hacksaw to cut off her ring finger?"

"That's what Billy said," Joe said cautiously.

"She wants to cut off her ring finger to make sure she won't get married again?" said Todd. "None of that sounds familiar to you?"

"No," said Mike.

"Nor me," Joe said. Billy said nothing. He was biting his lip.

"It's fucking *famous*!" shouted Todd. "It's the opening scene! The first paragraph!"

He looked at their blank faces. Janis came in from the

kitchen, as she always did when the real shouting started.

"Oh my God," Todd said shrilly. "None of you knows what I'm talking about, do you? You haven't the foggiest fucking idea."

"We should continue this another time," said Joe, who felt he'd had enough. It was difficult listening to Todd like this when you had some idea what he was talking about. This was worse, because it was incomprehensible as well as unpleasant. "Mike, can you give Billy a ride, you're nearest."

Todd stood up. He tilted his head back.

"Hesitantly, the store clerk repeated to the woman what he thought he'd heard her say. 'You want to buy a handsaw so you can cut off your ring finger?' he said. 'That's right,' said the woman, and what scared the clerk was how calm she sounded. 'I can't do that, ma'am,' said the clerk and, because he was a fair man, he added, 'And what's more, I'm going to telephone to all the other stores around here to alert them concerning your attempted purchase.'"

Todd ceased reciting. He looked at the blank faces staring back at him.

"Jesus," he said. "You call yourselves writers."

He turned to Janis.

"You know it, don't you?"

Janis, startled to be asked her opinion, stammered out a no.

"Right. Okay. Not one of you has read, or heard of, *All My Colors*."

"All my what?" said Mike, emboldened by the room's general ignorance.

Todd turned to him. "*All My Colors*, Mike. *All My Colors*. By Jake Turner."

More blank looks.

"Oh, don't tell me you haven't heard of Jake fucking Turner," said Todd, his voice a weird mixture of sarcasm, contempt, and genuine bewilderment. "I mean, Joe, Mike, sure, your knowledge of literary history is woeful, but Billy..."

Billy looked up, fearfully.

"Jake Turner, Billy. He was a Kerouac junkie just like you, am I right?"

"I don't know of him," said Billy.

"Christ," said Todd. "Jake Turner!"

He addressed the room.

"*All My Colors*, Whitney Press, 1966. It was in the *New York Times* top ten list for two years. And not one of you has heard of it."

Todd sighed. He'd done enough for art and literature for one evening. And he was tired. Tired of being the smartest guy in the room. Tired of being surrounded by the ignorant.

"Get out," he said, waving a dismissive hand.

Janis hurried everyone to the door, and no one lingered.

"You think I was too hard on them?" said Todd as he brushed his teeth at the bathroom mirror.

Janis was trying to unzip her own dress because if Todd did it, he'd break it.

"You're always too hard on them," she said. Todd heard it as praise.

"Maybe," he said. "But tonight, goddammit, that was classic. I mean, I expect you not to know it — you're all magazines and coffee table books—"

Janis, who always had a three-deep pile of library books by her bed, said nothing.

"But those guys... No wonder everything they write turns out shit."

Janis managed to slip out of the dress without tearing it.

"How's your book coming on?" she asked mildly.

Todd, immune to even the strongest sarcasm, frowned. It was a frown designed to invite sympathy and, even though it never achieved its purpose, Todd retained the habit.

"Oh, Jesus, it's hard," he said. "Sometimes the words flow like a tidal wave, and sometimes it's like God turned the stopcock off at the wall."

In fact, he thought to himself as Janis carefully replaced the catalog dress on its hanger, most times it's like that.

"I'm going to sleep in the spare room tonight," said Janis. "Early start tomorrow."

Todd nodded absently, unaware that Janis was trying to spare herself a night of him snoring, shouting in his sleep and whacking her in the face with a flailing arm. In fact, he was barely aware that Janis had left the bathroom.

Not for the first time, Todd Milstead was thinking about a book.

Janis woke up. A thumping noise was coming from downstairs. A repetitive, low thumping noise, like someone banging shot glasses onto a wooden table or—and for a moment an almost hopeful vision filled her mind—like someone repeatedly shoving her husband's face against a door. She got up, found a long and heavy flashlight under the bed, and, putting on a dressing-gown, went downstairs.

The door to Todd's study was open (he called it a study, but as all he ever did was read *Penthouse* in it, Janis thought of it as his jerk-off room) and the light was on. Janis approached it, trying not to be scared. As she did so, she could hear swearing.

"Mother*fucker*!"

It was Todd. She relaxed from the relief, but now she found that she was angry. He knew she was up early the next day. And here he was, up in the middle of the night, making an awful racket. Janis was very tired and suddenly it all seemed too much.

She went into the jerk-off room. Todd was standing by his bookcase. The house was full of bookcases, but this was Todd's special bookcase, where he kept the Good Stuff. Todd even called it the Good Stuff, like it was fine liquor and all Janis's dumb paperbacks (he never used the word in front of Janis, but then he didn't have to: she knew) were rotgut. *Rotbrain*, she found herself thinking as she stood in Todd's study, watching Todd attack his own bookcase. Now she could see the cause of the noise that had woken her: Todd was pulling books out and throwing them at the desk—*thud! thud!*—like a maniac.

"What are you doing?" she said.

Todd whirled around. "You startled me," he said accusingly.

"You woke me," she countered. "Todd, it's two in the morning."

"Now we're a clock," said Todd, which Janis thought made little sense. "I know what time it is, Janis."

"Go back to bed," she said. "You've got—"

Janis couldn't for the life of her think what it was that Todd had to do the next morning. Pull his pud until lunch, no doubt.

"Stuff," she said. "Todd, it's too late for this."

"What do you mean, it's too late?" he slurred, and Janis realized that Todd had started drinking again after she'd gone to bed. She was very tired. Bone tired and brain tired.

"Todd, I asked you once already," she said. "What are you doing?"

Todd *thudded* a few more books at the desk. Janis saw a second edition Bellow crease and fall to the carpet.

"I'm looking for that fucking book," he said.

"What—" said Janis. Then she realized. "That book."

"Yeah, that book," said Todd. "I figured it out. You jerks." He sniffed. *Oh great*, Janis thought, *he found some coke.* Cocaine was hard to find in their small town, but Todd could be quite determined when it came to himself and his needs, as he was now proving.

"What do you mean, you figured it out?" Janis sat down. She would rather have lain down, but the floor was stiff with literature.

"You all got together," said Todd. "One of you had an idea, to torment old Todd. Pretend you never heard of *All My Colors* or Jake Turner. So, you got Billy to tell that story—although knowing Billy, the poor ass probably thinks it really did happen—for bait, and then you all pretended you didn't know the book. Messing with my mind."

"I have never heard of that book," said Janis. "Honestly, Todd. Now please stop and go to bed. You're— you're tipsy, and somehow you think this thing is real. It's not real, Todd."

Like talking to a child who was having a tantrum, she thought.

"If it's not real," said Todd, staggering past a Herman Melville, "then how come I remember it?"

And, before she could stop him, he tilted his head back (did he need to do this to remember things, Janis wondered, or was it another affectation) and began to recite:

"At first, she thought she must be the luckiest woman alive, but as time went by, Helen came to realize that she was anything but that. Luck, the good kind anyway, was a commodity she was desperately in need of but forbidden, like a patient in hospital refused the one drug that might cure her."

Todd looked at Janis, his lips flecked with spit (or cocaine, she thought).

"Did I make that up, Janis?" he said. "Did I just make all that up?"

Janis looked at Todd. Suddenly, out of nowhere, a crossroads in her life was looming up. She wasn't sure if she was at the crossroads yet, but she could see it. It didn't look like a threatening crossroads either, the kind with a gallows at the roadside and the devil next to it. It looked like a promising sort of crossroads. But she wasn't there yet.

Not quite.

"No, you didn't make that up," Janis said. "Because it was quite good."

Todd glowered at her.

"Not great, I grant you. But it was quite good."

Todd's eyes seemed to glow. His face certainly did, fire engine cherry red. He took a step forward. He raised his hand.

Janis also took a step forward. She took Todd's hand.

"I want you to stop acting like a jerk," she said. "I want

you to be my husband, and be an adult. And—"

She let go Todd's hand and it fell to his waist.

"—I want you to stop screwing Sara Hotchkiss."

Before Todd could reply, Janis had walked out of the room. She didn't sleep long that night—it was nearly three now—but she slept well.

Sunday was a quiet day at the Milsteads'. Janis cleared up the mess in the living room and was going to leave the dirty glasses and crockery for Todd when she realized he'd be so hungover that he'd probably smash everything to pieces. So, she compromised: she cleaned up everything but Todd's study. If he wanted to wade ankle-deep in the great American novel, that was up to him.

After she'd cleared up, she went to visit a gallery with a friend, and came home about four to find that Todd had shut himself in his study and was—by the sound of it—making notes on his new book. She knew when he was making notes because he would spend hours getting everything just right—finding the perfect pencil, sharpening it, getting out his yellow legal pad, aligning everything so it was parallel to the sides of the desk—and then do jack shit until dinnertime.

The evening passed without incident. Janis and Todd watched TV in uncompanionable silence. Every so often, Todd would look at her with a puzzled expression as though he had something important to ask her, like *where do baby rabbits come from* or *how do I get red wine stains out of a white carpet*, but then his face would go blank and he'd stare at the TV again.

Next morning Janis was out bright and early to buy groceries. Todd was up neither bright nor early but he too had somewhere to go. After a light breakfast of cornflakes and toast (he had never got around to discovering how eggs worked), he drove into town in his old Volvo. In a perfect world, Todd would have owned a Porsche but that wasn't going to be happening any time soon, and beside he liked the Volvo because it was Scandinavian like Ibsen or something, and it looked like the kind of a car a writer would drive.

Todd rarely made trips into town. Janis ran all the errands and did the shopping, and Todd met Sara in motels out by the highway. Sometimes Todd might have a night with the gang in a local bar, but money for booze came from Janis (her dead old dad still holding the purse strings) and bartenders didn't like it when Todd started shouting. But today was special; today was *writerly*. Todd was going to the local bookstore.

Legolas Books was small, cramped, and unpopular, but Todd liked it. Timothy, the owner of Legolas, was a former hippy who'd taken advantage of premature baldness and myopia to remodel himself as an archetypal bookstore-owner, complete with bald head, gold-rimmed glasses and the benevolent look of a man who has lived his life among books rather than taking too much acid. His devotion to the wholesale faking-up of whatever a bookstore should be— shelves in disorder to create the impression of *too many books*, cups of awful coffee to encourage *chats*, unnecessary step ladders and a framed, hand-written copy of the *Desiderata*— had extended to his own attire of moleskin waistcoat and collarless shirt. Anywhere else, Timothy would have been roughed up and thrown into a storm drain, but here in his book-lined kingdom, he could be himself with impunity.

Timothy's attitude to literature appealed to Todd, who had himself been faking a life in books for some years. Todd was particularly drawn to Timothy because the shine-pated bookseller had decided for some reason that Todd was a real writer, in the same way that Timothy was a real bookman. They could stand for hours, Todd and Timothy, on either side of Timothy's counter, discussing books and their contents until finally interrupted by an angry cough from some idiot who wanted to actually buy a book. Timothy didn't mind at all: he knew that Todd was as likely to write a great novel as he was to piss diamonds, but Todd was part of the bookstore's color. "See that fellow, browsing among the Hemingways?" he'd say to a tourist who'd come in to buy a map, "Local author. We're kind of proud of him." And the tourist would feel ashamed at not being more artistic, and buy something expensive by a dead guy.

Today as usual Timothy was behind the counter, or rather beside it, sitting on a high stool, nose in a book, ready to peer over his glasses at any approaching customers. When the shop bell rang as Todd entered, Timothy closed the book without marking his place—it was, being the first book he'd picked up, an empty notebook with an attractive marbled cover and as such had no actual words in it—and greeted Todd.

"Good morning, scribe," he said. "How fares the struggle?"

Even Todd would normally have had difficulty responding to this without headbutting Timothy, but today he was hardly listening.

"Got a specific request for you today," he said.

"Well," said Timothy, "like it says in the men's room—
'We aim to please. You aim too, please.'"

He beamed at his salty sally. Todd just looked at him.
What the fuck was the old prick on about?

"I need a copy of *All My Colors*," he said.

Timothy looked confused.

"I don't think I recollect that one," he said. "Is it new?"

"Oh, not you as well," replied Todd. "Has my wife been
down here, is that it?"

"Your wife?" said Timothy. "No, haven't seen Janis since
your last birthday. She came in and bought that facsimile
copy of *Tropic of Capricorn* for you."

"You sure?" said Todd, a hint of menace in his voice.

"Yes, I'm sure," Timothy said, more firmly. He might be
an old fraud, but he was also a nasty heartless old fraud and
Todd didn't exactly scare him. "Now what was the name of
that book again?"

Todd backed down. "Sorry, Timothy, I'm having a weird
time lately."

Timothy was about to tell Todd that the times they were
a-changing when he realized that this was a heap of bullshit
too far, even for him. Instead he said, "Just tell me the name,
author and publisher and let's see if we can track that bugger
down for you."

A few minutes later, having searched the FICTION shelves,
both hardback and paperback, Todd and Timothy were in
the stockroom. A bare bulb shone above them and Timothy
was consulting his ledgers.

"Nothing," he said. "Not the book you wanted nor anything by this Jake Turner."

Todd grabbed the ledger from him. Timothy took it back.

"I know my own stock," he said. "And I know books. If you weren't so darned fervent, Todd, I'd be so bold as to say that there ain't no such book."

But I've seen it, Todd wanted to say. *I recall the cover—it's a woman's head, and she's looking out of the cover, and her hair is like a hydra's. No*, he corrected himself. *It's a rainbow. It's all her colors. Kind of literal, but it works.* Todd found himself remembering more lines from the book. Dialogue. Plot. Even chapter titles. He said none of this to Timothy. He didn't want the Mayor of fucking Hobbiton telling people that Todd Milstead was losing his mind.

"Okay, Timothy," he said finally. "I guess I got it mixed up with some other book."

"I guess you did at that," said Timothy. "I'll keep an eye out for it, Todd, and anything else by this Turner fellow, and call you if something turns up."

Somehow Todd knew that nothing was going to turn up, just as he knew that there would be no copy of *All My Colors* or any other books by Jake Turner at the local library, or the main library in the city, or the new giant bookstore out of town, or anywhere in the world. But he also knew that *All My Colors* was real, that he'd seen it, he'd read it, he'd owned it, for Christ's sake. He couldn't understand how two entirely different things could be true, but they were, and there was nothing he could do about it.

"See you 'round, Todd," said Timothy as Todd headed out the door. He picked up his empty but beautifully bound book. *Stupid fucker's finally gone crazy*, he thought to himself as he flicked through its blank pages.

If Timothy could have seen Todd forty-five minutes later, he would not have changed his opinion. Todd was sitting in the driver's seat of the Volvo, both hands clamped onto the wheel, and he was talking to himself. He had been talking to himself since he'd got into the car half an hour ago and he showed no signs of stopping.

"*Chapter Two*," Todd was now intoning, "*A Sunrise and a Sunset.*"

His eyes were focused on the car's immobile windshield wipers, but they weren't seeing anything.

"*Helen woke that morning with a feeling she could not explain,*" Todd told the windshield wipers. "*She could not tell if she had ever felt like that before, but as she could no longer remember feelings or anything that wasn't part of her daily routine, this was not surprising…*"

He stopped. A woman, passing in front of the car with her child in a shopping cart, was staring at him. Todd looked at himself in the rearview mirror and saw what the woman saw: a staring-eyed maniac, holding the wheel of a car that wasn't moving, and talking to himself without stopping. Todd stared back until she moved on, saying something to the child. Then he addressed the mirror.

"What the fuck," he asked, "is in me?"

What the fuck is in me? It was a question Todd couldn't stop asking himself all the way home. The answer was simple. It was a book, called *All My Colors*, by a man called Jake Turner, only the man didn't exist, and nor did the book. He was going to go through all his encyclopedias of literature and dictionaries of biography and copies of *The Writer's Gazette* and if necessary the *Yellow Pages*, but he already knew what he would find. Nothing. There was no such writer as Jake Turner, and there was no such book as *All My Colors.*

So what the fuck is in me?

Todd got home, threw the keys in the wooden bowl by the door—once he'd dreamed of beautiful undergraduates and even the occasional professor's wife doing the same, at swinging parties where everyone drank Todd's whiskey and laughed at his jokes and Todd always went home with the most beautiful wife, but Todd never got a professor's job because he'd never been *published*, and wasn't that a loaded word. But anyway, it was a nice bowl—and went into the kitchen to find something to drink. As he opened the fridge, the phone began to ring.

Todd picked up the extension. Maybe it was Timothy, ringing to apologize and offer him a compensatory copy of—

"Todd, this is Sara."

"Oh, Sara. This isn't a great time."

"It never is, unless you're drunk and I'm naked."

"Sara, can I call you from my study?"

"No, you can't. Todd, I just had *Janis* on the phone."

"What did she want, a recipe?" Todd almost laughed at his own witticism, then remembered the conversation he'd had with Janis the night before.

"No," said Sara, "she wanted to tell me to stay away from you. I told her I didn't know what she was talking about—"

"Good," said Todd, who had located a carton of V8 but was now thinking of trading up to a beer.

"—but she knew I did, so that was a waste of breath. So, I just let her talk."

"I bet that was fun."

"Actually, it was interesting."

"Janis?"

"What she said. I thought she was going to give me both barrels, and she started out that way, like she was about to scream at me and call me a whore, but then she just went calm."

"'Went calm'?" asked Todd.

"Yes," said Sara. "She went calm. Her voice changed and then she said:

"I'm not going to warn you off or any nonsense like that. I'm just going to ask you to do me one favor."

"What?" said Sara, anticipating a *Go fuck yourself*. Maybe not that: Janis never swore. *Go screw yourself*, then.

"I don't see why I should be the one who has to do all the work. I want you to call the house and tell Todd I'm leaving him."

"You want me to—"

"Yes," said Janis. "I figure you owe me that at least. Can you do that, Sara? It's not much to ask after what you did. Call Todd up and tell him I'm leaving."

"I can do that."

"Great. Oh, and Sara? When you've done that—"

"Yes?"

"Go fuck yourself."

●

"Janis said that?" Todd repeated, amazed. "Janis told you to go fuck yourself?"

"She did," Sara replied. "But I think she mostly wanted me to convey to you the fact that she is leaving you."

"Because of us? You and me?"

"No, Todd," said Sara. "Because of you." And she rang off.

Todd sat in front of the TV with a beer. There was nothing on TV but afternoon soaps and even Todd couldn't make a case for afternoon soaps having stories or characters that any writer could learn from (although one episode of *As The World Turns* contained more ideas, plot and character development than all of Todd's unpublished work to date). So Todd sat there, suckling at his beer like a baby, waiting for someone to do something.

Todd liked to tell the gang that there were two kinds of people in the world, those who do and those who don't. Todd was a do-er and they were don't-ers. The fact that Joe was a high school teacher, the fact that Mike had two jobs because his mother was in an expensive nursing home, and the fact that Billy was the only one of the gang who'd ever had anything published—these things were irrelevant. There were do-ers and don't-ers, and Todd was a do-er.

If pressed, and it was his booze so he was never pressed, Todd would have found it hard to produce any examples of doing. Janis cooked and cleaned and dealt with bills and maintenance. Todd had some intermittent income from—yes—teaching writing at the community college, but that had tailed off lately as Todd had a habit of giving outlandishly good grades to the girl students, while simultaneously putting down any talented young males (in this respect, and this respect only, Todd was an early proponent of positive discrimination).

Generally, however, Todd Milstead was not an active man. He had designed his life to be this way, as it gave him more time for writing. The only problem was that Todd very rarely did any writing. He would get up, shower, breakfast, and go into his study. He would organize all his writing materials and sometimes even tidy his collection of authorly items: the framed and signed photograph of John Steinbeck (Todd had bought it at auction and it was signed *To Beverley* but hey, it was authorly), the quill-and-ink brass paperweight that Janis had thought was cute and bought for him, the inspirational Bob Dylan quote he'd typed out himself and taped to the wall—these were all the tokens of his author-ness, what Todd (but only to himself, which was wise) sometimes liked to call "the handmaidens of brilliance."

But once this was done, the straightening and the tidying, that was it. Nothing happened. Todd could sit there for hours, waiting for the Muse to strike. But if she was striking, it felt to Todd like she was doing so for few er hours and more pay. Todd waited and waited. He took down books and scoured them for inspiration. He quoted his favorite lines to himself. Sometimes phrases came into his head, and he would start writing them down and expanding them into paragraphs until he realized that he was just transcribing passages that he remembered (he remembered them perfectly, but that wasn't really the point). And he'd pull the paper out of the machine and screw it up into a ball and throw the ball into the corner with the others, and then he'd pull out a copy of *Playboy*.

And that would be it until lunchtime, when he'd wander into the kitchen, look at whatever Janis had left him to heat up, and then phone for a pizza because he didn't cook. Todd was a man who'd always rather someone else did it for him, and now he was waiting for Janis to come home and tell him how his marriage was going to end.

Janis came home toward the end of Todd's second beer, which was just as well. If she'd come home during the third beer, conversation—rational conversation, anyway—would have been risky. Todd tended to get angry after beer in the afternoon.

Janis saw the two beers and decided to keep it short.

"Did she call?" she asked.

Todd thought about pretending he didn't know who Janis meant. Then he thought again, and said, "Yes," as briskly as he could.

"Good," said Janis. "Then you know where we stand."

"I suppose so," Todd replied. He had no idea in fact where either of them stood, but he was going to let Janis do this for him, and so he kept his answers short.

"This house belongs to me, you know that," Janis said. "You're at fault in this situation, I guess you know that too."

Todd said nothing.

"Any lawyer will tell you that you've got no chance of turning this around in your favor, so I wouldn't waste your breath or your money."

"We'll see," said Todd, and wondered why he'd said it.

"Fine, and good luck with that," said Janis. "Now. I want you out of here, for reasons already stated. You can have six weeks to get your stuff together and get moved out of here. After that, I'll pitch it."

Todd turned around at that.

"Six weeks is plenty of time, Todd," Janis said.

"Okay," said Todd.

If Janis was disappointed at Todd's lack of response, she didn't register it. Instead she turned and left the room.

"You fucking *cow*," Todd whispered to his beer.

Todd's response to his wife's advice was to ignore it. The very next day he went to see Pete Fenton, the man he called his lawyer. Pete wasn't really Todd's lawyer, but a few years back he'd advised Todd on a contract Todd had been offered by a vanity publishing company (he'd told Todd it was a piece of crap, but Todd signed it anyway, and then the company went bust), and Todd had been impressed by his frankness and his low rates.

Pete wasn't pleased to see Todd, who he remembered without fondness, but he'd had an appointment make a late cancellation and it was a shame to waste the slot, so here they were, Pete telling Todd how it was, and Todd not being very happy with how it was.

"She's got me by the balls," Todd said.

"Others might see it differently," said Pete. "Your wife's character appears to be spotless. The sole difficulty a judge would have with her testimony is staying awake during a description of Janis's day. Whereas you—"

Pete's large hands spread.

"You're a heavy drinker, you have affairs, you contribute nothing to the marriage... it's a tough one. Even forty years ago, when a husband could do pretty much what he liked, you'd have had trouble fighting this one."

Todd said, "But it's a no-fault divorce, right? I don't mean there *is* no fault, I admit my failings... I mean, if she's not going to take me to court, then it's a fifty-fifty split. Isn't it?"

Pete almost laughed. "A fifty-fifty split of what? Janis owns the property outright and pretty much everything else. Your half, if you can call it that, is whatever you can get in the back of a van."

"So you're saying I don't have much of a chance?"

"I'm saying you have no chance at all, Mr. Milstead. The only way you could fight this is if you had a great deal of money."

Pete looked at Todd. He knew the answer to his question already but what the hell, he was going to get some enjoyment out of this.

"*Do* you have a great deal of money, Mr. Milstead?"

Todd's defeated headshake almost made Pete Fenton feel sorry for him.

The Volvo was parked at an angle to Scully's Bar, blocking the sidewalk. Inside Scully's Bar, Todd was also parked at an angle, trying to stay on his bar stool without holding on to it. He was explaining to the barman for perhaps the third time why life had conspired against him to such an extent.

"It's because I'm a real man," he announced. The barman ignored him, choosing instead to wipe something. "She's scared of that, you see," Todd continued. "She knows there's something inside of me, something good, something real strong, and she's scared of letting it out."

"Maybe you should go home and write about it," said the barman.

Todd frowned at him.

"How do you know I'm a writer?"

"You told me," said the barman. "But seriously. Everybody's got a novel inside them."

"I know I do," Todd said, and giggled. "A big one, too. A bestseller."

"Well, like I say, go home, get some sleep, and when you wake up, write it," the barman said.

"I can't," said Todd. "It's not mine to write."

"You're not making any sense," the barman said. "Time to go."

Todd looked at his diminished store of dollar bills. He scooped them all up, dropped some coins back on the counter, and picked himself off the bar stool.

"Real man," he announced to the empty bar and left.

Todd's journey home was packed with incident. He ran one red light, drove down a street closed for building works, crushed a bike that someone had left on the sidewalk, and parked in a neighbor's drive before realizing his mistake and reversing back into his own.

After he'd managed to find both his door key and his front door, Todd let himself into the house and collapsed onto the sofa and then, as it was made from an untextured leather-like substance, slid off again onto the rug. He remained there in a sort of crumple until two o'clock in the morning, when cold and cramp woke him and he was able to get up and make his way to the spare room.

The next morning, Todd waited until he heard Janis's car drive away (he imagined her reversing past the Volvo, which was parked half on the lawn and half on the drive) before deciding that he should stay in bed an hour or two more.

Ten minutes later, Todd was out of bed and into his clothes.

Sometimes Todd surprised himself with how methodical he was. Right now he was surprising himself to an extraordinary extent, as he pulled out folder after folder of writing. Once he'd got all the folders down, pastel blue and pastel pink and pastel red, he got on a chair to reach up to the top of the bookshelves and brought down two boxes marked JUVENILIA. Then, just to make sure, he went through every drawer in the desk.

Todd was pretty sure he had everything out. He stood in the middle of the room, surrounded by folders and boxes.

"My fucking career," he said, and got down on his knees.

Everyone needs an audit, whatever they do for a living, and Todd's personal audit was way overdue. He methodically opened folders, reunited pieces of paper with other pieces of paper, put stories with other stories, and then did the same with the boxes. When he'd done that, he made a pyramid of all the manuscripts, notebooks, and bulldog-clipped writings. It was less than six inches high. Todd, who'd started writing when he was seventeen and was now hitting forty, worked it out. Half an inch a year, and most of that written before he was thirty.

Todd sat down in the middle of his career and started to read.

None of it was any good. None of it was finished, for a start: there were novels that were one or two chapters long, there were short stories that were so short they were barely paragraphs, there were movie treatments which were three pages long but neglected to mention what the story or characters were... and there was a play. Todd could barely bring himself to read the play, but it seemed wrong to single it out for special treatment, so he dove in. After three pages, he went to get a drink. After six more pages, he got another drink. Eight pages later, the play ended, halfway through a speech by a character called The Fisherman, and Todd was so glad that he had to get another drink.

He piled it all back up again. Then, after a moment's thought, he slid the lot into a waste bin. He took a box of matches, lit a match and dropped it in. His career took flame (for the first time, Todd thought wryly) and Todd sat there, bathed in the hot glow of his own failure.

After a while, the fire went out. Todd stuck the bin under a faucet and tipped the contents into the yard. Then he fetched a bottle of whiskey and Janis's sleeping pills into his study and set them down next to his yellow legal pad. He set the whiskey and the pill bottle on his left and the pad and the pen on his right, then took a dime from his packet

"Okay," he said to the dime. "Heads for my right hand, tails for my left."

Todd flipped the dime into the air. It leapt toward him and went down the top of his shirt.

"Motherfucker," said Todd, and fished the dime out.

He flipped it again, this time slapping it down onto the back of his other hand. He looked at it. Tails.

Todd wasn't a brave man. "Best of three," he said. "And I'm saying the first one was heads."

He flipped again. He looked. Heads.

"Dame Fate is a kind mistress," said Todd, inaccurately. He pushed the whiskey and the pills to one side, thought again, grabbed the whiskey and took a swig from the bottle. Then he picked up his pen and—for the first and only time in his life—wrote from the heart.

I have no money and no talent, Todd scribbled. He looked at what he'd written. It was harsh, but fair. He wrote again.

I need money. This was true. He wrote again *but I have no talent. I can't write*.

Todd had never looked into his own soul. It was exciting, like looking over Niagara Falls. He examined every nook and cranny of his being, seeing himself naked on a wheel like the Leonardo da Vinci drawing of the cross-looking guy. Todd inspected his soul from every angle, and it wasn't good. He stole a glance at the pill bottle again.

Todd Milstead, who had an opinion for every occasion and an occasion for every opinion, found that he had nothing. *Now what?* he wrote and put the pen down. He looked at the pill bottle. He swiveled in his swivel chair and looked at the Steinbeck portrait dedicated to Beverley. He gazed at the window, through which the sun, improbably, was now coming up.

"*A new day for some is a new beginning,*" he intoned. "*But for others it is the appearance of the jailer, bringing bread and water and fresh hurt.*"

Where the hell had *that* come from, thought Todd. He remembered almost at once: the fucking book. He started laughing; how fantastically useless it was he had managed to retain a very complete memory of something that didn't exist. Like a man dreaming a film in perfect detail that had never been made, or someone waking up to find a fully formed melody in their head, just waiting to be…

Todd sat up straight. That was it. Just waiting there. Just waiting to be written down. He'd read in *Playboy* about the Beatles song, "Yesterday," and how Paul had dreamed the song, or some shit, and spent a year humming the tune to people and asking them if they'd heard it before, until he realized that nobody had and the song was his, all his.

I don't have a fucking year, thought Todd. He reached for the legal pad again. Then—*why waste time?*—he pushed away the pad and took the cover off the typewriter. He ripped out whatever crap was in there, slipped in a fresh sheet, and began to write.

ALL MY COLORS
by Todd Milstead

Chapter One

The hardware store was empty. Jimmy the store clerk was clearing away some boxes when he noticed the woman standing at the counter. She was in her early

thirties, good-looking with blonde hair and wearing a
blue print dress.

"Can I help you?" Jimmy asked.

"Yes," she said. "I want to buy a hacksaw."

TWO

Billy Cairns woke up sweating. This wasn't a big surprise—Billy always woke up sweating. Sometimes he woke up sweating because he'd been drinking the night before, and sometimes he woke up sweating because he hadn't been drinking the night before. But today was different. Today Billy was sweating through his ancient pajamas because he'd had a dream.

Normally Billy paid no heed to his dreams. In a decade when people were always being told in self-help books to follow their dreams, Billy was an exception. He would no more follow one of his dreams than he would follow a serpent with the face of his father who wanted to eat him; coincidentally, this was one of Billy's recurring dreams. And in a decade where dreams were constantly being scanned for meaning and dissected for their relevance, Billy had no need for interpretation. He knew exactly what his dreams meant. They meant that his subconscious hated him.

Last night's dream had been no exception. Or rather, it had started out as no exception, being the usual parade of Bosch-type living torsos, many-eyed bartenders and childhood friends in awkward sexual positions, but all of a sudden it had shifted somehow. Like a TV picture which has been flicking between random stations with lots of static and incoherent images but then settles into a program and stays there, the dream had become—for the first time since Billy's childhood perhaps—stable. A story even an old rumpot like Billy could follow.

Not that it was a reassuring story.

Billy found himself in a library. It was a huge place, with shelves piling up into the—the clouds? That couldn't be right. The library was domed somehow, and even the dome part had shelves going up, and each shelf was crammed with books. There wasn't an inch of wall that didn't have a shelf full of books leaning against it. Billy knew, he didn't know how, that every book ever written was here. If he'd been able to, he could have climbed a ladder and found books from every era of human history, from medieval manuscripts to Egyptian scrolls to Babylonian clay tablets. Billy even had a feeling that Moses' two tablets of stone were in here somewhere, along with *The Adventures of Tom Sawyer* and *The Canterbury Tales* and—Billy suspected—the manuscript for Billy's own unfinished novel, which he'd lost, along with everything else he owned, ten years ago in an apartment fire.

Once, Billy would have loved to spend a lifetime in this library, pulling out volumes of Dickens and Thackeray and Ginsberg to his sober heart's content. But now, even though it was a dream, he just wanted to get out. There was something claustrophobic about the place. No windows, he noticed, while the book-lined dome seemed to loom over him like a monster made of spines.

Billy was about to look for an exit when he saw the counter. It seemed sensible to him to approach the counter and ask the person behind it for help. So Billy approached the counter, and as he did so, he noticed that there was someone already there, engaged in conversation with what he presumed was the librarian. As he got closer, he recognized the someone. It was Todd. Todd didn't see Billy, perhaps because he seemed het up about something, which was about as surprising as Billy's waking up sweating.

"You must have it!" said Todd.

"I'm sorry, sir," said the librarian who wasn't dressed much like a librarian, being clad in overalls with a pencil behind his ear. "We do not have the book you are requesting."

As Todd went redder and redder in the face, Billy realized he knew the librarian from somewhere.

"Be with you in a moment, sir," said the librarian.

"No rush," said Billy, and felt foolish.

Todd still hadn't noticed him, a fact that Billy was relieved about. Todd in a fury was never a good thing.

"Why not?" Todd shouted. "Why don't you have the book?"

The librarian smiled and gestured around him.

"Because this is a hardware store," he said.

Todd looked around. Billy did the same. The librarian—and Billy now saw he wasn't a librarian at all, he was the clerk from the hardware store—was right. The whole place was full of saws, and ladders, and boxes of nails and screws. There were tin kettles, and steel buckets, and a strong odor of linseed oil. It was a hardware store all right.

"You haven't heard the last of this!" Todd bellowed—and Billy marveled how, even in a dream, Todd behaved entirely true to type—and he stormed off toward the outside world.

The store clerk turned to Billy. "Sorry about that," he said.

"No problem," Billy found himself saying.

"Now," said the store clerk, "how can I help you?"

He smiled, and his teeth were the teeth of a hacksaw. They glinted, gray and steely, in the light of a bare bulb.

Billy screamed and woke. He turned on his bedside lamp and fumbled on the floor by the bed for the glass of Old Times he'd left there the night before in case of emergencies. His hand caught something else, knocked the glass over and sent it skittering across the floor. Billy cursed, and looked at his hand. It was bleeding after coming in contact with whatever it was he'd touched on the floor.

He put on his glasses and peered over the side of the bed. On the floor, amongst the dust bunnies, was a shiny new hacksaw blade.

Billy screamed again.

Todd woke with a start. His neck hurt like hell. He opened his eyes and was surprised to find himself in his office, sitting at his desk. He stretched, and as he did so, his eye fell on the neat pile of pages next to the typewriter. Todd picked up the pile and riffled through it. There were close to thirty pages here, neatly typed and, even at a cursory glance, clearly written with a sense of flow and direction that most writers would envy. Todd wasn't sure whether he should be feeling envy or not as he was the person who'd written these pages. Although in another, equally real sense, he wasn't.

"Well, if I didn't, who else did?" Todd reasoned to himself. He looked at the typewriter. There was a piece of paper in it, with words typed on it, two or three paragraphs that ended halfway through a word. Todd had written and written until he was forced to stop through sheer exhaustion. Other writers might have worried about picking up the thread again, but not Todd. He could, as it were, just rewind the tape in his head to the point where he'd left off, like a secretary taking dictation from her boss. Except in this case, Todd didn't know who the boss was.

He didn't want to think about that right now, though, and he certainly didn't want to write any more until he'd got some food and coffee inside him. So (while Billy Cairns was bent double over his own toilet and finding out just how empty an empty stomach can be) Todd got stiffly out of his seat, and went out to his car, which was still parked at a rakish angle across the lawn.

Todd liked driving. It was manly, it was American and it put words and phrases into his head that he approved of, like "road" and "motion" and "*Bildungsroman*." And besides, driving a car was a great feeling. There was the radio, which you could tune into jazz (hep, fifties), rock (still a young guy at heart), or classical (a thinker). Todd liked to twiddle his way across the dial and sample all these kinds of station, but invariably he would settle on a bland top forty station, ostensibly so he could feel that he was above this kind of pap, but really because he liked it.

Right now Todd was cruising into town with Kansas blasting out the Volvo's speakers, and composing an amusing riff that went *what is it about all these groups who are named after places? Kansas, Boston, Chicago... it's like America has to keep reminding itself that it's America*, a riff that ended when Todd was unable to think of any more bands who were named after places.

A light turned red and Todd stopped the car. He drummed his fingers on the steering wheel in vague time to the radio. It was a long light. Todd looked around. He saw cars and trucks. He saw a strip mall. A tire shop, and a diner with an optimistically large parking lot. A small brown car was pulling into the parking lot. Todd despised small cars, regarding them as somehow un-American (the Volvo might be European but it was big, like an oblong Cadillac), and this one was particularly contemptible, being small enough to be Japanese.

"A contemptible automobile," said Todd to himself, as the driver—a not especially tiny-looking person in a leather jacket—got out. He adopted the voice of Top Cat. "A... contemptible..."

He stopped. The driver of the contemptible automobile opened the passenger door and Janis got out. She smiled at the driver and they walked into the diner, hand in hand.

"Son of a—" exclaimed Todd. He squirmed in his seat, trying to get a good look at the person Janis was with, but no matter how he tried, he just couldn't get a fix. Behind him, car horns blasted. The lights were green. Todd stalled, started the engine again, and drove on. Then an idea occurred to him. Instead of going straight ahead, he made a sudden left and parked, not in the diner's lot (he wasn't that dumb), but outside the tire store next to the diner.

He thought for a moment, then got out the car and went into the tire store.

"Welcome to Bill's Tire," said the owner, presumably Bill. "Can I help you?"

Yes, I think my wife is fucking some other guy, Todd thought but did not say.

"I'm good," he said, and walked through the store to the side window which, he hoped, offered a good view of the diner. To keep Bill from bothering him, he pretended to look at car stereos. Across the way, he could see Janis ordering breakfast. He couldn't see the other guy's face, just his dumb leather jacket.

"That's a good one," said Bill, who had followed Todd over to the window.

"Is it?" said Todd, who had no idea what stereo he was supposed to be looking at.

"Yes, sir, got the FM and everything. Plays cassettes, about the only thing it don't do is drive the car for you." Bill guffawed. Todd made a kind of "heh" noise. Janis and the other guy were laughing at something now. Todd wished he'd brought a camera, to collect evidence. Evidence of what, he wasn't sure.

"You know those two?" said Bill suddenly.

"Excuse me?" said Todd.

"Those two people you're staring at," said Bill.

"I don't know what you're talking about," said Todd, at

the same time trying to look over Bill's shoulder. Now Janis was leaning over and saying something to the other guy.

"I don't enjoy people coming in here to stare at other people like some fucking kind of pervert," said Bill. "Now get out of here or I'll make you get out."

"Can you move please?" Todd said, which was ill-advised.

"Nobody fucking listens anymore," said Bill, and punched Todd in the stomach.

Todd doubled over.

"What the *fuck* did you do that for?"

"Plenty more where that came from," said Bill. "Now get out before I get the tire iron."

Clutching his stomach, Todd made for the door, casting one last glance at the diner. A shove from Bill propelled him into the lot. He staggered, tripped into some trashcans, pulled himself up, and pulled a trashcan over with a mighty crash.

A few feet away, Janis heard the crash and looked out the window to see her future ex-husband trying to clamber to his feet and cover his face as he skulked back to his car.

"Leave him," said her companion as they watched Todd brush garbage off himself and get back into the Volvo.

Janis, out of pure reflex, was about to defend Todd, but no words came, so she just smiled and shrugged.

"You are so beautiful when you smile," said her companion, and Janis smiled again.

Todd didn't even wait until he got home before calling Pete Fenton. He pulled over by the curb and jammed himself into a phone box.

"He's not here right now," said Pete's secretary, Alice. "He'll be back after lunch."

"Can I leave a message?" said Todd.

"Sure," said Alice. "What would you like me to tell him?"

"Tell him my wife's fucking some other guy."

There was a pause at the other end of the line, then Alice said frostily, "I'll be sure to pass that on," and put the phone down.

Todd drove to a bar to think things over. This time, remembering the drunken mess of two nights ago, he stuck to beer and, after even more thought, ordered some peanuts to soak up the booze. The problem as Todd saw it was one of fairness. Janis was divorcing him for—ugly word—adultery. That is, she knew he was fucking Sara, which by her lights was not only an offense, but a good reason for her to take all his money. Todd could understand her anger at the former— maybe if she'd been a little more willing in the bedroom department he might not have had to go elsewhere for his pleasure—but not the latter. Where for example in the Bible did it say that someone who had successfully coveted his neighbor's wife should pay for it financially? It didn't make any sense. "Hey, you fucked someone else, you have to give me all your money." People committed murder and they got to keep their money, didn't they? It was all wrong.

And what made it even more tits-up topsy-turvy was that this only applied to the man. Todd was a feminist as much as anyone, but surely this was discrimination. The man dips his wick, he gets caught, he has to pay a substantial fine known as alimony. The woman—whatever "dipping her wick" would be for a woman—the woman plays away from home, and what happens? She gets the alimony. The whole thing was like playing heads or tails with a two-headed coin. Whichever way it came down, the man lost. And the man in this case was Todd. *Shit*, he thought, *if I'd known I was going to get screwed this badly, I'd have fucked every woman in this town.*

With that happy if implausible thought in mind, Todd ordered one more beer for the road and sat back to suck the salt off his peanuts.

"Let me pay for this," said Janis's companion when the bill came.

Janis beamed. "Todd never pays for anything," she said. "He says this is an equal opportunities world now, so the man shouldn't pay for everything. But that just means—"

"You don't have to talk about Todd so much," said her companion.

"I'm sorry," said Janis. "It's just for the longest time he's been the only thing in my life. God," she said, looking away for a moment, "How sad is that? How freaking... *empty*."

"All that's over," her companion said, taking Janis's hand. "There's a new world for you now. If you want it."

Janis looked up. She saw a pair of strong blue eyes, and a mouth that disguised concern in a smile.

"I do," she said. "I do want it."

Todd got home, not too buzzed, and threw his keys at the wall. Then he checked his messages. Nothing from Janis, nothing from Sara, and then just a whole lot of rustling and breathing. He was about to erase the lot when he heard Billy's familiar voice rasp out his name.

"Todd," said Billy on the tape, "Todd, you need to call me. I had this—"

There was a pause long enough for Todd to feel irritated.

"I had this dream," said Billy's voice. "You were in it."

"Jesus, Billy." Todd winced. "I don't need you to tell me your erotic fantasies."

"Todd," said Billy, "it was more than a dream. It was a warning."

Todd sighed dramatically and erased the message.

"*Some people never realize the truth,*" he said out loud. "*But the truth is like the tide. It rolls in whether you know about it or not. And if you're standing in the way of it, you're going to get your feet wet.*"

He blinked.

"Time to get to work, I guess."

Todd was seated at his typewriter. He looked at the paper already in the machine, the word uncompleted on the paper, and was about to consider his next move when his fingers leapt at the keys and began hammering away as if of their own volition. Pages flowed out of Todd as he battered away, stopping only to put in fresh sheets of paper. A thin sweat broke out on his forehead, and his hands began to ache from the sheer mechanical act of typing, but he never stopped. After two hours, during which time Todd hadn't stood up, taken a drink of water or turned on the lights, his body was unable to go on.

He slumped in his seat. He looked at the fresh sheaf of words beside the typewriter.

"Who's writing who here?" he said out loud.

He frowned. What the hell did that mean?

After a few minutes, blood began to flow through his cramped muscles. Todd looked at his hands. They were flexing with eagerness to get back to work.

"All right, boys," he said. "Just let me get a sip of—"

But his hands jerked forward—*like a dowsing rod*, Todd thought—and began clattering at the keys again, and did not stop until it was too dark for Todd to see and then, after he had turned his lamp on, until Todd himself was too tired to see.

Todd woke in his chair again, but what woke him this time was not the ache in his neck, or the light of the morning sun, but his hands. He looked down. The things were virtually drumming a tattoo on the table.

Todd looked at his right hand. "Thank you, Thing," he said, but it didn't sound that funny and it also put an image into his head of his two hands, severed from his body, typing away quite happily while Todd sat there aghast, blood pumping from his useless wrists.

"I need to eat," he said to his hands, not feeling as dumb as he would have expected. "I need to take a dump, I need to wash, and I need to sleep in my own bed."

At once his hands relaxed. Todd lifted his arms and examined them. They seemed somehow *his* again.

An hour later, full of oatmeal, showered but not shaved, and rested after a brief nap, Todd found himself at the typewriter again. His hands virtually flew at the keys, like he was a deranged virtuoso pianist performing the concert of his life.

As his fingers typed and typed and more and more sheets of paper were added to the pile, Todd was reminded of a movie he'd seen with Janis—a movie Janis had made him go and see with her—some English crud about a dancer who put on some magic ballet shoes and couldn't stop dancing. At the time Todd had entertained himself, if not Janis, by laughingly asking why the dancer didn't just shout, "SOMEBODY GET THESE DAMN SHOES OFF ME!" at the audience, but that too didn't seem so funny now. Or so Todd thought as his fingers battered away at the keys.

When he was able, as he was slotting another sheet of paper into the machine, Todd stole a glance at his fingers. They were red and swollen, as though he had been climbing a rock face with them. He wondered if he could get a bowl of warm water to bathe them in but the moment the paper was in the typewriter his hands were off again, like seagulls whirling relentlessly around and around.

A passerby peering in through the study window would have seen an encouraging sight—Todd Milstead, would-be author, finally applying himself to his craft, writing solidly for hour after hour. The same passerby might wonder that Todd never seemed to worry about where the next word was coming from, and wrote at a consistent, but also maniacal speed, like he had so much to get out of himself and hardly any time to do so. They might also note that from time to time, Todd would open his mouth and emit a wordless yell, like someone trapped on a switchback.

But there was no passerby, nobody for Todd to say *get these damned shoes off me* to, and no respite.

•

Seven hours passed, at which point Todd noticed that two of his fingers were bleeding.

"Stop, dammit," he said. "I need to get a Band-Aid."

In the bathroom, his hands twitched impatiently as Todd rummaged through the first aid kit. Inspired, he thrust them into his pockets, where they comprehensively thumped his thighs in frustration.

"Oh darn," he said in what he hoped was a convincingly flat tone, "We seem to be out of Band-Aids. I better drive to the store and get some."

And without a moment's delay, he turned and walked downstairs and out of the house.

Todd's hands were his again, which was good news for Todd, as he was currently using them to drive his car. He had no idea how long this would last (maybe forever, he thought. Maybe it would be his fate to be a conduit for every lost book ever written, and one day they would find his skeleton slumped over a previously unpublished Jane Austen novel), so he was determined to make the most of it. Which in this case meant visiting a Burger King drive-in and ordering the largest meal they had.

"I have to eat," he reasoned out loud as he maneuvered a Whopper to his mouth at the traffic lights. His hands seemed to have no argument with this, and even let him enjoy his fries with ketchup.

Todd was so encouraged by this development he decided to take a chance and make his next destination not the drug store but the nearest bar.

•

It didn't go well. As soon as he made a left instead of a right, Todd found himself making an extremely abrupt U-turn, to the accompaniment of furious horns, and then having a major fight on his hands, or rather with his hands, to regain control of the parking brake. There was a crunch. Todd's car was stalled right in the middle of the road. He tugged at the parking brake, but to no avail.

After a while a police car came by. Its driver got out.

"Having trouble?" he said.

"I stalled just as I was about to overtake someone," Todd lied.

The cop said, "You can't stay here, pal. This is the middle of the road."

"I know that," said Todd, testily. "I'm sorry," he added. He felt his hands loosen.

"Just get going," said the cop. Todd started the engine, Todd's hands released the brake, and the car drove off again.

Todd sat behind the wheel, sweating. His life was—he could see the cliché coming—out of his hands. As if to confirm the thought, he saw his hands turn the wheel and make a U-turn in the middle of the road.

A few minutes later, they were at the drug store.

"Now what?" Todd said to himself as he collected a cart from the entrance. He began walking, looking for Band-Aids. But his hands had other concerns. Or so he eventually worked out after he started slapping himself in the face. After a while he realized with a sick lurch that he was being directed by his own hands—left side of face for left, right side for right, and both sides for stop.

Todd walked around the store, slapping himself like a

maniac, and pausing only to look at shelves and work out what it was he was supposed to be buying. After a few minutes, he had several packs of aspirin and paracetamol, some long-life milk, several bottles of water, a box of energy bars, and—

"Oh no," said Todd. "The fuck no."

He was standing in front of a shelf of adult diapers. His hands reached out for a family pack (a *family* pack?) and placed it in the cart. Todd knew then that this was going to be a big book.

Back home, Todd found himself arranging the food and drink on the desk in front of him (he had already, against his will, put on the adult diapers, an experience he hoped he might one day forget) and sitting down at the typewriter. He'd been able to bathe his fingers in alcohol (sadly not the kind you could drink, although Billy Cairns might have had something to say about that), which he hoped would relieve the pain (he was wrong about that, but the paracetamol helped a little).

Todd pulled a fresh pack of typing paper from a drawer—he had literally reams of the stuff lying around, just in case he ever had an idea that would sustain more than a chapter—checked that the typewriter ribbon was okay for a few more miles—*make that "a few hundred more miles,"* he thought grimly—and slid in a new sheet of paper.

This time his head didn't so much tilt back as jerk back like Todd had been shot, and his fingers went into overdrive. A passerby going past this time would have been horrified by the sight of a man leaning backward at an alarming angle, mouth agape and fingers smashing away at a typewriter, and would, had they not been too busy calling 911, have been put in mind of the keyboard player from a progressive rock band caught up in the throes of a complicated synthesizer solo.

How long this went on for, Todd could not say. He dined where he sat, he slept where he sat, he crapped where he sat: despite frequent diaper changes, Todd could feel the sores blooming on his butt and groin. His beard grew and grew into a tangled, matty bush. His teeth remained uncleaned and his sweat started to smell of nail varnish remover, as by now Todd was borderline starving and his body had begun to release acetone.

He looked like a hermit writing his memoirs. He also looked like shit. Todd had read about the billionaire Howard Hughes ending his days as a recluse, thin as a rail with long white hair, collecting his own fingernail clippings and pissing into jars. Todd looked down at his etiolated frame. *At least he had a jar*, he thought. *Fucking rich guys got it all.*

Surprisingly often, the phone rang. Sometimes it was Janis, telling him to get in touch with her lawyer over some legal detail or other. Sometimes it was Sara, mouth close to the receiver in a way that a long time ago Todd would have found very sexy, asking where he was and what he thought he was doing. A couple of times it was Mike wondering when the old gang was going to get together. But mostly it was Billy Cairns.

Initially, Todd did not enjoy Billy's calls, but as time went by, they became part of his new life. Just as every TV watcher has shows they like and shows they hate, so Todd found he had callers he liked and callers he didn't. Callers he didn't included Janis—*"You can hide out all you like, Todd. It's just going to cost you more is all"*—and Sara—*"Todd, I need you to call me. I think someone tipped off Terry."* Callers he did comprised of Billy.

Billy's early work, in Todd's opinion, was not his best. It followed a predictable pattern (probably because Billy's mind was so fried he almost certainly had no memory of his previous calls). The answering machine would click on, Janis's weary voice would ask the caller to leave a message, and then, after the beep, there would be several seconds of frightening, gulping breathing. And then, just when it seemed he would never speak, Billy would say:

"Todd? 'S me, Billy."

Todd could almost see Billy looking around, as though fearful of being spotted. He imagined him leaning into the phone, flecking the mouthpiece with 100 percent proof saliva. Then:

"Todd, I had the dream again. The dream where you'n'me were in the libe-aree."

If Todd had been blessed with empathy for other human beings, he might have felt something for a man who'd once been touted as a promising young author, but was now such a lush that he could no longer pronounce the name of the place where books were kept. Instead, whenever Billy called and said, *"in the libe-aree,"* Todd would generally call out, "'Library,' Billy. It's pronounced 'library.'"

After revealing that the dream featured Todd and Billy in the libe-aree, Billy would generally start muttering fearfully to himself, and Todd would shout, "Speak up, Bill!" But then Billy would have rung off, having spooked himself back into a terrified silence.

The calls went on like this for a while, but then, like all long-running shows, they began to evolve. This second iteration was in many ways Todd's favorite, not least because the calls seemed to coincide with Todd's rest periods. Todd would be sitting back in his chair, enjoying some once-sparkling water or gnawing on an energy bar, when the phone would ring, Janis would invite the caller to speak after the tone, and then Billy would step in and get right to it.

"Todd, Billy," he'd say. *"I got to tell you about the dream. I got to do it."*

"Do it, Billy!" Todd would shout as he tried to soothe his groin with a wet tissue before diapering up again.

"Todd," Billy would say, *"The libe-aree. It was you'n'me in the libe-aree."*

"With the lead pipe, yeah, you said," shouted Todd. "Get to it, Bill."

"Except it wasn't the libe-aree," Billy would say. *"Todd, it wasn't the libe-aree."*

"You just said it was the libe-aree," Todd would sing out as he eased his ravaged body back into his seat and loaded more paper into what he now called the Iron Maiden. "Was it the libe-aree or was it not the libe-aree, Billy?"

"Todd, I know you ain't going to believe me—"

"Aren't going to," corrected Todd as he watched his bruised and blistered fingers get ready to go again.

"But that place was the hardware store, Todd. The one I told you about."

"It's okay, Billy," Todd would say, more to himself than out loud, because the old eidetic generator was powering up inside him. "I suppose I could have used that info a while back. But right now"—and suddenly his fingers flew out at the keyboard like bats from an increasingly crowded belfry—"I got problems of my own."

The third set of calls were, Todd supposed, like the last days of a former hit show, the kind where all the original writers and producers are long gone, but some of the cast are still hanging in there, and loyal fans still tune in, but the magic has dried up. There were only three or four of these calls, and they were pretty short. Mostly they went like this:

Janis would invite the caller to speak after the beep. There would be the longest pause. And then Billy would just start crying. Sometimes he'd cry for a few seconds, sniffle and then hang up. Sometimes he'd cry and gulp and try and speak and then hang up. And sometimes he'd just cry and cry and cry for so long that the tape would beep and cut him off.

Todd didn't say much during these calls. They were distressing, even for him. And also he was getting tired, and needed to direct all his effort into his writing. The typewriter was an Iron Maiden that never seemed to get any less hungry, whereas Todd was running low on energy bars and, indeed, energy. So he just sat there while Billy huffed and sniffed and cried. And sometimes Todd cried too.

There was one final call, and it was not like the others. Billy sounded different again. Weak, but determined, like a kitten at the bottom of a well that was doing its darnedest to get out again.

"Todd," he said. *"I know you're there 'cos I can see you."*

Todd started. He looked out the window, but it was night and there was nothing there but the moon.

"I know you're listening right now, too," Billy said. *"I can see you, sitting at that thing, letting it use you."*

Todd actually looked around. "Billy," he said, and immediately felt foolish.

"I suspect I don't have much time," said Billy. *"It's got—"*

And he giggled. It wasn't a very nice giggle.

"It's got its teeth into me," he said.

Todd felt his guts freeze at that. He had no idea what Billy meant, but he doubted he was talking about his drink problem. Todd was pretty sure Billy was using neither metaphor nor simile. He was talking about real fucking teeth.

"So I'll just say this," Billy went on. *"Whatever you're doing, you better stop now. I know you're going to say you can't stop. Listen to me, you fucking jerk. I loathe you. I always did. But what I say now I say for the good of your soul. Which I maintain is a separate and more deserving entity."*

Todd remained silent. He had never heard Billy talk like this. Probably nobody had since about 1957.

"Stop it now. Walk away. It'll hurt, but you can do it. If you don't…"

The giggle again.

"Well," said Billy. *"It's got plenty of teeth for everyone."* And he rang off.

After that, there were no more calls.

The next day, Todd was surprised to wake up in his own bed. He had no idea how he'd got there, but he wasn't too fussed. Somehow he had gotten into bed and slept. He still felt like he'd been pushed off a cliff, and he was still wearing an (apparently full) adult diaper, but he'd had worse hangovers and, more importantly, he wasn't sitting in his study typing.

He examined his fingers in the mid-morning light. They were battered, bloody, and looked like he'd used them to claw his way out of a lead coffin. But they were his again.

Todd slowly lowered himself out of the bed, trying not to look at the sores on his thigh, and ran his hand absently over his beard. It felt filthy and dull, as did the rest of his hair.

"Time for a bath," he said, and made his way gingerly into the bathroom.

As the bath was running, Todd treated himself to a few minutes on the toilet, enjoying—despite his very painful ass—his first unfettered bowel movement since he didn't know when. He drained a tooth glass full of cool clear tap water. He got up, flushed, and went into the bathroom to brush his teeth.

The face in the mirror was not a pretty one.

"Shit," Todd said. "I look like Charles Manson."

He rummaged in a drawer for a pair of Janis's scissors and began to hack away at his facial hair. He went over to the bath and poured in everything fragrant that he could find. He turned the bath off and got in.

Immediately an orchestra of pain started a symphony in his nether regions. Todd just gritted his teeth and waited for the agony to subside. When it finally did, he closed his eyes, ducked his head under water, and counted to a hundred. Then with a gasp he sat upright in the bath again. He repeated this process several times until he was sure he could now run his hands through his hair to wash it.

An hour later, washed, shaved, and with enough antiseptic cream on his nethers to stifle a horse, Todd felt able to venture back into his study, cautiously like a man who fears there might be a dead body in the room. What he saw was a far from pleasing sight. The desk and floor were littered with crumpled wrappers, empty bottles, and crushed cartons. There were spots of blood on the rug and on the typewriter. And the place stank. It stank of Todd, and what came out of Todd.

Todd was about to throw open every window he could find when he stopped. Next to the typewriter, stacked with an almost inhuman neatness, was a thick pile of paper, the size of a large cornflake packet. Todd approached it gingerly, as though it were going to (*teeth*) bite him. He picked up the first sheet.

ALL MY COLORS
by Todd Milstead

Todd flicked through the sheets of paper. They were impeccably typed, neatly laid out and the product of a more orderly mind than his. After a moment's thought, he flipped the stack over and pulled out the last page. It said simply:

The End

Todd was about to go back and read the last part of the story when something (*teeth*) made him stop. He put the paper back in the right order, found a clean and empty cardboard box—the kind with thick sides and even thicker staples to hold it together—to store it in, and put the box and manuscript on a high shelf, just for safety. Then he threw open every window he could find.

"Now what?" Todd said out loud and his inner voice answered, *a smoke'd be nice.* Todd realized as the words came into his mind that he hadn't had tobacco since he'd started writing the book. He'd had no cravings either, which was weird because normally after ten minutes without his pipe or a cigarette, Todd would be jonesing for a tobacco hit. But he was feeling the itch again, the irritation which meant it was time to light up.

Todd found a pouch of tobacco and his pipe and was looking for some matches or a lighter when the phone rang again. He was tempted to let the answerphone take it, just for old times' sake, but that was too much a reminder of how he'd been spending the last few—the last few days or weeks, he had no idea, but the last few anyway. So Todd lifted the receiver and said:

"Milstead residence, Todd Milstead speaking."

"Milstead? This is Pete Fenton."

Todd's mind had been so far away from reality lately that for a moment he had no idea who Pete Fenton might be. Then it came to him. The lawyer.

"Mr. Fenton, good to hear from you—"

"I doubt that. Milstead, before we go on, I want you to speak to Alice."

"Alice?"

"My secretary. You used profanities down the line to her

last time you called here. I would like you to apologize to her, personally."

Jeez, lighten up, Todd thought. In truth, he had no memory of speaking to Alice, let alone swearing at her, but what the fuck, if this born-again douche with a broom-handle up his rear end was so pussy-whipped as to let his secretary push him around, what business was that of Todd's? So he waited while Alice huffed onto the line and he said:

"Alice, this is Todd Milstead. I'm very sorry if anything I said or did may have offended you."

There was a moment of silence while the uptight old spinster processed Todd's words and then she said, "That's all right. Thank you, Mr. Milstead."

Fenton came back on the line. "Okay," he said.

"Okay," echoed Todd. *Some people,* he thought as he filled his briar.

"I understand from Alice," said Fenton, in a voice way more formal than he'd used last time they spoke, "that you have some information concerning your wife's activities."

"Yes I do," said Todd, finally discerning the real reason for the call. *Money.* "I witnessed something which I feel may alter the nature of the divorce... settlement."

"I see," said Fenton. "According to my secretary, what you witnessed was—and I quote—'My wife's fucking some other guy.'"

"Yeah," said Todd. "I didn't actually see her fu— sleep with him, but I did see them go into a diner together."

"A diner?" said Fenton. "And after they went into the diner, is that when they fucked?"

"Excuse me?" said Todd. "No, of course not."

"The parking lot then?" said Fenton. "Did she fuck the other guy in the parking lot?"

"I don't know," said Todd. "I mean, no of course not. Fenton, whose side are you on?"

"Nobody's side, Mr. Milstead," said Fenton smoothly. "I'm a lawyer."

"Goddammit, you're my lawyer," snarled Todd.

"I haven't seen any documents to that effect," said Fenton. "And no money has changed hands."

"I'll bring over a check right away," Todd said, almost choking with rage.

"Okay then," said Fenton brightly. "Let's start again. You witnessed your wife and another man... being intimate."

Todd took a deep breath.

"I didn't exactly witness anything," he said. "But I implied it."

"You inferred it," said Fenton, immediately moving himself from Todd's mental list of assholes to his mental list of complete and utter assholes. "You saw your wife and another man go into the diner where they—what?"

"They ordered food together," said Todd, feeling foolish. "And the food arrived, and they began to eat it."

"Began to eat it?" asked Fenton. "Do you mean that something interrupted their meal?"

"Yes," said Todd, feeling more foolish. "It was me. I was—compelled—to step into the parking lot and they became... aware of me."

Fenton paused for a moment. Todd had a feeling the bastard was beginning to enjoy himself.

"A while back, I heard from a cop friend about a little

fracas outside Bill's Tire Shop," he said. "Which is next to Roberta's Diner, I believe."

"What of it?" said Todd.

"Oh, nothing," Fenton said. "Just interesting. I know from Alice that Janis goes there sometimes. Wondered if it might be the same place. That's all."

Todd said nothing.

"Apparently, or so the cop told me, Bill had to punch a guy because he was some kind of peeping Tom," Fenton continued, almost blithely. "But I guess these are two isolated incidents."

Todd's knuckles were as white as ivory.

"Could we," he said with what he hoped was calm restraint, "get back to me?"

"I'm sorry, I thought we were talking about you," said Fenton. "Concerning the incident you witnessed, I mean."

Todd put the receiver carefully down on the side table. He drew back his fist and punched the wall, hard enough to make a small crater in it. He paused to let the pain sink in and then picked up the receiver again.

"Sorry, Milstead, I thought I lost you for a moment there," said Fenton.

"I'm here," said Todd through gritted teeth.

"Look," said Fenton, tired of the weak sport and wanting to throw his catch back in now, "unless you have documentary evidence of your wife being with another man, this news of yours will have no effect whatsoever on your divorce settlement. And even then... the courts tend to favor a no-fault divorce these days, you know."

"They tend to favor the *bitch*!" shouted Todd, and

slammed the receiver down. The mouthpiece flew off and hit him in the eye.

"Motherfucker!" he shouted and slammed the entire phone into the wall again and again, hearing it ding senselessly before it smashed. Todd dropped it and slumped to the floor, head in hands.

There was no escape. That damn cow was going to take him for everything he had. He was going to be the loser he'd always secretly feared he might be. No friends, no money, no luck: this would be the Todd Milstead story from now on. Unless he could get the book published. Visions of dollar bills literally danced before Todd's eyes: like a cartoon character, he imagined himself signing book deals, receiving huge checks, being fellated by book groupies, and generally achieving undreamed-of levels of fame.

For a moment, he imagined himself being interviewed.

"Where do you get your ideas from?" asked the buxom young interviewer.

"Where does anyone get their ideas from?" replied Todd, no longer slumped against a wall but sitting relaxed in a TV studio. "Experience, practice, imagination…"

"And theft," said the buxom interviewer. "Do you remember this voice?"

Todd looked around. A voice filled the air. A bubbling, drunk voice.

"He stole 'em!" said the voice of Billy Cairns. "He took 'em from a book!"

Gasps in the studio audience as Billy walked in, carrying a heavy sack.

"He stole the whole thing," shouted Billy as he opened the bag

and, from it, took copies of a big thick book, which he threw into the audience. "He stole it from Jake Turner!"

A book hit Todd in the chest. ALL MY COLORS by JAKE TURNER it said.

"Billy!" Todd shouted as the audience began to boo. "I'm your friend! Why are you doing this to me?"

Billy turned to Todd, and for the first time Todd saw Billy's face properly. It was a mass of tiny bloody marks, miniature gashes, like some small animal had been gnawing at it, with its small, sharp, unrelenting teeth.

"Thief!" shouted Billy. "Thief!" the audience joined in. "Thief!" every voice in the room shouted. Except for one voice. One small, sharp, unrelenting voice.

It wasn't shouting, "Thief!" It was shouting, "Teeth!"

Todd came to, sweating.

One thing about Todd Milstead, he knew when to ignore a hint. Put Todd Milstead in a Victorian Christmas story, have him visited by three Christmas ghosts, and at the very last he'd still be maintaining it was someone else's fault and what the fuck was Bob Cratchit bitching about anyway.

Todd went into his study. He got down the boxed manuscript. Then he got out his secondhand copy of the *American Publishers' Directory*, and began flicking through it and writing down telephone numbers.

The first number Todd rang was out of service. The second was answered by a woman who said they didn't take unsolicited manuscripts and, when Todd asked how you could get a book published without sending it to people who you didn't know already, put the phone down. The third said they would happily take Todd's manuscript for a reader's fee, and when Todd asked what a reader's fee was and they told him, Todd put the phone down.

The fourth person was helpful.

"We would need to see the first three chapters," she said. "Or the first ten thousand words, it's really up to you."

"I can do that," Todd said. "I have the whole thing written."

Something in Todd's tone must have made her wary, or else she was used to people telling her that all the time. Either way the smile in her voice sounded more strained when she said, "You need to enclose a self-addressed envelope for return of the manuscript and, if it is lost in transit, we can accept no responsibility."

Todd made five or six more calls, and realized quite quickly that this was the standard response to unsolicited authors. Which was fine. He knew *All My Colors* would be accepted straightaway.

After all, he thought, *it's already been published once.*

Todd took himself to Staples, where he asked for and was given directions to the photocopier. He spent a large part of his remaining disposable income making six copies of his manuscript, and a slightly smaller portion mailing them out to the more reputable-sounding publishers.

Coming out of the post office, he almost bumped into Pete Fenton with Alice. If Todd thought it was unusual for a lawyer to take afternoon walks with his secretary, he said nothing: he knew there was a Mrs. Fenton but what was that to do with him? Todd considered himself a liberal and broadminded sort and besides, Alice turned out to be less frowsty-looking in the flesh.

Pete must have read something in Todd's expression, because he said, "Mr. Milstead, I've been thinking about your situation."

"How kind of you," said Todd.

"I know Mrs. Milstead's lawyer. Kevin Coughlan," said Pete. "And he's a 'grab 'em by the throat' kind of guy. I've known women go to him wanting nothing from the divorce but to get away from their husbands. Some of them are even prepared to let the man keep the kids. And they come out of his office swearing they'll take their husband for everything he's got."

Alice tutted sympathetically. So did Todd, whose own view on kids was that they should be raised on distant farms until they were old enough to work.

"What's your point, may I ask?" he said, politely enough.

"This," said Fenton. "Given Coughlan's reputation, and your own situation as regards Janis—your adultery, your drinking, and so on…"

Todd didn't like the "and so on" but he said nothing.

"… it seems likely that Coughlan is going to advise Janis to, er, take you down."

"Take me down?" echoed Todd.

"Take you down like a lion takes down a warthog," said Alice. Todd looked at her and she smiled back sweetly.

"He'll take you for all you've got and then some," added Pete. "Unless—"

"Unless?" said Todd, who was wearying of his apparent

role as Greek chorus to the all-wise Fenton.

"Unless," and here Fenton shot a guilty look at Alice, "unless there really is something in this story of yours about her and another man."

"What about all that *no fault* stuff you were coming out with before?" said Todd.

"I'll see you later, Pete," said Alice, and at that moment Todd suspected he was coming between them. He didn't give a fuck.

"It's reputation," said Fenton. "This is a small town. If you had some dirt on Janis, it wouldn't matter if a divorce court gave her the house and the money. Might even make it look worse. If you can prove that she's seeing someone else, it makes her look like a slut."

"But what about me seeing someone else?" said Todd.

"You've got nothing to lose, Janis does," said Fenton. "Like I say. Reputation."

Fenton was looking worriedly in Alice's direction now.

"I have to go," he said. "Here. Call this guy."

He thrust a card into Todd's hand and strode off. Todd looked at the card.

JACK BEHM, it read. **PRIVATE INVESTIGATIONS.**

THREE

As a connoisseur of film noir, Todd was pleased with Jack Behm's office. Everything was in place: the wooden desk with drawers presumably containing both revolver and whiskey bottle, the filing cabinet full of case notes, the dirty windows overlooking some mean streets, and best of all, in a standard-issue 1950s swivel chair, Jack Behm himself.

Behm looked more hard-boiled than an egg with a drinking problem. His eyes were narrow and red, his cheekbones high and stubbled, and his bony yellow fingers were constantly lifting cigarettes to a narrow and suspicious-looking mouth. He looked at Todd with an expression that was both interested and keen to show a complete lack of interest. Todd liked him immediately.

"How'd you get my number?" said Behm, and began coughing. It was a horrible cough, like an old car being started up, and it didn't end for what seemed like minutes. When he'd finished, and wiped his mouth with the back of his hand, Behm looked up at Todd, still waiting for an answer.

"My lawyer," said Todd, "Pete Fenton."

"That asshole," said Behm encouragingly. Todd had no disagreement with this point of view.

"Sit down," said Behm. Todd waited for Behm to pour him a slug or whatever private eyes were supposed to do next, but no slug was forthcoming. Instead Behm drew heavily on his almost extinct cigarette and said, "Pete Fenton," in a thoughtful voice.

"That's right," said Todd, wondering if this conversation was going to take all night, "Pete Fenton."

"You fucking his wife?" said Behm.

"No," said Todd.

"Okay," said Behm. "Good to know."

"Why would—"

"You fucking him?"

"No!" Todd said.

"Calm down," said Behm. "Just checking there's no loose threads that might unravel later."

Todd was not consoled.

"I'm not that way inclined," he said.

"Like I care," said Behm. "Besides, I know he's fucking his secretary. So why are you here?"

I'm starting to wonder, thought Todd. But he said, "I believe you can help me."

And he unrolled the whole sorry tale, playing down the part where he and Sara were having an affair, and talking up the part where he thought Janis was having an affair. All the while he talked, Behm took no notes, and stared intently at Todd.

"I see," he said when Todd had finally finished talking. "You're not telling me everything."

"I am—" Todd began.

"About the affair, if that's what it is, yeah," said Behm. "But you're not telling me *everything*."

"You want to know the name of my first date?" said Todd. "Where I went to school? The first time I got drunk?"

"No," said Behm. "Just whatever it is you don't want me to know. Doesn't matter. I'll find out. I usually do."

Yeah, right, Todd thought, *and good luck with that*. He smiled and said, "Whatever you say, Mr. Behm. How much do you charge?"

Behm told him. Todd didn't like it. He didn't have a choice, though.

"You like whiskey," said Behm.

"Yeah, why do you ask?" said Todd.

"It wasn't a question," said Behm, and got up from behind his desk. Todd noticed that he had a pronounced limp. *L-I-M-P, pronounced limp*, he thought to himself. Behm dragged a tatty hat from a coat stand and headed for the door.

"Come on," he said, and Todd followed him out the door.

"See," said Behm as they settled themselves in a leatherette booth in a local bar Todd had never noticed before, "I like to get to know my clients. Find out what's behind the mask, so to speak."

"I just want you to do some surveillance," said Todd.

"I know you do," said Behm. "Everybody does. They think I'm gonna hide across the street from some bastard's house, take pictures with the car window down, and produce *evidence*."

"That's pretty much what I'm looking for," said Todd. "What's wrong with that?"

"What's wrong with *evidence*?" said Behm, harshly. "*Evidence* is just—" He made a chopping gesture with his hand. "—just a slice of time. A knife through the air. Take this, for example," he said, and pulled a crumpled snapshot from his wallet.

Todd, who knew a man with a hobbyhorse when he saw one, took the photograph by its edges and studied it.

"What do you think you're looking at there?" said Behm.

"A man and a woman, naked, lying on a bed," said Todd. "You collect these?"

"First off, don't ever cheek me," said Behm. "Second, I don't collect anything except maybe headaches, one of which you are currently giving me. And third, you're wrong. That's not a man and a woman, it's a woman and a boy. Not even a bed either, not that it matters. It's a ditch full of snow. Looks a bit like a counterpane, I guess."

Todd handed the photograph back.

"You've made your point," he said, irritated. "Things are not always what they seem. Thank you for that insight."

"I'm getting another headache," said Behm. "Yeah, things are not what they seem. Things can be misinterpreted, manipulated, changed. A photograph, even a film, can be altered or just read wrong. More whiskey."

When he'd worked out that the last part of Behm's speech wasn't connected to the first, Todd bought more whiskey.

"Your case is boring," said Behm. "You were fucking someone so your wife wants out. So you want people to

76

believe she's fucking someone else."

"She is fucking someone else," Todd insisted.

"Sure," said Behm. "Even if it's true, it's boring. And you still aren't telling me something,"

Todd said nothing. He really had nowhere to start with that.

"But that's okay, I'm not your mother," said Behm. "Or your shrink. I'm just saying, I can't get to the bottom of this unless I have all the facts."

"All right," said Todd. "I have no money, I have no prospects and my wife's going to screw me."

"That feels like a prelude to me," said Behm.

Todd took a deep breath. "You wouldn't believe me," he said.

"I don't believe anybody," said Behm. He drained his glass. "Time to go. I'll take your case, because there's something in there that interests me. Maybe when we get to know each other better, you'll tell me."

He got up. Todd thought for a moment. "What about the woman and the boy? In the snow?"

"It's just a picture I carry around," said Behm, and left.

Time passed. Todd sat around at home. There were messages from Janis (but not, thank God, from Billy). No publishers rang. Behm didn't ring. Every so often, Todd would slide a sheet of paper into the typewriter and wait for something to happen. Nothing did. Days went by like this.

And then one morning, there was a knock on Todd's door. Todd all but ran into the hall and yanked the front door open.

"Delivery for you," said the person at the door. It was Sara, and she was holding three large packages. "I found this on the step," she added.

Todd took them.

"Thanks," he said, and turned the first package over. It was from one of the publishers he'd written to. So were the others. *Return to sender*, Todd thought.

"Can I come in?" said Sara, after Todd had stared grimly at the packages for almost a minute.

"What? Sure, I guess so," said Todd, still numb from rejection.

"Gosh, thank you," said Sara as she followed Todd into the house.

"Are you okay?" Sara said when she'd got Todd a beer from the fridge and a glass of water for herself.

"Sure," said Todd. "Why do you ask?"

"Gee, I don't know," said Sara. "Maybe it's because you didn't return my calls. Maybe it's because you're acting like you can hardly see me. Maybe it's because you lost fifteen pounds. Maybe it's because nobody's seen you for weeks. Or maybe it's all of that."

She leaned toward Todd, and touched his face.

"Besides, you pompous, vain, arrogant, self-obsessed, rude bastard," she said, "I missed you."

Half an hour later, Todd rolled over in bed.

"You're a lot lighter now," said Sara approvingly. "I like being able to get my legs around your waist."

Something was troubling Todd. "Have you had any calls from Janis lately?" he said.

"You old romantic," said Sara, and there was an edge beneath the breeziness. "No, Janis is staying away. Maybe—" and the breeziness was back, "she's playing away as well."

"That's what I'm counting on," said Todd, and he told Sara about what he'd seen at the diner.

"Wow, Janis, you dog," said Sara. "Jesus, if word gets out that Lockjaw Janis is getting some, the universe might just explode in shock."

"Lockjaw Janis?" said Todd.

"Some of us call her that," Sara said, "On account of she never smiles."

She rolled over on Todd, and poked a rib just below his right nipple.

"Guess she's got something to smile about now," said Sara, and moved her hand down toward Todd's crotch.

Todd stopped her, a fact which came as a surprise to both of them.

"What are you doing—"

"You know what I'm doing," said Sara.

"—here," finished Todd.

Sara frowned.

"I'm doing what we always do. We don't do anything else."

"Sara, I haven't seen you since I don't know when," said Todd. "Last time we spoke, you were freaking out about Terry finding out, and Janis making life hard for you. And now here you are, all calm and relaxed."

Todd reached for his beer to clear his throat. It was probably the longest speech he'd made since the Saturday nights of yore.

Sara was looking less breezy now. "I just thought you might want some company," she said. "Janis is gone, and I guess I missed you. You were out of circulation a *long* time."

This was another topic that interested Todd.

"How long exactly?" he said.

"A month," Sara said. "Six weeks maybe."

"Six weeks?" said Todd. *So that's how long it takes to write the Great American Novel*, he thought.

"Yeah," said Sara. "At first I thought you were out of town, but then Yvonne Morris said she thought she saw you driving to the drug store, so I figured sooner or later you'd get back in touch," said Sara. "And here we are."

Todd furrowed his brow in a rare moment of concentration.

"One name you haven't mentioned," he said. "Terry."

There was a moment's silence.

"Terry's gone," said Sara.

Todd flopped onto his back.

"That's not why I'm here!" Sara said.

"Really," said Todd. "Terry moves out, and you come looking for a sugar daddy."

Sara began to shake. Her eyes watered. For a moment Todd thought she might be having some kind of seizure, then he realized she was laughing. A minute or so later, when she had stopped, Sara said:

"Todd, believe me, you are no one's idea of a sugar daddy."

"Then why are you here?" said Todd, revealing new levels of low self-esteem.

"Because I like you," said Sara. "Is that so hard to believe?"

Yes, said a voice inside Todd.

"Look," said Sara. "I can hardly believe it myself, but

I'm glad I'm here, Todd. You know why? Because you're different. I don't just mean different to the other jerks in this town—and I *do* mean 'other jerks'—I mean you're different to how you were."

"Oh really," said Todd. "How so?"

"Well, apart from the sparkling repartee," said Sara dryly, "there's a change in you. I can see it in your face."

She looked into his eyes.

"And not just your face," said Sara.

"No?" said Todd.

"No," said Sara. "It's written all over you."

Sara was in the kitchen making coffee when Todd walked in. He wrapped his robe around him, vaguely noticing that the belt required more tightening than before.

"There he is," said Sara brightly. "The great man. Does the great man want coffee?"

"Yes please," said Todd, and almost exclaimed. It had been a long time since the "p" word had left his lips.

"Todd Milstead is at home to Mr. Manners," said Sara. "I never thought I'd see the day."

She handed him a mug of coffee.

"I feel different, you know," said Todd.

"You do?" Sara said.

"Yeah," said Todd. *Maybe it's getting laid*, said the voice inside him. Todd chose to ignore it.

"A lot of things have happened lately..." he began. *Like you stole someone's book, and your own hands made you poop at your desk, and you hired a detective to follow Janis, oh, and something ate Billy*, said the voice. (Todd chose to continue ignoring it.)

"I know they have," said Sara. "But we're going to sweep all that under the carpet for now."

Easier said than done, said the voice.

That night, as they rested after what Todd reckoned was certainly the most sex, as well as the best sex, he'd ever had, he felt it was safe to ask the one question that could safely be asked.

"I hate to bring it up," he said, "but—"

"Terry," said Sara. "I guess you have a right to know."

"I don't, but thank you," said Todd, and almost bit his lip at this latest burst of niceness.

"I came home the other night," said Sara in the rhythmic tones of someone who had been rehearsing a speech in the car and wanted to get all the details right, "and I found Terry in the front room, packing his bags. Which was kind of odd, because nobody packs in the front room. I mean, that's what bedrooms are for, right? That's where the closets are."

She stopped. "Jesus, I'm rambling already," she said.

"Take your time," said the new, improved, patient-like-a-saint Todd.

"I asked him if he was going on a trip, but I knew he wasn't, because he'd just got back from one," Sara continued. "He didn't say anything at first, just carried on folding shirts. I'll say one thing for Terry, that man can fold clothes like a laundress. If ever the business goes under, he could— I'm rambling again."

She took a sip of Todd's coffee and looked out the window for a moment.

"He put the shirts in the suitcase and closed the lid. Then he stood up, and he said, 'I'm leaving you, Sara.' I asked him why, and he said, 'There's someone else.' At first I thought he meant you, but the way he wasn't catching my eye, I realized, he meant he was seeing someone else."

"Oh, the irony," Todd said.

"Right," said Sara. "Here I am, wondering if I'm about to be hauled over the coals, when Terry gets up and spills his own beans. By now, I'm so surprised I don't know what to say. I mean, Terry? He was okay when I met him but he's let himself go."

"So who is it?" said Todd. "Do I know her?"

"The lucky lady?" said Sara. "You'll have seen her, all right. You may have even spoken to her. Not that you'll remember." For the first time, there was a note of bitterness in her voice.

She turned to Todd. "It's one of his checkout girls," she said. "She's twenty, Todd. She's twenty and she's pregnant."

"Jesus," he said, in disbelief.

"I couldn't believe it," said Sara. "He won't tell me her name, in case, I dunno, I go into the store where she works and start screaming. Like I would do that to a child. A child who's…" Sara began to weep.

"It's okay," Todd said, and put his arm around her. Part of his mind was calculating that this was the most time he had gone without being a dick since high school.

Sara began to sob properly now.

"He's forty-eight," she said. "He's old enough to be her dad. He's old enough to be the baby's granddad. He told me he didn't want kids."

"The bastard," said Todd, and was surprised to find that he meant it.

"She's got him by the balls," said Sara. "He isn't going to know what hit him."

"What about—" Todd hesitated. "What about your future?" he said.

"He says he'll see me right," said Sara. "And I believe him. He's got enough money to do that, and to look after the kid. I mean—"

"I know what you mean," said Todd.

Sara stood up straight and looked into Todd's eyes.

"So you see," she said, "I'm not after a sugar daddy. I'm not after your millions, Todd Milstead. I just want you."

She smiled.

"Stranger things have happened," she said.

"I guess so," said Todd. For a moment, though, he couldn't think of any. He embraced her.

"Stick with me, kid," he said in a voice that sounded quite like Humphrey Bogart's, "You'll be okay."

Todd believed it, too.

Sara wouldn't move in with Todd, even though there was room now that Janis had moved out (a U-Haul had been and gone with all her things, although Todd had no memory of this happening). She didn't want Todd coming to her house, either, because Terry was still fussing in and out, living out of suitcases in a hotel somewhere, before finding a permanent place for himself and his future child bride to live. So Todd found himself in a strange state of suspended bachelorhood, where Sara would stay over, and leave again, and come back, and stay over, and leave again.

Days passed, and turned into weeks. Nothing much happened. It was the quiet time.

Behm called.

"Mr. Milstead, I think I'm wasting your money here," he said. "There's nothing."

"Okay," said Todd.

"Do you want me to continue?"

Todd shrugged, then remembered he was on the phone. "I don't know," he said. Sara was coming over in a half hour. He hadn't even thought of Janis, he realized.

"I was hoping for a more decisive reply," said Behm.

"Where are we financially?" said Todd.

"Well, I haven't spent all your money yet if that's what you mean," said Behm.

"I guess that is what I mean," said Todd. He laughed. "Okay, keep going until the check's spent."

"Sure thing," said Behm, and hung up.

Two more manuscripts came back in the post. Todd was about to throw them away unopened when Sara said, "At least read the letters."

Todd opened the packets, read the letters and ripped them up.

"Okay then," said Sara.

"Nothing I haven't read before," explained Todd.

"Can I at least look at what you wrote?" said Sara.

Todd took her by the shoulders.

"You know in *On the Waterfront* when the guy says he could have been a contender?" he said.

"Yeah," said Sara. "Are you going to tell me you're that guy?"

"I wish," said Todd. He stole a glance at the manuscripts lying on the counter top. "I'm the guy who couldn't have been a contender. Which is fine."

"Really?" said Sara.

"I am," said Todd. He kissed her. "I'm a lover, not a writer," he said. Sara laughed, and kissed him back.

Later that night, just to be sure, Todd took all the manuscripts out back and burned them on a small bonfire. After a moment's thought, he went inside and brought out everything he could find that he'd written, and threw that on the fire too.

Todd watched the pile of paper and card set light and topple to one side, a burning tower of failure.

"We're gonna need a bigger bonfire," he said, and set about looking for more wood.

Janis's lawyer called.

"This is Kevin Coughlan," he said. "I need you to come into my office and sign some papers to begin the process."

Todd thought "the process" sounded a little bit medical. He supposed it was in a way, the extraction of a person from a marriage, or the severing of two conjoined twins. He was about to say yes when he remembered his conversation with Behm.

"I need a little more time," he said.

"Time for what?" said Coughlan. "Mrs. Milstead is very anxious to conclude matters."

"I'll get back to you," said Todd and put the phone down.

Billy called. At least, it could have been Billy. It could have been anyone, really. Or anything. The sound coming from the telephone receiver was like something swallowing. *Or*, Todd thought, *being swallowed*.

"I saw Terry today," said Sara.

"You okay?" Todd asked.

"I guess," she said. "He says he's going to sign the house over to me, as well as make good with the alimony."

"What did you say?" said Todd.

"I said, all right then," said Sara.

"All right then," said Todd.

Mike called.

"Hey, Todd!" he cried, almost delighted, when Todd picked up. "Long time, no speak."

"I've been busy," said Todd, not unpleasantly.

If Mike caught the unexpected tone of not-unpleasantness in Todd's voice, he was careful not to mention it.

"I heard. Buddy, you have been through the mill," he said. "Listen, Joe and I were talking. We understand that you might not want to revive the old literary soirees like we used to have, but it would be…"

Mike was clearly searching for the right word.

"*Good* to see you," he concluded.

Todd thought for a minute.

"Okay," he said.

"Okay what?" said Mike.

"Come over," said Todd. "Saturday night."

"Really?" said Mike.

"You and Joe," said Todd and then, for the hell of it, "And Billy."

"We haven't seen Billy for quite a while," said Mike.

I'll bet, thought Todd.

"You sure about this, Todd?" said Mike.

"Saturday night, seven P.M.," Todd said. "It'll be just like old times."

"Wow," said Sara when he told her that night. "I guess you want me to rustle up a delicious selection of buffet foods."

"No," said Todd. "We can buy some chips and dips, and get some booze. Not too much though."

Sara gave him a weird look, half approval, half appraisal.

"Are you quite yourself?" she asked.

"And maybe some rat poison," said Todd. "Watch the ungrateful motherfuckers puke their guts up."

"That's the Todd I know and love," said Sara.

The funny thing was, Todd thought later, that he was quite himself. Maybe not spending every night mired in whiskey was helping. Maybe the weight loss—which seemed to have settled on the good side of healthy—was contributing to his sense of wellbeing as well as his actual wellbeing. Perhaps it was the ending of his marriage (although there were some loose ends there), or the start of something new with Sara. Quite possibly it was all of these things. All Todd knew was that things had changed, and for the better.

He ran the tap and filled a glass with water.

"To the future!" he said.

"That better be vodka," said Sara, and went back to her list.

No more manuscripts came back. Todd went out in the yard and swept up the ash where his writing career had been. It didn't take long.

Mike called again, to check that Saturday night was still on. He still didn't quite seem to believe Todd when Todd said it was.

Behm called again.

"Has the money gone?" said Todd.

"It's not that," said Behm. "Mr. Milstead, I've been following that lady for weeks now and she's done nothing more exciting than visit her sister."

There was silence on Todd's end of the line.

"Mr. Milstead?" said Behm.

"Janis doesn't have a sister," Todd said.

"I guess we're still on then," said Behm.

There was a knock at the door, and then the bell rang; the person at the door wanted to make really sure that their presence was being registered.

Todd opened the door. Mike was standing there. He looked both nervous and eager.

"I don't have any candy for you," said Todd.

"What?" said Mike.

"You look like a kid trick or treating," said Todd. "Where's Joe?"

Mike looked briefly uncomfortable.

"He couldn't make it," he said.

"I forgive him," said Todd, "I guess. Say, those flowers for me?"

Mike was clutching a small bunch of flowers, wrapped in cellophane.

"These are for you," Mike said to Sara.

"Thanks, Mike," said Sara. "I'll go put them in something."

Mike stood in the hallway, looking expectant.

"This way," said Todd, pushing him into the lounge.

"Will you relax?" Todd said. "Sit back in the seat or something. You're making me feel like someone died and you came to tell me."

Mike's smile was a rictus.

"Sorry, Todd," he said. "It's just been a while."

"He's not used to you being polite," Sara said. "Insult him. Call him a fucking jackass or something."

"Mike, you're a fucking jackass," said Todd, but his heart wasn't in it.

In truth, nobody's heart was in it. The evening went by in fits and starts. Conversations went into cul-de-sacs. There wasn't enough booze (there wasn't *any* whiskey, to Mike's distress). The absence of Janis and the substitution of Sara, who clearly had no intention of spending the evening in the kitchen, reduced the flow of both conversation and snacks. Billy's absence, while a relief in some ways—as Mike would say to Joe a few days later, it changed the air in the room.

And then there was Todd. Only a lunatic would say that they preferred Todd the way he used to be, cawing and carping and mocking and holding forth, but this new Todd—he was unsettling the way he seemed to be listening to what people were saying, rather than waiting until they'd finished speaking so he could jump in with a sarcastic putdown or a prepared witticism. Todd seemed interested in Mike but—if they were honest—he also seemed to be appraising him, like tonight was a test. A test of what, nobody knew.

When eleven came and Sara started yawning, everybody was relieved to take it as a cue to head on home.

"That went well, I think," said Todd as he helped Sara clear the bowls of snack food and the beer cans from the lounge.

"That was weird," Mike said to Joe the next day, when they went for a beer together.

"That was amazing," said Sara lying in bed and stroking Todd's chest.

Billy Cairns didn't say anything. How could he? There was no longer any part of Billy capable of speaking.

"Where are we going?" said Sara as Todd opened the Volvo's passenger door for her.

"I just feel like going for a drive," said Todd.

"I see the holiday mood is continuing," Sara teased. Todd smiled back, a little tensely. A holiday was something that couldn't last.

"A penny for your thoughts," Sara said, as Todd got in the car.

"I was just thinking about an old joke," Todd said, starting the engine and pulling out into the road.

"And now Todd Milstead is telling jokes," said Sara. "Wonders will never cease."

"Guy goes to Hell," said Todd, "and Satan shows him two fields, both full of shit. Like four feet deep in actual shit."

"Charming."

"One field of shit is full of people standing on their heads, and in the other, all the people are also in shit but they're standing up and drinking coffee and eating donuts."

"I don't think that's in Dante."

"And Satan says to the guy, which field would you like to go in? And the guy's not dumb, he says, the field where everyone is standing up, drinking coffee and eating donuts."

"Reasonable."

"In the blink of an eye, the guy finds himself in that field. And he's just about to say hi to his neighbor when Satan grabs a loud hailer and shouts, 'THAT'S IT, FOLKS! COFFEE BREAK'S OVER!'"

A few minutes later, they were driving into town when Todd had an idea.

"I've never bought you anything," he said.

"You bought me dinner," said Sara. "And a few cocktails."

"Come on," said Todd, and turned into a side street.

"Wow," said Sara. "I haven't been here in a long time. Is that old fraud still running the place?"

"Sure is," said Todd. He parked opposite Legolas Books and got out.

"I guess by now anybody else would have torched the

place for the insurance," Sara said as they crossed the road to the store.

The bell tinkled behind them as they went in, giving Timothy time to put away the calculator he was using to add up the previous week's sales and to instead pick up a slim volume of Carlos Castaneda.

"Hey, pilgrim!" he greeted Todd. "I see you brought a friend."

"Morning, Timothy," said Todd, moving off immediately toward the shelves.

"And how can I help a beautiful lady on a beautiful day?" asked Timothy, whose interest in ladies, beautiful or otherwise, was largely confined to photographs of them in specialist European publications.

"I have no idea why I'm here," said Sara. "But it certainly is a pleasure to be inside this marvelously quaint old store."

Fuck you, thought Timothy, who was no stranger to sarcasm with a smile. "Why, thank you," he said. "'Tis a small thing, but all mine own. To quote the poet."

Timothy had no idea which poet he was quoting, or even if he was quoting: as far as he knew, he could be saying the first weak shit that came into his shiny bald head. But it must have done the trick, because the woman looked impressed.

"You still looking for that mystery tome?" Timothy said and was surprised to see Todd turn around abruptly, as if about to— what? Tell him to shut up?

"No," said Todd, forcing a smile. "I found it, actually."

"Really?" said Timothy. "Have you been seeing... other bookstores?"

"Of course not," Todd said, apparently not caring to join

in the merry banter. "As it turns out, I had it at home all the time."

"Well, there we go," Timothy said. "A man with so many books, he doesn't know what's in his own library. I know the feeling!"

And Timothy gestured around the store, as if to say, "This may not be the Great Library of Alexandria but to me it is the finest repository of books in all the world." He even thought of actually saying it, but decided that it might be some bull too far.

"How then can I help you today?" he said.

"I'm looking for a book for this lady," said Todd.

"I was hoping for jewels, or furs," said Sara. "But I guess a book will do. I'm joking," she added to Timothy. "I love books."

"Well, you've come to the right place," said Timothy. He made a decision. "This may not be the Great Library of Alexandria but to me it is the finest repository of books in all the world."

"Isn't that wonderful?" said Sara, clearly possessed of a bullshit detector of her own.

Timothy decided to ignore the cow.

"Did you have a particular book in mind, sir?" he asked mock-genteelly.

"Yes," said Todd.

"Here we go," Sara said. "The books men buy for women. *Fear of Flying. The Joy of Sex. Jonathan Livingston Seagull*."

"All classics of their kind," said Timothy, who would have gone under in 1972 without *Jonathan Livingston Seagull*. "May I enquire as to your own tastes?"

Sara was too wise to fall for this. "Oh, I have no tastes," she said. "Or taste. Right, Todd?"

She laughed, but Todd wasn't laughing back. Instead he was standing beside her, an old hardback in his hand.

"Where the heck did *that* come from?" said Timothy.

"I found it on the cart," said Todd.

"Old stock," said Timothy. "All that stuff is destined for the dumper."

"Not the goodwill?" said Sara. "Not the old folks' home or the prison library?"

Timothy, who was actually going to sell his old stock as a job lot at auction next month, suspected he might actually hate Sara.

"Good idea, miss," he said in his kindly old fucker voice. "I might just do that."

"Well, if you're giving your old stock away," said Sara, with just a hint of a smile in her voice, "you should let Todd have this one for nothing."

Timothy almost swallowed his own tongue in anger.

"*Another* good idea!" he cried, feeling bile mingle with saliva in his mouth. "And Mr. Milstead's been such a good customer over the years that I'm sure the gods of literature won't begrudge him one small—"

"Thank you," said Sara, cutting Timothy off mid-flow.

"Thanks, Timothy," Todd said, sounding as though he meant it, too. He handed the book to Sara. "It's old, I know, and it's been around the block, and—let me finish, please— and I'm *sure* you've read it, be a bit weird if you hadn't, but this is the book that made me want to be..."

He stopped. "—well, it's an important book. To me, anyway."

Sara looked at the book.

"*The Catcher in the Rye*," she said. "Wow, I haven't read this since high school. Thank you, Todd."

She kissed him. Then she opened the book.

"It's a first edition," she said to Timothy. "Lucky Todd saved it from the dumper."

"I couldn't possibly give it to you, I'm afraid," Timothy began.

Sara's face fell.

"But you said I could take anything," she said. She looked stricken.

"I did say that," Timothy agreed. "But—"

"You did say that," Todd intervened.

"Folks," Timothy said, agitated, "I really don't know what to say, but that fu— that book is not leaving this store."

"Relax, I'm kidding," Sara said. "It's not a first edition." She opened it and showed Timothy. "You only had to look," she added, putting the book in her bag.

Timothy was too much gripped by fury and hate to respond. Todd opened the door for Sara and they exited to the silvery tinkle of the bookstore bell. Timothy shut the door, flipped the OPEN sign to CLOSED and spent a few minutes in the bathroom shouting obscenities into the toilet until he felt a little better.

"You fucked him over," said Todd, admiringly. "You fucked Timothy over."

He looked at Sara in amazement.

"Guess I'd better read it now," said Sara.

"What?"

"Look at your face. You look like my mom did when I told her I had smoked dope."

"You smoke dope?" said Todd.

"Yeah, want me to get some?" Sara said.

Todd was about to reply when he saw someone standing outside the house. It was Behm.

"Excuse me a moment," he said, and walked up to the front door.

"Hi there," said Behm, and coughed up a fusillade.

"Is everything all right?" Todd asked.

"I'm sorry to come up to the house," Behm said. "But I couldn't get you on the phone and I needed to see you in person."

"All right," said Todd.

He walked back to the car.

"Do you know that guy?" said Sara.

"In a manner of speaking," Todd said.

"He looks like he returned from the grave and he can't wait to get back there," Sara said.

"I have to speak to him for a moment."

Sara gave Todd an appraising look.

"Okay," she said. "I have some things to do at home. Call me later?"

"I only meant I need to talk to this guy for a—"

"I know." Sara was already retreating. "Call me!"

Todd went back to the house. Behm was lighting a cigarette.

"She the new lady?" he said.

"Mind your own business," Todd said.

"No problem," said Behm and followed Todd into the house.

Todd gave Behm an ashtray and a glass of water. Behm put the glass to one side and set the ashtray in front of him at the kitchen table. Then he pulled out a thin buff envelope from his jacket and dropped it onto the table.

"What's this?" said Todd, although he had a pretty good idea what it was.

"What you pay me for," said Behm. "Open it."

Inside was a set of grainy black and white photographs. Todd flipped through them.

"When were these— when did you take these?" he asked Behm.

"Over the course of three, four days," said Behm. "All over town."

Todd nodded. "Night shots, too?"

"I spend your dollar wisely," Behm said.

Todd picked up a print. "Where's this?"

"Outside a bar in midtown."

"Janis doesn't go to bars."

"Maybe she just likes to stand outside them."

"You didn't follow her in?"

"I would have stood out."

Todd looked at Behm. "I don't get you."

Behm pulled out two more prints.

"You don't really know this town, do you, Mr. Milstead?"

"I've lived here most of my life," Todd said.

Behm pointed to a photograph of Janis outside a different bar. "That's Janis outside Flagg's Bar," he said.

"Never heard of it," said Todd.

"No reason why you should," Behm said. He picked up another print.

"Laura's Place," he said. "Doubt you heard of that one either."

Todd shrugged. "Where are we going with this?" he asked.

In answer, Behm took a red matchbook from his pocket. LAURA'S PLACE it said in brutal black letters. He flipped it over. On the back was a drawing, not too badly executed, of two androgynous figures embracing.

"Laura's Place is a gay bar," said Behm. "So is Flagg's."

"Gay?" said Todd. "But Janis isn't a man."

Behm looked at him.

"Nor," he said, "is the person she's been seeing."

"Well, I think it's pretty cool," Sara said. Todd had gone straight around to hers after writing Behm another check.

"Explains a lot, I guess," said Todd.

"You mean she never liked you because she never liked guys?" said Sara. "I think that's a little simplistic, Todd."

"What other explanation could there be?" Todd said.

"Maybe we should go into this some other time," Sara said. "It's late."

Todd agreed. It was all too much for him.

"This guy you hired to follow Janis," said Sara. "Did he say who she is?"

"Who?" said Todd.

Sara raised an eyebrow. "The woman she's seeing, of course."

When Todd got home, he poured himself a whiskey for the first time in he didn't know when, drank it, thought about having another, decided against it, and went to bed. He tried to read for a while, but the only book he could find was an old paperback that Janis had left behind, and after wasting a half hour trying to find clues about her secret life by reading *Watership Down*, Todd gave up and drifted into uneasy slumber.

That night, Todd dreamed he was back in Legolas Books.

"Hi, Timothy," said Todd as the bell tinkled behind him.

But Timothy didn't reply. He was bent over something at the counter.

"Nose deep in a book as usual?" said Todd.

"Not exaffly," Timothy said in a muffled voice and turned around. He was face deep in Todd's copy of *The Catcher in the Rye*, shredding it with his teeth like a dog tearing into a ragdoll.

"Good book?" said Todd, taken aback. Timothy spat a few pages out. Todd could see his teeth, jagged and gunmetal gray.

"I'm devouring it," said Timothy, and grinned.

Todd woke early, remembered the dream, shuddered, shrugged, and went downstairs to make coffee. He put Behm's prints back in their envelope—that could all be dealt with later—and picked up the phone in the hall to call Sara. Then he hesitated. He picked up the envelope and spread the photos out on the table again.

There was something here he was missing. Todd was sure of it. But what? Todd looked from print to print. Janis outside Flagg's. Janis outside Laura's Place. Janis getting into her car... Then it came to him. They were all Janis. But

Behm had been clear: Janis was seeing someone else. So why wasn't the other person in the photos?

Todd was about to pick up the phone when it rang. He answered it at once.

"Hello, Milstead residence, Todd Milstead speaking?"

It was a woman. She sounded breathless.

"Mr. Milstead, this is Nora Franklyn."

"Hi."

"From Franklyn and Sullivan."

"I'm sorry—"

"The publishers. You sent us your manuscript? *All My Colors*."

"Oh, right. Did I not put a return address on the packet?"

"Mr. Milstead, we are very excited about *All My Colors* and we'd like you to come to New York to discuss it."

Todd held the phone out like it was a tiny crying baby.

"Excuse me?" he said.

Now Nora Franklyn was sounding slightly less breathless and slightly more tetchy, like a bringer of good news who feels that her good news-bringing is not getting the overwhelming joyful response that it deserves.

"Mr. Milstead, we feel that *All My Colors* is an extremely saleable work. I've already taken the liberty of showing it to one or two of my colleagues and I can confirm that they think the same as we do."

"Okay," said Todd, who wasn't so much lost for words as abandoned by words in a deep forest and left to the wolves. "I—when can you—when do you want to see me?"

"Tomorrow would be great," said Nora. "My secretary will call you with the details."

"New York tomorrow?" said Todd. "Okay," he added, again.

"Goodbye, Mr. Milstead. It's going to be a real pleasure working with you," said Nora Franklyn, and she put the phone down.

Todd continued to stare at the telephone receiver for several minutes, until eventually his arm began to ache and he had to put it down again.

"Yes, I wrote it," said To

"Then go out there ar

Sara kissed him on

Todd's flight

He declin

just suc

Sara drove Todd to the airport.

"I am nervous," Todd admitted.

"Don't be," Sara said. "They want your book, don't they? Your book," she teased, "that you wrote without telling anyone."

"I was going to tell someone," said Todd. "I just—didn't know if it would turn out."

"All that time, working on it," Sara said, marveling. "And all the time during the Saturday nights with the boys and all the trouble with Janis. No wonder you were kind of tetchy."

"Tetchy's one word for it," Todd said.

"Yeah well, I don't have time to list all the other words for it." Sara smiled. Todd tried to smile back.

"Todd," said Sara. She put her hands on his shoulders. "You wrote this book, didn't you?"

"Excuse me?" Todd almost stammered.

"It's a rhetorical question."

103

dd. "Of course I did."

d get 'em."

the lips.

as relatively short and not too uncomfortable. d a free drink and tried to nap instead. He had eeded when the plane began its descent.

Todd carried his sole bag through the concourse and was about to start looking for the transit stop when he saw a huge young man holding a piece of card with MILSTEAD written on it.

"Is that for me?" he asked. "I'm Todd Milstead."

"Then it's you," said the huge young man. "Welcome to New York. I'm Barry."

Barry took Todd's bag in a hand so large that the action reminded Todd of Gulliver picking up a barrel of beer. "Follow me," he said.

"New York's cold for the time of year," said Barry. He wasn't wrong. Everything around them was gray or white, except the sky, which was both. Barry led Todd to a large gray sedan, opened the trunk to let it swallow Todd's bag, and then opened the sedan's door for Todd.

Todd slid inside. Barry started the engine and the sedan nosed its way out of the airport parking lot.

"Ever been to New York before?" said Barry.

"Few times," said Todd, by which he meant he'd been once.

"Great city, despite what they say," Barry said.

Todd had to take his word for that, as they were now enveloped in rolling clouds of sleet. When he could see anything, it was boarded up and covered in angular, sprawling graffiti.

"Manhattan," said Barry as they cruised past Times Square. Now Todd could see through the snow, not the wealthy socialites of his favorite noir movies, but an entire city of people swathed up in huge coats, heads wrapped in what looked like gray rags, huddled around braziers, walking through clouds of steam belched from subways, and all dodging around hundreds—no, thousands—of yellow taxi cabs. Todd wondered how it was that there were so many cabs and yet so few people were having any luck hailing one.

Barry turned the sedan abruptly right and drew up outside a large building with a low gold-frosted frontage.

"The Excelsior," he said. "This is where you'll be staying tonight."

"I had planned to go home this evening," Todd said.

"Well, I guess you're welcome to do that," Barry said, "but I'm told the rooms here are terribly nice. I'll wait here while you check in and then I'll take you to your meeting."

Todd gave Barry two dollars—he had no idea if that was too little or too much—and checked in. His room was large, beige and had the kind of bed you could swim in. There was a minibar and a room service menu. The TV had a cord coming out of it with a remote control device on the end. There was a robe in the bathroom and a lot of tiny things wrapped up in perfumed paper.

The phone rang. Todd took a moment to work out that he was standing next to it.

"Hello, Milstead res— Todd Milstead," he said.

"Mr. Milstead," said Nora. "I just wanted to welcome you to New York and ask if your room is okay."

"I'd have preferred a suite," said Todd. "I'm joking," he added, and heard Nora breathe out. "It's magnificent," he said.

"Wonderful," said Nora. "We'll see you very soon."

Barry was waiting outside, massive on the sidewalk.

"Where are we going?" said Todd.

"The Schirmer Building," Barry said. "It's only a couple of blocks."

Twenty minutes later, after completing a journey slow enough to impress a funeral director, they were outside a tall gray-faced building with its own doorman. The handover of Todd from Barry to the doorman was smooth and efficient, and Todd found himself inside a moderately opulent lobby.

"Hi, I'm Carrie," said a woman, appearing from nowhere. She was tall, thin and nervous-looking with strong teeth, like a racehorse owner who'd spent too much time with her thoroughbreds. She was wearing, Todd noticed, a skinny tie and an Elvis Costello pin in her lapel.

"Todd," said Todd, and followed Carrie into the elevator.

"I read *All My Colors*," said Carrie. For a moment, Todd thought she meant the other *All My Colors*, the one he tried not to think about.

"You're a brilliant writer," Carrie continued. She went red. Todd smiled graciously.

"Thank you," he said. "My first compliment."

"Second," said Carrie. "After Nora."

They exited the lift into yet another reception. Todd was beginning to feel that New York was nothing more than a mass of reception areas and lobbies, each leading to even more reception areas and lobbies. But in this one stood a middle-aged woman, dressed elegantly but not, as Todd thought of it, wealthily.

"Todd Milstead," she said, extending her hand like a man. "Nora Franklyn."

"Nice to meet you," said Todd, wondering if there was anyone writing down these amazing bon mots of his.

"How was your flight?" said Nora.

"Fine," said Todd, Illinois' own Oscar Wilde.

"Excellent," said Nora. She turned to Carrie.

"For a writer, he's a man of few words," she said, then beamed at Todd. "I like that in a man. Norman Mailer, he just won't shut up."

"You know Norman Mailer?" said Todd.

"God, who doesn't?" said Nora. "Word of warning. Don't ever get in an elevator with him."

She laughed, and Carrie laughed too. Todd thought of rolling out his stock Mailer opinion, but decided against it. He'd only read Mailer: these people *knew* him.

Nora's office was a masterpiece of dissimulation. Even Todd could see that. Here, on the fourteenth floor of a modern block, some genius of an interior designer had recreated the interior of a Cambridge English tutor's study, complete with worn-out desk, shelves of jacketless books, and deep armchairs made of leather cracked like a riverbed after a drought. The whole room screamed TRUST US and WE

LOVE BOOKS. Only the presence of an electric typewriter, discreetly placed on a side table behind a couch, indicated that Todd was still in the twentieth century.

"Thank you for coming all this way," said Nora.

"Not at all," said Todd. "It's a great honor to be here."

"Let's get to it," said Nora. "We have lunch in an hour."

"Oh," said Todd. "You have a busy schedule."

Nora and Carrie laughed.

"Todd," Carrie said. "The lunch is for you."

"Oh," said Todd again, reduced to talking in vowels.

"I'll be brief, and not just because I'm hungry," said Nora. "We would like to publish you, Todd. We think *All My Colors* is not just fantastic, it's a surefire commercial success, and that's a great combination."

She leaned back in her seat.

"Naturally, you are free to entrust your work to another publisher, but we are the best."

"She's not kidding," said Carrie. "We're great."

They both laughed. Todd looked around the office. There were signed photographs of most of his literary heroes. Awards. Framed book jackets. The odd autographed menu.

"And you're sure you're not crooks?" he said.

Nora and Carrie laughed again.

"We're not crooks and this isn't a dream," said Nora.

"I don't have an agent," Todd said.

"We're happy to wait until you find one," Nora said.

If there was one word Todd didn't get along with, it was "wait." He figured he could delay giving someone fifteen percent of his hard-earned royalties.

"No need," Todd said. "Where do I sign?"

•

Barry was outside already when they came out of the Schirmer.

"Looks like you're one of the team now," he said.

"How did you know?" Todd said.

"I can always tell. They got a look."

"What kind of look?"

"The kind you got."

"Fair enough."

"Even for a writer, you're extremely quiet," Nora said. "Would you like a drink?"

Todd decided that he would like a drink and told Nora so. It seemed a shame not to, as the restaurant was as close to Todd's fantasies of sophistication as possible, without actually building a time machine and returning to the 1930s. Waiters brought actual Martinis and Manhattans (*Manhattans in Manhattan*, thought Todd, and immediately felt like a farmer), the menus were huge and oysters seemed to get into everything.

"I'll be honest, Todd," said Nora. "We don't do this for everybody."

"Why are you doing it for me?" said Todd, immediately wondering why he didn't just stick a piece of straw in his mouth and be done with it. Perhaps he should have worn his dungarees as well.

"Because," said Nora, an actual twinkle in her eye, "you are about to become our number one author, Mr. Milstead."

The food arrived. There was meat and fish and oysters.

Todd put his hand over his wine glass the second time the wine waiter passed by, then changed his mind. He had a feeling that this would be the only time anything like today would ever happen in his life, and he intended to savor it.

"Has any other publisher expressed interest in *All My Colors*?" asked Nora, and Todd fancied he could see a new steel in her eyes, like an adding machine under the skin.

Todd thought of the returned manuscripts. "No," he admitted.

"Readers," said Nora. "Half of them just skim the synopsis, and the rest can't even do that. This one—" and she indicated Carrie as a dowager lady might acknowledge her timid companion "—can read."

"We receive hundreds of manuscripts every week," Carrie said. "*All My Colors* just stood out immediately."

She waited to see if Nora was going to take over, then continued, "The first page—the scene in the hardware store—it's such a great opening. And then when she—"

"I don't think Mr. Milstead needs to have his entire novel told back to him," said Nora, and Carrie returned to silence. "One thing Carrie did say that we all agreed on is how well you write women."

"Thanks," Todd said, who had no memory of writing anybody.

"It's very unusual to meet a man who can convincingly portray women as well as men," said Carrie quickly, before gazing down into her salmon again.

"And we feel that's a major part of your appeal," said Nora. "*All My Colors* is one of those rare novels that both sexes can enjoy."

"Glad to hear it," said Todd, who at that moment wouldn't have been surprised to learn that the book was also one of those rare novels that featured a fight between a giant squid and a robot. The more he struggled to recall the book that had literally occupied his life all those weeks, the less he could remember any of it. It was as if that famous eidetic memory of his had been wiped like a cassette tape.

"I know this is an obvious thing to say," said Carrie, looking at Nora to make sure she wasn't going to squish her again. "But it's such an unusual novel, for any author to write. So I'm going to ask it anyway."

"Fire away," said Todd, draining the nearest glass to him.

"Where did you get the idea from?"

Todd paused. He lifted his glass to his lips, remembered that he'd just emptied it, then smiled.

"Where does anyone get their ideas from?" he said. "Sometimes they're just in the air, aren't they? And sometimes we draw on personal experience, always changing it, always tuning it so it becomes art, not autobiography. But always there is the idea at the core."

"Yes, that's very true," said Carrie. "But you're talking about ideas in general. I meant in this specific case, where did you get the idea?"

I stole the whole thing from a book that nobody else had heard of, thought Todd angrily, *and when I realized I could get away with it, I copied the whole thing out while crapping in a diaper in my own house. You know, like every writer does.*

Todd realized that the booze was making him feel a little bit too much like his old self again.

"I honestly don't know where it came from," he said,

then added, trying not to sound too cautious, "Why? Does it seem familiar to you in any way?"

Carrie, anxious now lest she had gone too far, said, "No! Not at all. It's just such a fresh concept I…"

She tailed off. Nora smiled a smile that Todd had seen somewhere before. *Oh my God*, he thought, *it's Endora from fucking* Bewitched. Todd smiled back, a Darren eager to please.

"I'm sure Todd doesn't want to spend all day dissecting his own work," she said. "We can leave that to the critics. Now who wants dessert?"

By the end of the meal, which had left Todd both dizzy and bloated, he was even more convinced that Nora Franklyn was the ideal person to publish him (the fact that she was the only person who wanted to represent him was long forgotten). He was ready to sign up on the spot and must have indicated as much, because, as the coffee cups were taken away, Carrie said nervously:

"We love the book unconditionally, Mr. Milstead, and we are very, very keen on being part of your future as an author. But I feel—" and here she exchanged a look with her boss "—that, as with every novel, we'd like to engage an editor."

"An editor?" said Todd. He felt the cold hand of terror on his throat.

"There are moments in the book which we feel could be usefully trimmed," said Nora, efficient now. "It's a marvelous book but we tend to find as publishers that every new manuscript benefits from a fresh eye. An eye ready to make cuts, and changes."

"I thought you said you liked it," he said.

"Oh, we do," Carrie hastened. "We love it. But—"

"We're not talking swingeing cuts," Nora butted in. "Just a few trims here and there. It's a big book and we like it that way. Also," she beamed, "There are sections we feel could be lengthened. For clarification."

"Some moments are obscure," agreed Carrie. "Which is charming, but in the current climate, we don't want to be obfuscatory."

"You do see what we mean," said Nora.

Todd was silent. His mind was racing. *I'm not editing this fucking book*, he thought. *I wouldn't know where to start. Or stop.*

He imagined himself in a butcher's apron, blindly slashing at the manuscript, with no idea if he was improving the novel or just hacking the life from it.

"I'm not sure," he said finally.

Nora crushed a cigarette Todd hadn't even noticed she'd been smoking.

"Todd," she said. "I hate to come over—heavy—but this is the twentieth century. A publisher has a duty to the retailer as well as the reader. We have to make sure the product—awful word—is as near to perfect as we can make it. This is a world of markets, Todd, and publishing is as much a market as anywhere else."

"No," Todd said, almost regretfully, "I get all that, I really do. But it's not that I don't want to change the book. It's that I can't."

And by can't, he thought, *I really do mean can't.*

Now Nora looked impatient.

"Not allowing an editor to work on your book is the kind of privilege we'd afford one of our long-standing clients," she said. "Someone who'd been with us for a number of years, someone who was selling decent amounts of books over a long period of time."

"And even then," said Carrie, "we'd have to be very, very careful. Authors are not always the best judges of their own work."

"Short version, everyone gets edited," Nora said. "Everyone."

"I feel like I'm being ganged up on," said Todd, laughing nervously.

"If we are, it's for your own good," said Nora. "We want to make sure that your work is interpreted the way it should be, and not misunderstood."

"I can assure you I spent a considerable amount of time making sure that my work is easy to understand," said Todd. He felt affronted that the book he'd ushered into this world was under attack. After all, wasn't he the only begetter of this novel? *Well, maybe not.*

Nora was looking at him sternly. Carrie was looking at Nora looking at him sternly.

"I'm going to be frank with you, Todd," said Nora. "We never, ever publish a manuscript from a new author in the state in which it was submitted to us."

"Well then," said Todd, and maybe it was the booze talking, or maybe it was something else, "I'm going to be frank with you. There is literally—and I am aware of the meaning of the word 'literally,' I'm a writer, you may recall—there is literally no way or circumstance in which I would change or allow to be changed a word of this book. It is what it is."

Silence fell. A waiter hovering for the check went and hovered somewhere else. Nora crushed out the already crushed-out cigarette some more. Carrie looked a little bit sick. Todd ran out of things to do with his hands and just let them rest flat on his lap.

"Excuse us a moment," said Nora. She flashed a look at Carrie and they both stood up. "Order yourself a cocktail, Todd. We shan't be a minute."

Nora and Carrie left the table. After two minutes, Todd waved at the waiter and asked for another Manhattan. He figured, why not, it could be the last time he ever had a free drink in New York.

Todd was just wondering if he could stretch to a third Manhattan when Carrie returned to the table. "Nora won't keep you," she said breathlessly, then, "This has never happened before."

"Is that right?" said Todd, wondering exactly which part of *this* had never happened before. "I don't mean to cause any trouble."

"Between you and me," Carrie said, "I think it's a smart move. Showing her who's boss. But you've got to be careful, Mr. Milstead. She's very good. And remember, her grandfather started the business."

Todd was still trying to work out the specific relevance of this last remark when Nora came back. She sat down, smiled like Agnes Moorehead in a hurry, and turned to Todd.

"Well, this is a first," she said.

"Carrie was just telling me," Todd said.

"We don't like it," said Nora. "And when I say we, I mean me. *I* don't like it. I have a way of doing things, a way that's worked for several years. Everyone benefits and nobody has ever questioned it."

"You make me sound like a troublemaker."

"Oh, you are a troublemaker," said Nora. "It's no good looking innocent and pretending you have no idea what you're doing. I know exactly what you're doing."

Perhaps you'd like to tell me, then, thought Todd.

"I just want to protect the integrity of the book," he said.

"Oh, surely," said Nora. "And we appreciate that. But we also appreciate a little power game too. Most of our authors are so simple. They come here, they eat the lunch and drink the cocktails and they don't say a damn thing when we mention editors, or rewrites. They just nod their heads because they're not listening. You know why?"

"Because they're drunk?" said Todd, and wished he hadn't. Nora's gaze was beyond steely now.

"Because they're waiting for us to mention the money. The advance. The royalty. They just want to know about their cut. But with you—we didn't even get that far."

She reduced the steeliness of her look by about fifty percent.

"Which is refreshing, Mr. Milstead. Because it means we can work together."

"It does?" said Todd, confused now.

"I called my grandfather," said Nora. "He's retired but he's also kind of a... a resource. And he said, and I quote, if the guy doesn't care about the money, he's an idiot."

"I didn't say I didn't *care* about the money," Todd said hurriedly.

"But if he doesn't care about the book, he's more of an idiot," finished Nora. "He advised me to offer you a pathetic advance, Mr. Milstead, as a tribute to your mulish tenacity, in return for which we will present your book to the world just as you wrote it."

Todd took a moment to realize what Nora had just said.

"Thanks," he said, then, "Thank you very much."

"It really will be a risible advance," said Nora.

"But advances are loans anyway," Carrie pointed out.

"You know what?" said Todd, suddenly elated. "I don't care."

And he didn't. For the first time in his life, Todd Milstead had followed his dream and his dream hadn't told him to go home.

"How about another Manhattan?" he said.

That night, Todd called Sara. She was, if anything, more elated than he was.

"So what happens now?" she said.

"I sign the contract tomorrow morning in their office and fly home," said Todd. "And then I guess I'm a published author."

"Published author." Sara savored the phrase. "That sounds *sexy*. Which reminds me, you going to hit the strip joints tonight?"

"No," said Todd.

"What? A night in New York and you're not going to Forty-second Street?"

"I am not."

"No titty bars for Todd? Not even a porno theater? I hear those places are bad."

"I'm sure they are," said Todd. "I'm just going to watch some TV and go to bed."

"Good for you, scout," said Sara. "Well, goodnight, author man. And hurry home."

"I will," said Todd.

And to his amazement, he did.

Waiting for something to happen is the surest way to make nothing happen. Waiting for someone else to do something is the longest haul in the world. Every day Todd would get up, have breakfast, call Mike (Joe having disappeared from the scene), and maybe drive down to Legolas Books.

Todd would later realize that he had little or no memory of this time. It wasn't the quiet time—there was too much anticipation for that—but it wasn't a memorable time either. Even Janis seemed to have—disappeared wasn't the right word, but she wasn't on Todd's personal radar. Todd pictured her with her mystery lover—for some reason he wanted to say *demon lover*—going to bars, watching strange specialty acts, and then maybe slowly vanishing into a kind of demi-monde underground about whose details he was enormously vague.

Mostly what Todd remembered about this time was the tension. Todd and Janis had never had kids—Todd never saw himself as a dad and after the first couple of years, Janis didn't see him as one either—but he found he could suddenly sympathize with expectant fathers in old movies, pacing around outside the delivery room, waiting for the happy event to occur so they could faint or hand around cigars. Except in Todd's case, the happy event wasn't going to be a bouncing baby but a big fat Great American Novel. And he was secretly worried—no, terrified—that the last few weeks had been nothing more than a phantom pregnancy.

Things had begun promisingly. In the days after his return from New York, Nora or Carrie had been in fairly regular phone contact.

"We've gotten a lot of positive reactions from retailers," Nora would say, or Carrie would tell him, "Everybody is so excited about *All My Colors*, it's ridiculous."

And then nothing would happen. There'd be a few bits of grain strewn his way—someone would pass on a favorable remark, or Carrie would say the cover design was coming along—but nothing was actually *happening*. It was like a moment in a stage play where an actor has forgotten a line and the prompt has lost her place in the script, so the cast are just staring at each other and saying things like, "Wonderful weather we're having for this time of year," as the prompt drops her script on the floor and utters a muffled curse. Except longer. Much longer.

Todd found himself gripped by the dilemma of the writer in limbo. Should he sit back and wait? Or should he call, or write, or even go to New York? He felt certain that if he intervened in person—gave someone a little nudge—he could get the ball rolling again. But the problem lay in the fact that he didn't know where the ball was or what it looked like or even if there was a ball. And he was also powerfully scared that if he did call, or write, someone would say, "Oh

God, did nobody tell you? We decided not to go ahead with your dumb book."

(There was also a part of Todd—located in a secret corner in his mind, in his memory, maybe even in the deepest, darkest place in his soul—which was terrified that he had been found out, that somebody had walked into Franklyn and Sullivan, picked up his manuscript and said, "But this isn't by Todd Milstead at all! It's stolen from that other guy! How come nobody noticed!" and everybody in the office would just wake up and go, "Jesus, he's right. This Milstead fellow is a rotten thief. Let's kill him!")

And then the call came.

"You're on the Fall list," said Nora with no introduction or preamble.

Todd was so thrown he just said, "Is that good?"

"It's good," said Nora. "Believe me, it's good."

"Fall next year?" said Todd. He was a little disappointed. "That's a way off."

"Fall this year," said Nora. "I know, it's insane, it's like tomorrow, but they are very eager to get it out there. And for you to promote the book."

"I don't know what that means," said Todd. "Will I be on local radio?"

"Maybe," laughed Nora. "Think bigger."

"NPR?" hazarded Todd.

"Radio, yes, and newspapers," said Nora. "But we're also pushing for TV."

"TV," said Todd. He stared at his reflection in the hall mirror. Did he look authorial enough for television, he wondered.

As if reading his mind, Nora said, "Relax, Todd. With that firm American jaw and a tweed jacket, you'll look the part to a tee."

"TV," said Todd again. Like everyone who'd ever wanted to be a writer, his secret fear and desire was television.

"Did they give you any dates yet?" he said. His mind was racing so fast he almost forgot his diary was an aching empty void. *Not for long*, he thought.

But *not for long* was a way off. There were delays with the proofs, and then there were delays with the galleys (Todd had no idea what the difference was) and then there was a delay with the cover, and then the galleys looked like they'd been proofread by the Marx Brothers and nothing seemed to go right and Todd just completely freaked at seeing the whole damn book typeset like it was real, which of course it was, it was extremely real.

Either way, it was all too freaking much for Todd and he was seriously thinking of taking a long weekend or maybe a long week or just getting very, very drunk when one morning there was a knock at his front door and he opened it and there was Behm, coughing into his fist like it was a microphone and he was testing it.

"Mr. Behm," said Todd, once Behm had finished coughing. "To what do I owe the pleasure?"

Behm looked up, and Todd saw that he was, for the first time since they had met, uncertain.

"I need to speak to you," Behm said. "Can I come in?"

"I guess so," said Todd, but Behm was already inside the house.

Behm stood in the kitchen and pulled from his jacket

—which seemed, Todd noted, even more threadbare than last time—another yellow envelope.

"You found her?" said Todd. "I wondered where Janis had got to."

"This isn't about Janis," said Behm, and scattered three prints on the table. Todd looked at them. One was taken outside a gas station at night. One was of an undistinguished stretch of grass and trees that Todd recognized as being part of a local park. And the third was taken through the window of a diner on the way to the highway.

"Landscape shots," said Todd. "Branching out into regular photography. You thinking of going straight?"

Behm didn't even bother to pretend to smile.

"Nobody in those pictures, right?" he said. "Thought so."

"Wait a minute," said Todd. "You came here to ask me if there were any—what's going on?"

"Those are just three examples," said Behm. "I must have twenty more back at the office."

"Examples of what?" said Todd.

"I've been surveilling your wife for weeks now," said Behm. "And her routine is unchanging and unvaried. So I thought that I would try to find out a little more about her lady friend."

Maybe it was the phrase *lady friend* that chilled Todd. He felt a strong and cold unease as he waited for Behm to continue.

"I started following her," said Behm. "And that was a little trickier than following Janis, let me tell you."

"Hardly surprising," said Todd. "She may have something to lose by being found out. Maybe she's got a family at home."

"Thank you, the great detective," said Behm. "That's what I thought. Except she doesn't appear to have a home."

"What?" said Todd. "Everybody's got a home. Except," he added stupidly, "homeless people."

"This lady don't sleep rough," said Behm. "So far as I can tell, she don't sleep at all."

"I'm really not following any of this," Todd said.

"I went where she went," said Behm slowly. "It wasn't easy. She knew how to get me off her trail. I'd be right behind her and she'd just—vanish. I'd turn my head and she'd be gone. Real professional."

"So she's done this before," Todd said. "Broken up a few marriages, got good at shaking the private dick."

"Nobody shakes me," said Behm. "I spent three months following a Viet Cong once."

"In the war?" asked Todd.

"Baltimore," said Behm. "So I didn't feel that your wife's girlfriend was going to be a problem."

"Guess you were wrong," Todd said.

"Guess I was," said Behm.

There was a moment of silence.

"Well, it's been good catching up," said Todd. "But I have to get on with my day. Call me when you have something new, won't you?"

He handed Behm his photos. Behm shook his head.

"I haven't told you yet," he said.

"Told me what?"

"Those photos… they're her."

Todd took a photo, the one from the park. He scoured it. There were a couple of people in the far distance.

"She one of them?" he said.

"No," said Behm. "She's right square in the middle of the shot. Or at least she should be."

He pointed to the middle of the photograph. There was nothing there.

"Same as these two pictures. Same as all of them. She was in them all, Mr. Milstead."

"I don't see anyone," said Todd. He was starting to wonder if Behm was okay in the head.

"I know you don't," said Behm, in the tones of a man who is about to lose his patience. "Because I don't see anyone either. The difference is, when I took those shots, she was there. Right in front of me. She was there," he repeated, his finger stabbing at the prints. "*There.*"

Todd backed away a little. "Maybe there's a fault with your camera, or the lab," he said.

Behm shook his head. "No kind of fault does that, Mr. Milstead. And no kind of fault does *this.*"

As he spoke he pulled one more photo from his jacket. *Great, conjuror's tricks now*, thought Todd. Then he saw the photo. It showed Janis, walking down the street, talking. Talking in a relaxed way, happy even, like she was talking to someone she cared about, someone who probably cared about her.

The only thing was, whoever that person might be, they weren't in the photograph. Janis was talking to thin air.

"You beginning to see what I mean now, Mr. Milstead?" said Behm.

"You did something to them," Todd said.

"Why would I do that?" Behm said.

Todd didn't have an answer.

"Okay," he said. "Then someone else did."

"What, you think I send my films to Kodak to be printed? I develop my own pictures."

"Then I don't know."

"Nope, nor do I."

Todd and Behm looked at the picture of Janis again.

"She looks happy, talking to that air," Behm said. "Mr. Milstead, we have no evidence that your wife's lover exists. Only the evidence of our own eyes."

Todd thought for a moment.

"Can you draw?" he said.

"No," said Behm. "And even if I could, what good would that be? I could hire a fucking sketch artist and get them to come with me on a stakeout and they could draw her. But so what? I'd just have a drawing. And drawings aren't evidence."

"I could show it to Janis," said Todd.

"If you wanted to," Behm said. "But she'd just think you were crazy. And she'd have a point."

"I don't believe this," Todd said. "We're this close to nailing her."

"Not sure what you mean by nailing," said Behm. "Like I said, evidence of adultery itself won't help you in court. Especially given you were the first offender, as it were. And even if we did find some magical court with a judge and jury who were all crazy down on women, and we had film of Mrs. Milstead and her pal sitting in a diner together, so what? We've got proof that she knows another woman. Big deal."

"Can we get footage?" said Todd, seizing on the first thing Behm had said that made sense to him. "Not of them in a diner."

"What, film them in bed?"

"Fucking, yeah."

"You think a film camera will work when a photographic camera won't?"

Todd said nothing. Behm took a deep breath.

"Mr. Milstead, I'm biting the hand that feeds me here," he said. "But my advice? You need to drop this."

Todd felt something tighten inside his chest.

"I'm not going to drop this," he said. "I've got to nail her."

Behm was about to reply when the phone rang. Todd grabbed it.

"Not *now*!" he shouted.

Sara said, "Todd, it's me."

Todd held the receiver out. He inhaled.

"Sara," he said. "It's not a good time."

"I accept your apology," Sara said, and rang off.

Todd breathed deeply. He fixed Behm with an angry glare.

"I want you to carry on with this," he said.

"There's no point," said Behm.

"Just do it," said Todd. "I'll pay."

Behm considered the man before him. Todd was breathing heavily. His eyes were round and staring. He looked like he was barely in control of his emotions.

"No," he said.

Todd lunged at him. Behm stepped to one side and Todd crashed into the table.

"Shit," he moaned. He sat down heavily on a stool. "I'm sorry," he said. "I don't know what came over me."

"I'm sure you're under a lot of pressure," said Behm, not sounding too sympathetic. "And I've had worse. You weren't even armed. But I'm not going on with this, Mr. Milstead. It's too fucking—"

The word came into Todd's head just as Behm said it.

"—*weird*."

Todd said goodbye to Behm. Then he called Sara.

"Hi, it's me."

"Oh. Hi."

"Sara, I'm really sorry. I'm under a lot of pressure."

"Hey, who isn't?"

"I'm really sorry. How can I make it up to you?"

There was a pause.

"I guess by not doing it in the first place. Look, can we talk later?" Todd continued.

"I thought you called me."

"That was then. This is—"

A huge crash of something resounded in Todd's ear.

"What the hell was that? Are you okay?"

Sara sighed.

"Terry is moving the rest of his stuff out today. That was some of his stuff."

"I see."

"I'll come over later. At this rate Terry's stuff is going to be shrapnel."

"I didn't know you cared."

"I have floorboards. They're being dented. Look—"

There was another crash.

"Call me later."

"You got it."

Time went by. Todd visited Sara in her now-empty home. Mike came around, not every Saturday night, but oftenish. Behm didn't call.

Todd still had a knot in his stomach, a knot that remained there until one morning he got a knock on his door and the UPS guy was there, looking stressed.

"That is a huge package," said Sara. "And for once I don't mean you, big guy."

Todd didn't get it at first and when he did, he was slightly embarrassed (Janis never talked dirty, not to him anyway).

"It's from New York," he said, setting the long, heavy box down on the table. Sara found scissors and they began cutting into it.

"Oh my God," said Sara. She reached into the box, and then stopped.

"Sorry," she said. "This is your moment."

Todd pulled back the flaps atop the box and put both his hands in. Then, like a medic assisting at a birth, he pulled out a book.

"*All My Colors*," said Sara, almost reverently. "My Lord, Todd, look at it."

Todd held up the hardback. Its jacket featured the head of a woman in profile and around it, almost like an Afro, a rainbow.

"By Todd Milstead," he read out loud. He dove back into the box and pulled out another copy, then another, then another. Sara joined in, and within a few moments they had pulled out every single copy of the book.

"Now what do we do?" said Todd. He found he was crying. Sara wiped his eyes.

"Tricky," she said. "I mean, we can't fuck on 'em, they're too hard."

In the end, they settled for fucking on the bed, with a copy of the book on the bedside, so they could look at it. It was weird, but it was funny, too, and they both enjoyed it, a lot.

Afterward, Todd was getting dressed again when his old pal the telephone started ringing. He picked it up and this time it was Carrie. Todd zipped his pants up—he always felt strange talking to people on the telephone in a state of undress—as Carrie said, "Did it come?"

"Excuse me?" said Todd. "Oh. Oh, yes it did. Thank you, it's great. I didn't know I'd get so many copies. I sure don't think I know enough people to give 'em to."

"Firstly, you'll be surprised. People if they know you, no matter that they never read a book in their lives, they'll want a copy," said Carrie. "Secondly, take my advice. Put the whole box under the bed."

"You think they'll come in handy one rainy day?"

"Todd. These are *first editions* of your book," Carrie said. "They're going to come in more than handy. They're going to be *valuable*."

Todd went and looked at the books again. It seemed less bizarre now to have a table covered in identical books, a miniature ziggurat with his name written on every brick. But he knew then that there'd always be a little frisson whenever he saw a copy of *All My Colors*, in a store or maybe in someone else's hand.

"Oh yes," he might say to the person looking at his book, "I wrote that. The name? Todd Milstead."

For some reason, the idea didn't feel as satisfying as he'd imagined.

It didn't feel entirely real.

It didn't feel entirely *right*.

Later on, he took Carrie's advice, and put the whole lot under the bed—after giving Sara a copy ("*To the amazing Sara, with all my love, Todd*"), one to Mike ("*To an old friend, with thanks, Todd*"), and, after some reflection, one to Timothy at Legolas Books ("*To Timothy at Legolas Books, from Todd Milstead*"). Then he sat down with the telephone in one hand and a pen in the other as Carrie began to discuss possible dates for his book tour with him. It was an interesting conversation from Todd's point of view. First of all, there was the sheer volume of appearances.

"This is a huge country," said Carrie. "Even if you appeared in one city in each state, that'd be fifty appearances. But Franklyn and Sullivan want to break this book."

"Feels more like they want to break me," said Todd, as he wrote down the name of another city he'd never heard of outside the atlas.

"Think of yourself as a rock star," said Carrie, and Todd remembered the Elvis Costello pin she'd been wearing at their first meeting. "You're taking on America. And America is not going to win."

Todd couldn't argue with that. He was too busy being

fascinated by the concept of a full schedule. He watched, almost distantly, as his hands wrote out an itinerary that didn't so much straddle the U.S. as spiral around it, crossing coasts and circling into the Midwest and out again via cities in the South which might be sympathetic to him, and then out to the coasts again.

Sara plotted everything on a big gas station map for him, and blocked out the dates on the calendar.

"Wow," she said. "Guess I won't be seeing you before Christmas."

"That's a point," said Todd. "Where shall we spend it? Christmas, I mean."

"What's wrong with here?" said Sara, putting her arms around him, and giving him a royal boner.

"Too many memories," said Todd. "I feel like it's time we moved on."

"Together, I hope," said Sara, and she wriggled closer to him. The royal boner became imperial.

"Of course together," said Todd. "How else?"

Todd's itinerary was further complicated (for him, anyway) by the fact that, while some of it would be undertaken in the luxury he'd sort of assumed was his new birthright when he'd signed to Franklyn and Sullivan—for example, when he made appearances in New York and Los Angeles, he'd be put up in a fancy hotel and wined and dined by the local publishers' representatives—a lot of it would not be.

"We can pay for flights to, you know, far-flung places like Nevada," said Carrie. "But a lot of the time I'm afraid you'll be driving yourself and checking into motels."

"I guess that's okay," said Todd.

"We'll reimburse you for gas and accommodation, of course," said Carrie apologetically.

"Of course," said Todd. "Don't worry about it."

"Hey," Carrie said, "this is going to be the last time you ever go tourist class, Todd. Savor it."

Savor my hot balls, thought Todd, and felt rather shocked.

"I'll remember these days and laugh," he told Carrie, and rang off.

Truth be told, the old Todd was coming more and more to the surface these days. The novelty of normal life was wearing off—he'd been with Sara for months now, for goodness sake, and a man can only take so many friendly smiles at breakfast and long walks in the park. Plus, wasn't he a published author now? There was a world of fame and money out there and Todd was champing at the bit to get at it. Saturday nights with Mike were all very well (they weren't all very well, they were fucking *dull*), but where were the Saturday nights with, Todd didn't know, Anthony Burgess and Herman Wouk? Maybe throw Farrah Fawcett in the mix too, why not. If he was honest, Todd had no idea what the life of an author was like, but he did remember that the guy who wrote *Death of a Salesman* had been married to Marilyn Monroe and that sounded like a good starting point. Of course, that guy was a playwright and they got out more, but Todd bet writing a number one bestseller put you in a position to meet swimwear models. He had no idea where this might happen; maybe on a chat show.

Yeah, that sounds about right, Todd thought. *Go on Johnny*

Carson and make 'em all laugh, and then afterward screw the swimwear girl.

Todd's view of celebrity was a simple one.

Old Todd was still in there, but new Todd was the boss. New Todd liked to sit on the couch, Sara on his lap, flicking through the book pages in the Sunday papers and wondering what it'd be like to be in them. New Todd drank his one glass of wine with dinner and helped with the washing-up (he got through *that* by imagining he was being photographed for a magazine feature—*"I'm no macho pig," says Todd Milstead*).

Life was sweet and Todd liked it that way. In his head he was planning an itinerary for his life. Get rich and famous from the book, move out of DeKalb—Chicago seemed a good bet, being familiar and a decent city with enough of a cultural scene to sustain his pretensions (and also, he was fully aware, slightly more robust and Todd-like than Los Angeles or New York). Divorce Janis and give her the chump change she was still whining about. Marry Sara (because he loved her) and try not to screw around (see reason above). Become richer and more famous, travel around the world and die from a massive heart attack sustained during fellatio on a bed made of solid gold at the age of a hundred and two. There were worse ways to go.

Some reviews trickled out. Not the thundering tidal wave of wonder-struck praise that Todd had hoped for, but they were by and large favorable. Unfortunately they were in low-mass circulation periodicals like *Books Now,*

The Penman's Review and—Todd's personal favorite—*The New American Librarian*, a bi-annual magazine devoted to covering only books that were being sent out to libraries (Todd joked to Sara that they should call the thing *Don't Bother Buying These Books, We Got 'Em For You Free*). But he was grateful for the coverage.

Sara clipped all the reviews out and pasted them in a scrapbook.

"You should have bought a smaller scrapbook," said Todd, when he saw them all together, bravely trying to fill an entire page.

"This is just the advance guard," said Sara. "Soon this thing's going to be bulging. Give it time."

Todd's local paper—the *Beacon* (known to one and all as the *Beaconfused*)—ran a page on Todd. They sent a photographer and everything. The piece looked nice.

LOCAL MAN WRITES NOVEL

"I guess I'm just lucky," says Todd Milstead. Milstead, who lives out on Hinckley Road, never dreamed of seeing his name in print, let alone on the front of a book. But after "a lot of perseverance," Todd's first book *All My Colors* is out now.

"You know that saying about how it takes ninety percent perspiration and ten percent inspiration to write a novel?" jokes Todd, "Well, in my case, it was more like ninety percent perspiration. I'm not kidding, I sat in this room and I almost literally sweated this book out."

Milstead, who teaches part-time in the area, says he wants nothing from the book but "the satisfaction of a job well done and maybe the chance to see a few copies in the local bookstore under a sign saying 'local author.'" That said, he is hitting the road for the next few months to promote *All My Colors* "at the insistence of my publisher. I'm really a homebody," says Todd, breaking into the kind of boyish grin that's sure to win him a few new female fans.

"I thought you said a guy wrote this," said Sara.

"Did I?" said Todd. "No, the photographer was a guy. The journalist was a woman. I think."

"Right," said Sara. "You think. You're not fooling anyone. I bet you forgot she was eighteen and blonde, too."

"I really can't remember," said Todd who, immediately after the wide-eyed young woman had gazed into his eyes for the duration of the whole interview and made him feel like the smartest stud in the world, had gone into the bathroom and jerked off.

"Timothy's not going to be pleased," said Sara.

"Timothy's never pleased," Todd said. "But why exactly this time?"

"Look at the part at the end," said Sara. Todd skimmed down to the bottom of the page.

"Uh oh," he said.

All My Colors *by Todd Milstead is published by Franklyn and Sullivan and is available from Legolamb Books, DeKalb.*

Timothy affected to be not pissed off at all.

"Maybe if I'd called the place Books 'R' Us they would have got the name right," he beamed. "After all, it's not like I've been putting the same goshdarned ad in the paper every week for twenty years."

"I take your point," said Todd, who'd lost interest in whatever the twinkly old fuckstick had been saying after "Maybe." "Listen, I just wanted to thank you for your support and say that anything I can do to pay you back, just let me know."

Timothy was well aware that his support had consisted entirely of encouraging Todd in his delusions of authorness, but he had no intention of saying so. Especially now he'd begun reading *All My Colors* and recognized it for what it was—the real deal. Timothy had no idea how a moron like Milstead—worse, a sloth like Milstead, who probably took six months to write a goddamn check, and even then had to lie down for a week afterward—had come to write a novel that was the real deal, but with no evidence to the contrary, he had to swallow his loathing of the man and concede (but only to himself) that maybe he had talent.

"Well," he said to Todd now, "a few signed copies for the store would be nice. And maybe—" Timothy swallowed the acid gall of envy. "—a reading. If you're not too busy."

"A reading!" said Todd. "That's a great idea. This place would be perfect for me to practice for my book tour."

Timothy's smile hid knives.

"It would be an honor, kind sir, to be the sounding board for your greater endeavors," he said. "Why, to think that one day soon, the words you haltingly uttered here would echo in the greater halls of our cities... it humbles me."

Timothy wondered if he'd gone too far, but Todd's expression—akin to that of the dog in the *Garfield* strip—suggested that he had lapped it up and would have been happy to hear more.

"Thanks, Timothy," said Todd. "I'll work up a few passages to read and then we'll give it a whirl."

"Great," said Timothy. "Let's set a date and I'll print up a few posters. I'll even write 'em myself." He smiled, tightly. "So as to get the name of the store right."

•

Todd worked hard on his presentation.

"You're going to be on for about an hour," said Carrie, which had terrified Todd until she broke it down for him. The hour would consist in a brief but comprehensive introduction to the book and explanation of who he was, interspersed with two readings from *All My Colors* of about ten minutes' duration, and a question and answer session which could be anything from twenty to forty minutes long.

"So you see," Carrie said, "you'll hardly be speaking at all."

Todd picked up a copy of *All My Colors*. He was no longer able to remember whole chapters and sections like he'd been able to a few months back: it was becoming a *book* now, an object rather than something that had once flowed out of him. He supposed this happened to all authors, once the work had entered the real world. Like a child growing up, the book would soon have an independent life of its own.

So he worked his way through the pages, seeking dramatic scenes and exciting chapters which, while not giving away too much of the story, would also work in isolation. It was trickier than it sounded: the book was so well woven together, its themes and narrative so neatly combined, that Todd found it difficult to find a part that didn't contain a necessary revelation or a major plot twist.

In the end he decided the first reading should, logically and inevitably, be the opening section. The second reading caused Todd more deliberation until he found the perfect selection. It was the beginning of Chapter Four, and a passage he should have remembered (*from my diaper days*, said his brain, unbidden) because it was one of the most important moments in the book, combining drama and menace in equal quantities.

Todd sat down and read his two sections out loud to himself, and saw that they were good. Then he read them to Sara, and she was impressed and said so.

Everything was going to go well. How could it not?

The night of the reading at Legolas came faster than Todd had expected. He scarcely had time to scribble down a few words about himself on a piece of card before Sara—self-designated driver for the evening—was at the door.

"Got everything?" she said, like a mom.

"Notes, check. Book, check," said Todd.

"Let's go," said Sara.

There were, Todd was slightly sad to note, no enormous crowds outside Legolas Books. He hadn't expected there to be, but in every author's mind lurks the irrational hope that somehow everyone in the world has gotten hold of their book and has gone nuts for it. As *All My Colors* was not actually out yet, this was not so much unlikely as impossible. But still, Todd would have liked a mob.

Instead, there was a small cloud of people outside the store (Timothy had closed the store ostensibly "to prepare for the grand event" but really to smoke an old doobie he'd found in a drawer). Todd moved past them with the half-embarrassed grace of someone who everybody had come to see but nobody actually knew.

Sara knocked on the glass door and a slightly unsteady Timothy let them in.

"I set you up here," he said, indicating a small lectern in the middle of the space where the gardening books normally lurked. Four optimistic rows of chairs faced the lectern and to one side was a table with at least three bottles of wine on it.

"That's perfect," said Todd. "You've done a fantastic job, old pal."

Timothy, pleased and furious to be called "old pal," smiled horribly.

"Not at all," he said. "Well, better cry havoc and let slip the dogs of—whatever!"

He opened the door and the small cloud of people drifted in. Sara took a seat in a chair at the back and smiled up at Todd, who made his way to the lectern to fiddle with his notes. When he looked up a few seconds later, he saw that three of the rows of chairs were full up. Todd smiled back, wanly. He was starting to feel more than a little nervous.

Sara smiled at him as Timothy got up and stood in front of Todd.

"Ladies and gentlemen, good people and fair," he said, and immediately Todd wanted to grab him by the hair and smash him into the glass window, "welcome to Legolas Books. 'Tis a small thing but all mine own. And tonight," and now Timothy gestured a little wildly at Todd, "I am honored to share it with a very special guest, someone who I have been privileged to know for many years: Todd Milstead."

There was some applause, the kind there is when people haven't actually been served up anything yet but want to be nice. Todd stepped forward, but Timothy wasn't done yet.

"Todd is known to many of us here as friend, colleague, buddy, acquaintance," he began, having apparently been at the thesaurus as well as the Mary Jane, "but tonight he is here in a new capacity. One that he has been hiding from us all these many years. That of scribe."

Todd gripped the lectern and, in his mind, beat Timothy to death with it.

"For tonight a poet walks among us," said Timothy, an edge in his voice. Then he smiled again, swaying slightly.

"Folks," he said, "I'll level with you. It was de la Rochefoucauld who said, 'It is not enough for me to succeed. My best friend must also fail.' And he wasn't joking. But," Timothy went on, "I am joking. Kind of. Todd Milstead is my pal, my best pal"—this was news to Todd—"and I have read his book and I am *jealous as hell*."

Timothy smiled again, seemed to forget where he was, looked around, remembered, and said:

"Ladies and gentlemen—Todd Milstead!"

And he staggered to one side as Todd clapped him on the shoulder a little too hard.

"Wow," said Todd. "What an introduction. I don't know how I can follow that."

He looked at his notes. The room was silent now.

"My name," he began, "is Todd Milstead. And I wrote *All My Colors...*"

How the time went by, Todd could not have said. He read his extracts, and felt that the audience was with him. He talked easily, if dishonestly, about the genesis of the book, and the process of writing it. He talked about what he thought the book was, and what it meant to him, and if it seemed to his audience that he was talking about the book so objectively that it was almost as if he hadn't written it, well, wasn't that the point with books?

He was drawing to a close now. He looked up and saw Sara pointing at her watch.

"I've allotted a few minutes for questions," he said. "I mean, if there are any."

To his immense surprise, six or so hands went up. Todd took a moment to gather himself, then pointed at a woman in the crowd. She was about forty, and despite the time of year was wearing a rainbow-colored scarf and matching tam o'shanter.

"I loved it," she said. "What you read, I mean."

Todd waited for more, but there wasn't any.

"Thank you," he said. "That's not strictly a question but it is nice to hear."

He beamed. More hands shot up. Todd looked around the room and saw a familiar face.

Mike.

I didn't see him come in, Todd thought. *He must have arrived late.*

Mike's hand hit the air, in a somewhat loose manner.

Arrived late from a bar, thought Todd.

"You," said Timothy, pointing at Mike.

Mike beamed.

"That was great," he said, slurring a little. "I just have one question."

"Fire away," said Todd. "Mike is an old friend of mine," he told the room. "So I bet this is going to be *harsh*."

There was laughter now. Todd looked back at Mike, waiting for God knows what question.

But Mike was gone.

In his place was Billy Cairns.

Billy didn't look good. His cheeks were all chewed up and in ribbons. Billy looked like he'd fallen into a shredder, or like he'd tried to make his own gills and botched it. Through the slits in Billy's cheeks, Todd could see the cause of all the trouble: Billy's new teeth. They were a dull blue-gray, and serrated. Todd could see tiny bolts where someone (or *something*) had fixed them to Billy's gums. The bolts were rusty red with dried blood.

Todd was amazed that Billy could talk at all, but talk he did.

Billy fixed Todd with a kind of dead/not dead stare and started to speak, his diction understandably mushy (Todd reckoned Billy's tongue had taken a few hits from those blade-teeth).

"Hi Todd," said Billy. "I have a question for you." Only the way he said it, it came out "kessshun," like a rat sneezing.

"What's the difference between a hawk—" began Billy. But he could get no further as he was consumed by a horrible, blood-and-spittle flecked coughing fit, and bits of tongue and cheek flew out of his mouth.

Todd would have screamed had his own tongue not frozen in his mouth.

"Todd?" said Mike. "Todd!"

"Guess he's thinking about it," someone said, and everybody laughed.

Todd blinked. The room was as it had been before. There was no Billy, just Mike, and the sound of genial, complicit laughter.

142

"I'm sorry, Mike," said Todd. "Could you repeat the question?"

"I think Todd has been at the complimentary wine," said Timothy.

"I may have had one glass too many," said Todd, who hadn't touched the wine.

"I said," Mike shouted when the merriment had died down, "where do you get your ideas from?"

The room murmured to itself. This was an excellent question, the room clearly believed, and one that struck right to the heart of the matter.

"I guess I better get used to that one," said Todd. "I think that every writer gets asked it."

"And I'm asking it now!" shouted Mike, who seemed to be on the verge of hysteria. Maybe he was just beginning to realize that, if all went well, he would be trading his long-time role as *that drunk guy* for a more lucrative position as *that drunk guy who knows the famous guy*.

"Okay," said Todd. "As I was saying, a lot of people have been asked that question. Do you take your ideas from real life, do you make it up, do you use a pair of dice?"

Laughter, but the kind where people are waiting for you to quit making gags and answer the question.

"I don't have a pair of dice," said Todd. "But what I do have is—"

An eidetic memory, his brain said, *which enabled me to remember wholesale an entire novel, which by great and weird chance no other fucker in the world has ever heard of. You know the Great Dictator? I'm the Great Dictated-To.*

"—a creative mind," said Todd. "And don't ask me if

143

that's something I was born with, or something I learned how to cultivate. Maybe it's a little bit of both, I don't know. But someone once said, genius is ninety percent perspiration and ten percent inspiration. Only I guess in my case…"

On Todd went, and on. Only Timothy guessed that Todd was talking the purest, most refined bullshit imaginable, because you can't bullshit a bullshitter. But not even Timothy could work out *how* it was bullshit, or *why*. He only knew that tonight, here, in his bookstore, a new strain of bullshit was being unleashed on the world for the first time.

And not, thought Timothy to himself, *for the last*.

The evening finally wound up, a full two hours after it was supposed to. Todd signed all the advance copies that the publisher had sent, shook a lot of hands, and listened to a lot of people say they were looking forward to reading *All My Colors*, if those two bits he read out were anything to go by. Todd assured everyone that they were something to go by, allowed himself a glass of Timothy's Chateau Execrable, and finally said goodbye at eleven thirty.

Sara drove them back. She kept throwing glances at him from behind the wheel.

"Do I have something on my face?" Todd asked. "Because you keep staring at me."

"I'm storing up memories," she said. "Of the old Todd."

"Oh, come on," said Todd, although he was pleased.

"Todd, I saw you tonight," said Sara, "and you were great. You were funny, you were kind, you were serious… Not that you can't be all those things normally… but tonight you were all of them at the same time."

"I was just enjoying myself," said Todd. "Everyone was great, weren't they? The reading went well, the questions"— *apart from Billy, chewing his own face off*—"it was all great."

"I think it's the book," said Sara. "I don't know how else to explain it. But ever since you got that book out of you, you've been... don't take this wrong, Todd, but you've been better."

"I suppose writing a book is like excavating something from one's soul," said Todd, and Sara laughed so hard she almost changed lanes.

"Please," she said, spluttering. "Please don't ever say that in a talk."

Then she got serious again.

"You know, maybe you're right. Maybe getting that book out of you got something else out too."

"Like gold in the rock?" asked Todd. "Or like poison from a wound?"

Sara didn't answer.

"You okay?" said Todd.

"Look," said Sara.

Todd looked. At first he couldn't see anything. Then he registered it. A police car, by the sidewalk. A cop talking to a broad woman in a housecoat.

"Isn't that Billy's place?" said Sara.

Drive on, Todd's mind said.

"You're right," Todd said. "Pull over."

Todd walked up to the cop.

"Can I help you, sir?" said the cop. He had a blond mustache and a really small nose.

"Is this something to do with Billy Cairns?" said Todd.

"Only I'm a friend of his."

"We both are," said Sara, slipping her arm in Todd's.

The cop narrowed his eyes.

"Yeah?" he said. "When's the last time you saw him?"

"Not for a while," said Todd. Sara nodded.

"You ain't kidding," said the cop. "He's been up there for weeks like that."

"Like what?" said Sara.

"Dead," said the woman in the housecoat, like she was trying to be helpful. "I found him. I'm his landlady."

"Oh no," said Sara. "Poor Billy."

"I guess you've been too busy to look in on him," said the cop. "Despite being friends and all."

"Hey," said Billy's landlady. "We all have things to do. I like to leave my tenants alone. Until, you know, they get too behind with the rent."

"Or they start to stink," said the cop. "And I do mean stink."

"Oh Lord," said Todd. He enfolded Sara with his arms. "Wait for me in the car," he murmured.

Todd watched Sara go. Then he turned to the landlady and said, "Pardon me for asking but—was there anything unusual about Billy's death?"

She looked at him quizzically. Todd felt an explanation was required.

"Because," he said, "it was weird for Billy not to be in touch. He was a buddy, you know? A pal. And it would have taken something big for him to stay away."

"There was something odd," said the landlady. "Apart from not leaving his apartment, that is."

146

"Save it for the station," said the cop. He turned to Todd. "This is a police matter."

Todd realized he had one chance. "What was odd?" he asked Billy's landlady.

"When I went in," she said, "there was all rice on the floor."

"Save it for—" said the cop.

"Be quiet, you," said Billy's landlady.

"Rice?" said Todd.

"I thought it was rice, anyway," said Billy's landlady. "It looked like rice, and it felt like rice under my feet. But when I bent down, I saw it couldn't be. It was too big, and too hard."

She shivered, cold under her housecoat.

"It wasn't rice at all," she said. "It was teeth. It was Billy's teeth."

The next day, Todd felt pretty subdued. The success of the reading seemed a long way in the past, and also kind of empty after what had happened with Billy. Sara had offered to stay over, but Todd felt he needed to be on his own, and Sara was okay with that (by the time Todd realized he should have asked Sara if she was also okay being on her own, she was gone).

One or two people called up to talk about the reading and how great it was, which didn't help. Todd couldn't stop thinking about Billy lying there for weeks, undiscovered and, frankly, un-given-a-shit-about.

What was it that Billy, or the thing that had once been Billy, had said to him? Todd tried to remember. Something about a hawk. Todd thought it might be a quote. In fact, he was damn sure it was a quote. He went into his study—now a tidier, cleaner place—and pulled down a few reference books. *The Oxford Dictionary Of Quotations. Brewer's Dictionary of Phrase and Fable. The Everyman Literary Encyclopedia. The World Encyclopedia.* And, finally, a book he'd guiltily used more than any of the others, a cheerful-looking hardback emblazoned with pictures of both writers and celebrities called *Who Said It?*

The dictionaries and encyclopedias confirmed that the question Billy had tried, and failed, to ask Todd was indeed part of a quotation. But it wasn't one that made a lot of sense to Todd:

Hamlet, Act II, Scene 2.

HAMLET: I am but mad north-north-west. When the
          wind is southerly, I know a hawk from a handsaw.

Which was interesting but made no sense, in context or, apparently, out of it. Todd decided there was nothing for it but to screw the highbrows and consult the oracle. He opened *Who Said It?*, found "hawk" in the index, and turned to the relevant page. And there it was.

"A hawk from a handsaw." This is a line from Hamlet, *where the eponymous Prince of Denmark has gone crazy. The saying may be something to do with different kinds of bird, but is deliberately obscure, which is why a lot of people misquote it as "a hawk and a HACKsaw."*

Todd closed the book. *Great,* he thought, *just my luck to be persecuted from beyond the grave by something that can't quote properly.*

Carrie called.

"How did it go last night?" she asked.

Todd erased all images of Billy, alive or dead, from his mind.

"Really well!" he said.

"Well, that's a good omen," said Carrie.

"Hometown crowd," Todd pointed out.

"Todd, once people realize how good *All My Colors* is," said Carrie, "the whole country's going to be a hometown crowd."

Todd imagined an entire nation sitting at his feet as he read to them.

"I have your finalized itinerary," said Carrie. "We're going to send it over to you today."

"I'd better pack," said Todd.

"You haven't *packed* yet?" giggled Carrie. "Todd, you are the least prepared author we have."

"Is that a bad thing?" Todd asked. He had a feeling it was. Being unprepared didn't sound like a good place to be.

"Todd, stay just the way you are," said Carrie. "You'll find being yourself is the best protection there is."

"Protection against what?"

"Oh, you know," said Carrie. "The cruel tides of fate, and whatnot. Now go and pack! And pack a lot!"

Todd packed. Then he sat next to his suitcase on the bed and waited. For what, he didn't know. It was only when it began to get dark outside that he stood up stiffly, carried his case downstairs, and went into the front room to watch TV.

•

When Sara came around that night, she found him, sitting in the dark with the television on.

"You'll go blind," she said, turning the light on. Todd blinked but didn't move.

"Todd? Are you okay?"

Todd managed a smile.

"I'm fine," he said. "Never better."

"If this is you when you're never better, I'd hate to see you when you're worse," said Sara. "You look awful."

"Gee, thanks," said Todd. He forced a smile. It must have been a poor attempt because Sara all but flinched.

"I *thought* as it was our last night together that we could celebrate," she said. "I have some terrible Illinois champagne and a couple of steaks."

"Illinois champagne? Now you're talking," Todd laughed.

"Yeah, did you know that this state used to be famous for its vineyards? Before Prohibition. We used to make some great wines, or so the guy in the liquor store told me. And then they passed the Volstead Act and boom, we never got the magic back."

"You're really selling it to me."

"Well, the liquor store guy did a number on me, so now it's your turn."

Todd stood up. He put his hands on Sara's shoulders, gently.

"Somehow when I'm with you," he said, "those old gray clouds just vanish."

"So now I'm what?" said Sara. "The wind. Thanks."

Todd held her.

"You're the listening wind," he said. "There's a difference."

She looked at him, curiously. Todd threw back his head and began to quote:

"*Where the remote Bermudas ride in the ocean's bosom unespyed*," he said. "*From a small boat, that row'd along, the listening winds received this song.* Andrew Marvell."

"That's beautiful," said Sara. "Also," she noted, "I see that you're quoting again. It's been a while."

Todd realized that Sara was right. He'd wondered if his eidetic memory had gone forever.

"I must have remembered it just for you," he said. "Now we'd better get that Illinois fizz in the fridge."

"Yes, sir," said Sara. She even saluted him.

It was the end of the quiet time.

That night, Todd and Sara made love. It was probably the first time, thought Todd, that he had made love in the real sense of the word. Over the years, Todd had fucked, screwed, entered, had sex with, poked, porked, and performed acts of a non-euphemistic nature with many women, only one of whom he had been married to, but tonight was the first time he had been involved in what he was forced to admit was an act of romantic love.

It was also the first time, as he lay there in the dark, Sara sleeping on her side, that Todd found himself thinking of the women he'd been with before. He hadn't been what you'd call an inconsiderate lover, just an inconsiderate person. The sex was very attentive but the rest of it—the thoughtlessness, the botched relationships, the sheer inability to give a flying one about anybody else—was anything but.

Todd found himself thinking about Janis. He wondered what she'd ever got from their marriage. After a minute or two, he realized he'd come up with nothing and gave up wondering.

When I get back from this tour, he thought, *I'm going to call up Janis's lawyer and tell him I'll sign the damn document.*

Then he fell asleep, as at peace with himself as he ever had been or ever would be.

PART
TWO

FIVE

Todd wasn't sure about the etiquette of heading out on a book tour. He had envisaged himself slipping out of bed in the gray dawn, leaving a note for Sara and driving off in the cold morning fog. But in the end he woke up late and went downstairs to find that Sara was making French toast in the kitchen.

"I'm doing this as a displacement activity," she explained. "Making breakfast instead of crying."

"I'll be back before you know it," promised Todd. "And I'll call every night."

"I'd kind of rather you didn't," said Sara. "I think I'd find it hard to take. Send me postcards instead, why don't you? Like on that Bruce Springsteen album."

She tapped him on the chest with a spatula.

"Find me," she said, "the tackiest postcards you can. *Greetings from Stoolbend*. With all fancy lettering and a photo of the World's Largest Pumpkin."

"I will," said Todd, and he meant it.

"Now eat," said Sara.

Sara waved goodbye from the porch as Todd swung the Volvo into the road. He was going to honk cheerfully as he drove off, but for some reason this idea made him depressed, so he just took a final look back in the rear-view mirror, saw Sara close the door behind her, and lit out for the highway.

At the lights, Todd consulted his map. His first reading was a full day's drive from here; he would be driving for most of the day if he was going to get there in time and check in to his accommodation after the event. He was a good map-reader and not too concerned about getting lost. It was all just a question of keeping going.

Four hours later, Todd's bladder was painfully full while his stomach was almost as painfully empty. Todd looked at the Volvo's clock. He was making good time and there was a truck stop just up ahead.

Todd pulled off the highway and into the parking lot.

The stop was largely full of Mexican truckers, which explained the counter menu. After a happy visit to the bathroom, Todd drank a Coke and ate a burrito. He was about to head back to the car when he saw a rack of postcards. They were generic *Illinois: Home of* some damn thing or other cards, but they fulfilled Sara's tackiness requirements and besides, he didn't know when he would be able to pick up some more postcards.

He paid for them and walked out into the sunshine. Across the way, two people were laughing about something.

It was the kind of snapshot of time you want to preserve, what the TV ads called a Polaroid moment.

It ended a second later when Todd realized that one of the people laughing was Janis.

She looked different. Janis was wearing clothes that she would never have looked at six months ago: jeans and matching denim jacket. Her hair was cut short, almost like an old rock'n'roller. And she was wearing biker boots. Todd's Janis had hated boots, said they deformed her feet or something, but this Janis looked like, Todd thought uncharitably, the fucking Fonz. He had to admit, reluctantly, that it suited her.

Todd felt a bump at his shoulder. He turned, to see *her*. *The other woman*. She walked past him, not saying a word, and before Todd could see her face, slid a bike helmet over her head. She was wearing a leather jacket, jeans, and motorcycle boots. She slid her legs onto the pillion of a big black Harley, and when Janis walked over to the bike, reached down, and pulled a still laughing Janis on with her.

Todd stared as Janis wedged on her own helmet, and the Harley roared into full-throated life and peeled out onto the highway. He didn't notice his grip slacken on the brown paper bag of postcards before it fell to the floor. He walked back to the Volvo and sat behind the wheel, staring into space for half an hour.

What he'd seen just hadn't seemed *real*. Oh, sure, he was well aware of his prejudices and fears concerning Janis and her newfound desires. He was, ironically, man enough to admit that he felt threatened by the idea of Janis preferring a woman to him. The thought made him feel inadequate but he was not so dumb as to equate lesbians with dickless men. Todd had read, and even listened, enough to pick up on a few modern notions about gender and sexuality.

But there was something a little pat about what he'd seen. Todd had read an article in *Playboy* about a guy whose job it was to make movies set in the past look real. And one thing the guy said had stuck with him: it was that the worst thing you can do with a historical piece is—and this was the guy's word—*smother it*. By which he meant, don't overdo the period detail. "In the fifties, say," the guy said, "not everyone was dressing like it was the fifties. Not everyone. Some people were behind the times, like people are now. Not everyone was driving a brand new 1950s car. Not everyone had a color TV. We weren't all listening to Elvis. But in a bad period piece—everybody looks *too* period."

That was it. Todd was no movie-maker, but he bet that if someone had set out to make a movie about two lesbians going out on the road together and they'd wanted to *smother it* in the kind of details people associated with lesbians, they might have done something like what Todd had just witnessed. The clothes. The hair. The biker boots. The *bike*, for fuck's sake.

What Todd had seen had been as real as the fingers on his hand. But what he'd seen had, equally, been completely unreal.

After that, the rest of the journey felt pretty unreal, too. The miles slipped by, the highway signs changed, Todd was overtaken by cars and trucks (but never a black Harley) and in turn overtook other cars and trucks, and all the time his destination approached, but the sense of going somewhere had been replaced by a sense of—what, Todd didn't know. Not even movement.

As a child, Todd had owned an auto-racing game where the road was a continuous loop of cloth, like a caterpillar track, and the game's toy cars remained still while the track moved under them, creating a back-to-front illusion of forward motion. That was how he felt now, that the world was shifting around him to create an illusion of progress.

He was able to shake the feeling off when he finally saw his exit come up on the highway. Todd turned the Volvo onto the ramp and looped off toward a smaller road leading to his first destination.

Amber, Illinois was a college town, more populous than DeKalb but still hardly in the big leagues. At this time of year, it was busy, the new college year bringing an influx of freshmen still finding their way around and adjusting to the confusion and excitement of what Timothy would have called "the groves of Academe."

As it happened, the groves of Academe were completely deserted when Todd drove in that late afternoon. Most of the students were still in lectures, Todd supposed, while the rest of the town was at work. Todd wasn't too worried—he was in too much of a state of ignorance about the whole business of doing a book tour to have any real opinions about any of it—as his concerns were entirely practical. Like, were they going to feed him or should he get something to eat now? Was there in fact time for him to check in at his motel or should he not risk it? Whatever, he needed to freshen up or at least stretch a little—a day in a car was not the best preparation for appearing before an audience.

In the end, he decided the best thing to do would be to find the venue and make himself known to whoever was expecting him. Todd pulled out the blue folder Sara had given him to keep his itinerary in and extracted the first sheet of paper, which told him that he would be speaking at Action Books at 7:30 P.M. Checking the map, and noting that he had just under two hours before his event began, Todd started the Volvo up again and headed for Action Books.

The only college town bookstore that Todd knew well—Legolas—mostly took its heart and soul from the early 1970s, when whimsy, flowers, and dragons had been popular. Action Books was its polar opposite, a modern, jagged shrine to everything considered happening and now in the late seventies.

Where Legolas was a place of almost-quiet contemplation, with panpipe music emanating discreetly from Timothy's cassette player, Action was brash, modern, and noisy. New wave rock burst from wall-mounted speakers, and as Todd entered, a deafening song with a squawking saxophone riff was telling the customers to contort themselves. Where Legolas favored royal blue walls like some kind of throne room, the walls in Action were exposed brickwork painted with red and white diagonal stripes. And where Legolas featured the odd reproduction of an illustration from *Winnie-the-Pooh*, Action was a riot of Xeroxed band posters and political slogan art.

The whole place was just noise to Todd. He approached the counter where a girl wearing a plastic T-shirt with one cap sleeve torn off was talking to another, similarly dressed girl. After waiting a minute for her to notice him, Todd was forced to take matters into his own hands and cough loudly. Only then did the girl stop her conversation and look up.

"Hi," said Todd. "My name is Todd Milstead."

The girl stared at him.

"Hi," she said. "My name is Tina."

Todd swallowed his irritation.

"Hi, Tina," he said. "I'm here for the reading."

"Oh," said Tina.

"Yeah," said Todd. "So I was wondering—"

"The reading isn't until seven thirty," Tina said, and turned back to her friend.

"No," said Todd. "I am the reading. I mean, I'm the person doing the reading."

As Tina took this information in, Todd skimmed the walls wildly for some evidence of the reading's existence.

"There," he said, pointing to a small poster on the wall behind Tina.

"I don't book the events," she said.

"Then," said Todd, balling his fists inside his coat pocket, "may I please speak with the person who does?"

This had the effect of making Tina go into a sort of trance. She looked blankly at the wall behind Todd. Then, just as Todd was about to snap his fingers, she said, "Okay," and picked up the phone.

"He's here," she said into it. "The guy! Who else, Hitler?"

She put the phone down. "He's on his way," she said to Todd.

Ten minutes later, the door opened and a tall black man

with a large beard and enormous, owl-like glasses came in. He walked right up to Todd and shook his hand.

"I am so, so sorry," he said in what Todd took a moment to realize was a British accent. "Tina is a fucking idiot."

"Hey!" said Tina, but without much enthusiasm. Todd guessed she'd heard it before.

"Andrew Malcolm," said the tall man. "Thank you for coming, Mr. Milstead."

"Todd," said Todd.

"Has anyone offered you a— what am I saying, of course they haven't," said Andrew. "Screw this, let's go to the pub."

"Fine by me," said Todd.

The bartender brought them two drinks.

"What is this?" said Todd, looking down at the muddy drink in front of him.

"Bass," said Andrew.

"Like the fish?" said Todd.

"Yep," Andrew said. "It's imported. About the only thing I miss about the good old United Kingdom. Cheers."

And he drank half his Bass in one swig. Todd tried to follow suit, but the taste proved too pondish for him.

"It really is very good of you to come," Andrew said. "A lot of writers, when they look us up on the map and see how far we are from anywhere, phone up and cancel. Some of them don't even do that. They just fail to show."

"This is my first time," said Todd. "Besides, this is exciting. A new town."

"You're very kind," Andrew said. "Loved the book, by the way."

"You read it?" said Todd. "You have a copy?"

Andrew looked at him. "I have fifty copies," he said. "I run a bookstore."

"But," Todd said, sounding stupid even to himself, "it's not out yet. Is it?"

"This is your first novel, isn't it?" Andrew asked, not unkindly.

"Yes," said Todd. "I have to admit I'm new to this."

"Okay," said Andrew. "Your novel—your *excellent* novel—has been delivered to my store and, I'm guessing, hundreds of other stores. I'm surprised your publisher didn't tell you. Did you get your author copies?"

"Yes," said Todd.

"Well, that would be about the time they also sent out the rest of the books," said Andrew. "Mr. Milstead, your books are available all over America."

"America," marveled Todd, as though he'd previously thought his books were only available in Tierra del Fuego, or Holland.

"You knew that, right?" said Andrew.

"Of course!" said Todd. "I have a book tour, after all. I'm going to… at least four states."

"Four?" said Andrew. "As many as that?"

Todd had to look at him to ensure that he was joking.

"They're all quite big states," he said, defensively. "I mean, when I say big, I don't mean like Alaska, or Texas…" Todd was now almost standing outside his own body, seeing himself dig his own grave.

"I know what you mean," said Andrew. "Seems to me you need a drink. An American drink, this time."

And he fetched them two glasses of bourbon.

"When I came here," he said, "I was amazed at the size of the whiskey glasses. Back home, you barely get enough whiskey to bathe a contact lens in. But here—these things are like buckets."

"I'll drink to that," said Todd, who had just realized that all Andrew was doing was trying to calm his nerves.

They drank some bourbon, and went back to the bookstore.

"What the hell?" said Andrew.

"What's wrong?" said Todd.

"This is unprecedented," said Andrew.

He was looking at a line of people that extended down the street.

"Must be a great restaurant," said Todd.

"There's only one great restaurant here, and it's terrible," Andrew said. "Mr. Milstead, this line is for you."

"Me?" Todd said.

"Maybe they want refunds," Andrew said, then grinned. "Wow. For once in my life I'm going to sell some books that aren't on the college curriculum. Move over, Saul Bellow, and let Todd Milstead take over."

The line parted for them as Andrew opened the door and went inside.

Tina's eyes were wide and her nostrils were flared.

"There's hundreds of them!" she said. "I'm going home."

"Then you don't get paid," said Andrew. "Did you get the wine?"

"Yes, I got the wine," said Tina. "It's over there. And I laid out the books, and the chairs. It's ready. But I need to get out of here, I'm having such a panic attack."

"Breathe into this," Andrew said, handing her a brown paper bag with ACTION BOOKS written on the side. Tina subsided into vexed silence as Todd removed his coat, draped it over the tall chair he'd apparently be perched on, and waited for—what, he didn't know.

Slowly coming out of her pout, Tina put on a tape—*Bad Brains Live At The Knitting Factory*, just the kind of music to soothe an audience before a reading, Todd thought—and opened the door.

If the first reading had been okay, the second was even better. Better because it wasn't a home crowd. Because the room wasn't full of people who were only there because they knew him. Because there was a fair chance that some of the people here—*some of the very attractive young people here*, thought Todd—had read *All My Colors*, and were here because they liked it. And because this was real; they were real people in a real room, and Todd was, to all appearances, a real writer, with a real book to talk about. Whatever anyone might say, there was nobody more qualified to talk about this book than Todd, and anyway hadn't this book been written by the sweat of his brow, if nothing else?

The people (*kids*) in the room were rapt. Todd's readings induced attentive gazes in those who obviously hadn't read the book and nods of pleased recognition in those who had. Lines he hadn't expected to got laughs, lines he had expected to get laughs got sage nods. But mostly there was a hand, and it was his, and he had his audience in the palm of it.

The reading ended, and then there were questions

from the floor. These were surprisingly varied. There was the question about where he got his ideas from again, to which Todd gave the same answer. There were a couple of questions that weren't really questions, which was fine, because while they went on a bit, they did at least contain phrases like "I really loved your book" and even, "I gotta say, this is the best thing I ever read". That was particularly good, Todd felt, because the person who said it wasn't a fey young girl with too much Emily Dickinson in her system, but a big football player-looking guy who appeared entirely surprised and confused to be here, but was here, and stayed behind so Todd could autograph his book.

Todd autographed a lot of books, so many that his signature went from the full *Todd Milstead* that he signed his checks with, to a kind of abbreviated one-line yelp. Todd counted the books as he was signing them, and was surprised that there were more than fifty.

"People must be buying them in Barnes and Noble, the traitors, and bringing them here," said Andrew. "Oh well, more people in my store, can't be all bad. Buy some books!" he suddenly shouted. Todd reckoned that Andrew had been at the free wine. So had Tina, who was lurking behind Andrew. She suddenly darted out, said, "That was okay," and left the building.

"Wow," said Andrew. "The last thing she liked was *The Basketball Diaries*. You're in good company, Todd."

The store was empty now.

"That was great," said Andrew. He extended his hand. "One day I will be able to tell my grandchildren that I met the author of *All My Colors*."

"I guess," said Todd. He pulled a smile out of the hat. "Now what—" he began.

"I have to go," Andrew said. "I live a long way from here and my wife works. Got to be up with the lark to get the kids ready for school. Can I give you a ride to your accommodation?"

"No thanks," said Todd, who had been hoping for more Bass and bourbon. "My car is here so I can drive myself back." *And enjoy the pleasures of the candy bar machine in the corridor*, he thought.

"Well, great," said Andrew. "Good luck, Todd."

Todd watched as Andrew made his way back to his car. He had a desultory look around, in case there was a gang of new young teenage fans waiting to invite him to a crazy party, but there was no one. He trudged back to the Volvo and drove to his motel, hoping it wasn't too late to check in.

The motel receptionist—a motherly woman in her early fifties wearing a badge with WANDA written on it—was pleased to see Todd.

"I have been waiting up specially," said Wanda. She handed him a small sheaf of paper.

"What's this?" asked Todd.

"Your messages," Wanda said. "Somebody's been trying to call you since lunchtime."

Todd's first thought was Sara. He riffled through the sheaf. A New York number. Nora.

"Thanks," he said.

Wanda winked. "Next time, check in earlier," she said.

Todd stifled the urge to wink back at her. Instead he picked up his bag and headed for his room.

It was pleasant enough. There was a painting on the wall

of something brown. The TV had no remote but it worked fine. The bed was firm and the linen clean. And there was a telephone on the desk. Todd picked it up and called the number Nora had left. It was late in New York but Todd figured leaving that many messages meant he was supposed to call as soon as.

After three rings, Nora picked up.

"Todd!" she almost shouted.

"Hi, Nora," said Todd. "Is everything okay?"

"Shut up!" shouted Nora, and it took Todd a moment to realize she didn't mean him. "Sorry," she said. "I was just telling some other people to shut up talking."

Todd could hear now that Nora was a bit tipsy. "We're having a party," she explained. "To celebrate."

"Celebrate what?" asked Todd.

"Oh, that's right," Nora said. "You don't know."

Todd was now thoroughly confused, a condition not helped when Nora said:

"Todd Milstead is a voice to listen to, and a voice to listen out for."

"Thanks," said Todd, wondering just how drunk Nora was.

"*All My Colors* is a *tour de force*," said Nora, and Todd realized that she was quoting something. "But it's more than that. *Tours de force* come and go. This book is special. Find it. Buy it. Read it."

"What's that from?" said Todd. "Is it a press release? Because it's kind of over the top."

"It's not a press release," said Nora. "It's the *New York Times*."

Todd didn't understand at first. Then he got it.

"You mean a review?" he said. "You mean the *New York Times* reviewed my book?"

"Yes," said Nora, "that is exactly what I mean."

"How did they get hold of it? I mean... I'm sorry, I have no idea what I mean."

"A whole page," said Nora. "With your photograph. Which reminds me, Carrie," she said, her voice fading, "we need to get someone to Todd right away. The photo the *Times* used, I don't know where they got it from but— are you still there, Todd?"

"Yes," said Todd, looking at the painting of the brown thing. "I'm still here."

"This changes everything," said Nora. "Obviously we can't cancel the tour at this stage, so I'm afraid you'll still be circling the boondocks for a while. But we can set up more, and better, appearances now."

"Okay," said Todd, who until that second had no idea that he was circling the boondocks. *Come on*, the painting of the brown thing told his brain, *what could be more boondocks than this?*

"In the meantime, go to bed, get some sleep, and carry on as you were," said Nora. "Because tomorrow, you're going to wake up famous."

The next day, Todd woke up, and didn't feel particularly famous. Wanda pointed him in the direction of a local diner, and he enjoyed a hefty breakfast. Afterward, he looked for somewhere selling newspapers, but with no luck, so he checked out of the motel, and sat in the car inspecting his slightly random itinerary. His next stop, he was surprised to see, was Chicago. Not that Todd was a stranger to Chicago—it was the nearest drivable city and he went as often as he could—but it was different being invited to go there.

He got back in the Volvo, arranged his maps on the front seat, and nosed out onto the highway. He had time to find out where he was appearing and—he thought with a sudden, unusual thrill—time to hit a truck stop, pick up a *New York Times* and see just exactly how famous he was.

One of the great mysteries in life is that you can never find the newspaper you want when you really need it. It seemed to Todd as he scoured the periodical section of the truck stop that they had every paper and magazine known to mankind apart from the one he actually wanted. There were local papers, national papers, even foreign papers—Todd was convinced he saw a lone copy of *Pravda* in among the *USA Todays*—but no *New York Times*.

"Excuse me," he said to the clerk. "Do you have the *New York Times*?"

The clerk stared at him.

"No, then," said Todd, and left.

It was the same wherever he went. No truck stop, no roadside diner—Todd even searched a drive-in McDonald's from top to bottom for a discarded copy—nothing, and nowhere. Perhaps there was some turf war between the Chicago papers and New York. Perhaps there was an East Coast newspaper strike. Todd had, frankly, no idea. He got back in the Volvo and drove on.

By the time he reached Chicago, his unspoken fantasies—*A tickertape parade? For me? You shouldn't have!*—were packed away, and all he could think about was the bathroom break he should have taken forty minutes ago. At the first stop light, Todd glanced at his map. He was only a few blocks from his hotel. Todd hoped it was a decent hotel and not some motel that had somehow crawled into the city to die.

The Randall wasn't a fleapit and it didn't look like it had ever crawled anywhere. Even as Todd pulled up outside to see if there was somewhere to park, a man in a top hat was tapping on the Volvo's window to get his attention.

"May we park your car, sir?" said the man.

"Okay," said Todd, wondering how the man was going to get his top hat inside the car. But as he stepped out, Top Hat gave his keys to a much smaller man, who slid into the Volvo and drove away with enviable ease.

"Is this your only bag?" said Top Hat, and, without waiting for an answer, picked up Todd's grip and strode into the hotel with it. Todd followed, nearly losing an arm in the revolving door.

Reception was a huge counter. It reminded Todd of a late night movie he'd seen where the gateway to Heaven was like a huge hotel lobby. The counter seemed to stretch from one side of the street to the other, and was occupied, apparently, by former models. One of them smiled at Todd as he shambled up to her. He gave her his name and she ran a fountain pen down a list of printed names.

"Oh," she said. "There appears to be a— one moment please."

She picked up a phone and, still smiling at Todd without actually making eye contact, said, "Hello, this is reception.

I have a Mr. Milstead here but— I see."

She put the phone down and cranked up her smile to such a degree that Todd wondered if her face would actually split in half.

"Your room has been changed," she said. "Please follow Michael."

Todd turned to see a smiling man with one hand on a huge baggage trolley. On the trolley, looking ashamed to be there, was Todd's grip. Todd followed Michael to the lift.

After a very long time, the lift stopped and the doors opened. The corridor in front of Todd was a testament to the power of carpet. There was a lot of it, and it went on for miles. Eventually, just when Todd thought all he would ever hear was the soft hiss of the baggage cart's wheels, Michael took out a key, opened a door and led the way into a tiny room.

Todd inhaled until his ribs were creaking as he tried to squeeze in next to Michael and the baggage cart.

"If you could just wait here in the anteroom," said Michael, "I'll take the cart in first." And he pushed open another door.

Todd stepped in after Michael, and found himself in the largest room he'd ever seen that didn't actually have a sports game taking place inside it. There were several sofas dotted about, as if grazing, some escritoires in case the guest wanted to invite a few pals back to do some writing, and a huge TV that looked more like a glass-fronted truck than an actual television.

Todd noticed something.

"There's no bed," he said.

Michael gave him an odd look, and extended an arm

like a graceful traffic cop. He was pointing at yet another doorway, inside which was a bedroom containing a bed so large, so wide and—Todd soon discovered—so deep that it seemed to compel sleep rather than encourage it.

Michael showed Todd how a few things worked—the TV, the curtains, the air conditioning—and would, Todd felt, have gone on showing Todd how things worked—the windows, the bath, the pen and pad—if Todd hadn't suddenly remembered something and hastily pulled out his wallet.

"Thanks," he said and stuffed a crumpled note into Michael's hand. Michael nodded and was gone before Todd could register that he had just given him his last fifty dollars.

Todd did all the things people do in penthouse suites. He ran the bath, and emptied all the little bottles in the bathroom into it. He changed channels on the TV while eating pretzels in a toweling robe. He took a tiny bottle of bourbon out of the minibar, looked at the tariff and put it back again. Finally he unpacked his clothes, filled the washbasin with hot soapy water and dropped in a pair of dirty socks and his boxer shorts. It was only then that he felt able to lie down on the enormous bed and, before his head sank into the squashy grip of the enormous pillows, remember to pick up the phone and call Sara.

She answered on the second ring.

"Todd? Is that you?"

"How did you know?"

"I recognized the heavy breathing."

Todd laughed.

"How are you, Sara?"

"Oh, you know. Just trying to make my house look like a home again. I swear, I haven't been outside all day."

"I wish you were here."

"Believe me, I wish I was there too. How's it going?"

Todd looked around the room. It seemed to have no horizon.

"Okay, I think," he said. "All right so far, anyway."

Then he saw it. A low table, with a stack of magazines on it. Magazines, and newspapers.

"Good, I'm glad. So where are you now? Chicago, right?"

"Yeah," said Todd, vaguely. He was on his feet now, still holding the phone but moving toward the table.

"How's the hotel?"

"Good. It's good," said Todd. He could almost reach the table, but the phone cord was too short. He lay the receiver on the bed and crossed the short distance to the table. On top of the pile were a couple of newspapers.

The top one was the *Chicago Sun-Tribune*, but the one below it… *Yes*, thought Todd. The *New York Times*. He sat on the bed and was about to open it when he remembered the telephone.

"—not sure if I'm actually going to go ahead with it," Sara was saying. "What do you think?"

"Um," said Todd. "What do you think you should do?"

Silence for a second.

"You're tired," said Sara. "Maybe I should call back later."

"No!" Todd almost shouted. "I got distracted. I'm sorry."

"Are you alone in there?" asked Sara, teasingly.

"Of course," said Todd. "There's nobody here but me. I swear. Listen."

And he held the telephone mouthpiece up high.

"Well, that'd stand up in court," Sara said.

"Ho ho," said Todd. His eyes lit on the *New York Times* again.

"Listen, seriously, we should talk about the house," Sara said. "But not now. You're tired and I know you have an event."

"Sure thing," said Todd. "I better go. I—"

Another pause.

"You what?" said Sara.

"I... will see you soon," said Todd.

"And I will see you soon," Sara said, good-humouredly. "Bye, Todd."

She put the phone down.

"Okay then," said Todd, and opened the *New York Times*.

The book reviews were snuggled away in the heart of the paper, but it wasn't too hard for Todd to find what he was looking for. It was opposite a full page ad for a stage production of *Blithe Spirit*, and it was easy for Todd to find because right in the middle of the page was the same photograph of Todd that had been in the *Beacon* (the same, except that in the *Beaconfused*, the image had looked cool and stylish, whereas in the *Times*, Todd's picture looked like a hick who'd recently tunneled out of a hay bale). There was a large headline—"A Different Rainbow"—and a whole lot of words. In all his years of reading reviews, essays, and theses, Todd had never seen so many words aimed at just one book. He set about consuming the piece.

Ten minutes later, his mind ticking over, Todd was sated. According to the reviewer, *All My Colors* was the book of the year, if not the decade. It combined a modern attitude to life and society with an almost arch 1950s feel, "almost as if," the reviewer had written, "Mr. Milstead's novel had been transported from an earlier time, with a frank contemporary take on the war between men and women running through it like a seam of anachronistic yet fitting iron." Todd wasn't sure if iron could be anachronistic yet fitting but he didn't really mind. The short gist of the very long review was as Nora had said: the reviewer thought the book was great, and wanted everyone to know that. Todd didn't know the circulation figures of the *Times*, but he guessed that an awful lot of people would know about *All My Colors* now.

Todd looked at his watch. He had just enough time to shower and change before walking to the venue for his event that night. As he dressed afterward, he thought of calling Sara back—*hey, if you get a moment, you might want to step out and pick up a* New York Times *for yourself. Oh, no reason*—but decided she'd find out soon enough. Besides, he could pick up a few copies of the paper before tomorrow, as souvenirs.

Todd took the elevator down to street level and walked across the lobby. He wondered if anybody was looking at him and thinking, *hey, I just saw a picture of that guy in the paper* or even *wow, isn't that Todd Milstead, America's hottest new author?* He doubted it, but it was fun to imagine.

Tonight's venue was a bookstore by the name of Volume, and it was apparently not far from the old Water Tower. Todd located it easily. Volume lived up to its name by being enormous, at least four storeys high and dominating the small plaza that it overlooked. Todd strolled in, feeling reasonably relaxed. Volume had a large magazine section and Todd couldn't help walking past the newspapers and directing a mental *hello* at them, like an old friend seen out of the corner of one's eye.

Taped to a pillar was a picture of Todd—*the usual one*, he thought, mock-jaded—with the words TODD MILSTEAD AUTHOR OF ALL MY COLORS 7:30 MEZZANINE. Todd located a map of the store, found an escalator, and ascended to the mezzanine.

Todd had always thought that a mezzanine was a kind of half floor, more like a landing that had got slightly ahead of itself. But this mezzanine was almost regal in its ambitions. Bookshelf after bookshelf stretched out in front of Todd, interrupted only by outbreaks of couches. There was, Todd noted, a sort of canteen area, serving coffee and pastries for the benefit of people who liked to get food on their reading matter. And at the back of the mezzanine, in front of a large picture window overlooking the Tower, some people were setting up a microphone in front of a lectern.

Todd looked at his watch. Seven P.M. *Guess some people don't read the papers*, part of his brain grouchily announced to itself. *Oh, have you been in the paper?* responded another part of his brain. Wondering where everybody—anybody—was, Todd walked over to the lectern.

"He's here!" cried a young woman in enormous red glasses, walking toward him at the same time. Her companions stopped what they were doing, and moved toward Todd almost as if they planned to throw him to the ground. Instead they merely surrounded him and—it seemed to Todd—just stood there and *admired* him somehow.

"I'm Leah Hansen," said the woman in red glasses, "and I am so glad you could make it."

"Yeah," said a chubby man in a Cars T-shirt, "some of us thought that you'd get a better offer. On account of the *Times* review."

"It wasn't that bad a review, was it?" said Todd.

Everyone laughed as soon as they realized Todd was making a joke.

"We better get you in the office before the masses descend," said Leah.

"Where are they?" asked Todd. "These masses? I didn't see anyone as I came in."

Leah smiled. She led Todd to a large window on their right.

"That's because you used the front entrance," she said. "The cops told us to make everyone stand in line by the side entrance. Look down."

Todd looked down. There were at least a hundred people down there.

"That's a lot of people," he said.

If Leah thought the author of *All My Colors* might have had something more insightful to add, she didn't say anything.

"That's just the advance ticket holders," she said. "People have been calling all day. We're also expecting a big walkup. Which brings me on to my final point—"

Leah nodded at a large table nearby. Todd took a moment to let it sink in. It was piled to chest height with hardback copies of *All My Colors*.

"I really hope you like signing books," she said.

•

Todd sat in the office with Leah's copy of the new Joan Didion, which he found confusing, but the only other reading matter was his *New York Times*, and he was damned if he was going to be seen reading that in public (besides, his eidetic memory was almost back at full strength now, and he found himself quite able to recall whole chunks of the review).

Leah brought him a Coke and said, "I'm going to say a few words to introduce you and then you're on, if that's okay."

"Sure," said Todd. "When?"

"Now," Leah said.

Later, Todd could only think of the evening as a movie, the kind where everything unfolds in slow motion with elegiac music underneath all of the action.

As he walked across the carpet, the bookstore staff moved back to let him through, applauding as he neared the lectern. Leah said a few words and, at the sound of his name, there was a small eruption of clapping and cheering.

It was the best moment of his short career.

Todd took his place behind the lectern, smiled, pulled his notes from his pocket, and held them up semi-humorously as if to signal to the audience that this wasn't going to take all night. He looked over at Leah.

"I left my darn book at home," he said, and got a burst of *this guy's all right* laughter.

Then he placed his hands on either side of the lectern, and took a good look at the audience. There were plenty of them, mostly young, which was good, but one or two older people, a real mixture of men and women, and not all white faces either.

"I guess you all get the *New York Times* in Chicago," he said, and earned himself an easy, but warm, shot of laughter. "Okay," he went on, after the laughing died down. "I promise not to keep mentioning my full-page rave review."

There was more laughter, which Todd could see was also enough laughter.

"Good evening," he said. "My name is Todd Milstead, I'm from DeKalb, Illinois"—he paused for, and got, a whoop from a college boy—"and I am here tonight to read from my novel, *All My Colors*."

The mention of the book's title created a sudden stillness in the room. A snatch of poetry came into Todd's head, some bit of Victorian English nonsense. *There's a breathless hush in the Close to-night.* Todd had no idea what a close was, but tonight, in this room, there was definitely a breathless hush. And it was all for him.

"I'm going to begin tonight by assuming that not everybody has had a chance to read the book," he said. "So, instead of standing up here and explaining the whole thing, scene by scene, I'm just going to read the opening pages. If that's all right with everyone."

The room nodded.

"Okay," said Todd, and opened the book. "*All My Colors*, Chapter One…"

He finished the first reading. The audience was quiet, and for a moment, Todd thought he'd lost them, or maybe they just hated him and his book. But then he realized some people were smiling, and some were even crying, and then the room was swamped in a wave, that was exactly the right word, a rolling wave of applause, and cheering, and foot-stamping (and, of course, whooping from Whooping Guy).

"Wow," said Todd. "I can't wait to hear what you think of Chapter Two."

Warm, relaxed laughter followed that remark, as though everybody in the room was an old friend. *First we take Chicago*, thought Todd.

"I'm kidding, of course," he said. "I have no intention of reading the whole book. That's your job. What I'm going to do now is—"

Todd consulted his notes. They were long, and detailed, and, if he was being honest, incoherent. He made a snap decision, and raised his eyes from the paper.

"Talk about stuff," Todd said. "By which I mean, what this book is to me. Where it came from, how it came into existence, and how it fits into the world today."

If there was one thing Todd was good at, it was talking. Which is what he did, and did it so well that some of the audience that night wondered how he was able to keep such a *distance* from his subject matter. Why, they might have said to themselves as they lined up for Todd's autograph on their books, it was almost as if he was talking about someone else's book.

Todd talked. And talked. And talked, until Leah looked in his direction and tapped her watch.

"Wow," said Todd. "It seems I have gabbed away half the night. I better read my second extract."

As he said this, he looked at Leah. She nodded back.

"What I'm going to read now," said Todd, "is—"

He stopped, interrupted by a loud noise, like someone starting a motorbike.

"Excuse me," he said. "I'm going to read—"

The noise leapt in volume, like someone was starting up a bike right there in the room. But nobody reacted.

"Can anyone else hear that?" Todd asked.

There was a shaking of heads.

"Right," said Todd. "Sorry, I must be tired from the drive. Okay, here we go. I'm gonna read from Chapter Four, where—"

Now the noise was so loud Todd almost yelped. He tried to calm down. *It's just in your head*, he thought. *Ignore it and it'll go away.* He looked around the room.

"Nobody else can hear it?" he said. This was a mistake. Now the crowd was confused and unhappy. Having just fallen for the author of *All My Colors*, they very much did not want to learn that he was crazy.

"I'm sorry," said Todd. "I get these bouts, these bouts of tinnitus."

Relief in the room. Something they'd heard of, physical and containable. The guy wasn't nuts after all.

Todd smiled, put both hands back on the sides of the lectern. Miraculously, the noise stopped, as though someone had twisted a key in the ignition. He paused to make sure it was gone, then said, "Nerves. That's what brings it on."

"You got nothing to be nervous about!" shouted a friendly voice.

"Oh come on!" Todd laughed. "In this room? Surrounded by all these books?"

He waved an arm expansively around the room. It did actually seem to Todd that the shelves were forming a kind of ring around him, their spines pushed out like rectangular shields to hem him in.

"All these names!" he cried, improvising wildly. "Jane Austen and Iris Murdoch and—"

Lost for names, Todd looked at the nearest shelf for inspiration. *Staff Favorites,* it said.

"Margaret Atwood! Ursula LeGuin!" he shouted. "Are there any guys on this shelf?"

More laughter as Todd walked over to the shelf and made a show of peering at it intensely.

"James Joyce! There we go! Anthony Burgess! Jake Turner!"

As the audience gave out its warm laughter again, Todd did a mental double take. *Jake Turner? I know that name.* He looked more closely at the books.

Ulysses.

A Clockwork Orange.

All My Colors.

Todd froze. He pulled the book out.

Rainbow cover. Hardback. *All My Colors.* By Jake Turner.

Todd opened the book. *First published The Whitney Press 1966. The rights of Jake Turner to be identified as the author of this book are established.*

"Are you all right, Todd?" Leah was at his side.

Todd slammed the book back into its place so hard that *Ulysses* almost rattled.

"I'm fine," he said. "I just got carried away in a sea of literature!" he told the audience. "Please excuse me."

He returned to the lectern.

"Chapter Four," he said, and began to read.

The second reading, everyone who was there agreed afterward, was nowhere near as good as the first. It wasn't that the *extract* was no good—the chapter that Todd read out was excellent. It was more the actual reading. He kept stopping, looking over at the bookshelf, mumbling to himself, taking a sip—a big sip—of red wine, and then starting again, and stopping, and starting. The whole thing was a mess, people said afterward, and if the book hadn't been so damn good, they might have just gone home.

The Q&A part of the evening was, at Leah's suggestion, abandoned, much to the relief of several people in the audience who'd noted Todd's stammering, confused demeanor and had decided that tonight was not the night to ask him who his influences were or if he'd found it hard to write convincing female characters.

The signing was awkward. Some people who'd bought books earlier took them home without coming forward to get them signed, while those who did form a line for Todd's John Hancock—and there were plenty of them—found it hard to engage the author in conversation.

"I never read a deeper novel," said one middle-aged man with a ponytail who'd found himself looking down on a seated and exhausted-looking Todd.

"It's pretty deep all right," said Todd, signing the book.

"Can you put—" began the man with the ponytail, but Todd was already handing the book back to him.

"Next," said Todd, wearily.

"If I didn't know better," said a lady with dyed red hair,

coquettishly, "I'd say someone's wife wrote this novel."

"My wife is divorcing me," said Todd, as he scrawled something in her book.

"Okay," said Leah, "that's pretty much it for tonight. We have to close up now."

"It says event until nine thirty," said a whiny boy.

"Mr. Milstead will be signing store copies before he leaves," said Leah.

"But I bought a book already," said the whiny boy.

"Then write your name down on this," Leah said, shoving a flyer at him, "and Mr. Milstead will be sure to write you a fulsome dedication."

Right now, Todd looked like he could barely write an X. He looked confused and worried, and ready for nothing.

"Out!" shouted Leah, and the room emptied like the people in it were steam and someone had opened a window.

Leah made Todd sign fifty books (she was a woman of her word) and brought him coffee and a pastry.

"We had Charles Bukowski here last year," she said.

"Don't tell me," Todd replied. "He got high and attacked the audience with a cleaver."

"Actually, he was really polite and charming," said Leah.

"I take your point," Todd said. "I don't know what came over me."

"Apology accepted," Leah said. "Anyway, who cares? They'll remember Todd Milstead as a proper writer. Someone who gets moody and mumbles and," Leah removed a wine bottle from Todd's table, "gets drunk incredibly quickly. It's what people want from writers."

"I'm glad to confirm the stereotype," said Todd. He put the lid back on his pen and stretched out his arms.

"Good work," said Leah. "I think we sold a lot of books tonight, considering."

"Considering what?" said Todd.

"Considering you're a jerk," said Leah, and kissed him.

Todd didn't know how he ended up at his hotel with Leah, or how they got into bed together and fucked the night away, and he wasn't sure he wanted to. There had been a cab, a few fumblings, a fairly violent entrance into the room, door banging open and shut, more fumbling on the couch, and then the bed. None of it seemed to have any logic, or flow, and there was no talking, which was remarkable for Todd. Todd and Leah just fucked like there was no tomorrow.

The next day did not begin how Todd expected. Leah got out of bed and ordered room service. Then she took a long shower and proceeded to act like she owned the place. She sat on the bed, one leg crossed under the other, reading the morning papers. Todd had no idea where the papers had come from, but there were a lot more than there had been yesterday.

Leah flicked through the pile, pulling out the parts she didn't want and dropping them onto the floor. Soon she had filleted them to just the review sections, and was now dumping movies, television, and music.

"Those are my newspapers, you know," said Todd.

"Like you're going to read the theater section," said Leah, parachuting another sheaf into the air. "I'm just saving you time."

She leaned over. "You take the East Coast, I'll take the West."

Every paper had reviewed *All My Colors*. Every paper loved *All My Colors*. The *Atlanta Bugle* had, its reviewer confessed, initially had a few reservations but these were all, it reassured its uneasy readers, swept away by the end of the fourth chapter. All the reviews used words like "triumph," "success," and "tour de force."

None of them, Todd noted, used words like "blockbuster" or "bestseller."

"That's because these are literary reviews," explained Leah. "You don't want to descend to the level of the hoi polloi and start talking about money and success. But relax, Todd, this really is a bestseller. In hardback, too."

"Okay," said Todd.

"You say that a lot," said Leah. "'Okay,' and 'good,' and 'that's great.' It's like you're on hold or something."

"I don't know what you mean," Todd said.

"I feel like I don't really know who I'm talking to," Leah said. "Like there isn't a real Todd Milstead in there."

"This is the real me," Todd said. "Honestly."

"If you say so." Leah frowned. "Personally, I find that slightly more worrying."

Leah left for work a few minutes later without eating the breakfast she'd ordered or having any more sex with Todd. Todd picked at her fruit plate, playing back the events of the evening in his mind. *She seduced me*, was his first thought, although seduction in Todd's mind implied wine and dinner at least, not a sudden kiss and a lot of fumbling in a cab.

Okay then, she jumped me, he thought. *I had no choice but to go with the flow.* Todd imagined saying this to Sara. Then he imagined not saying it, and felt better.

Whoever's fault it was, Todd found the whole thing easy to explain, to himself at least. Yes, he was seeing Sara, but hadn't he also been seeing Sara when he was living with Janis? And hadn't Sara been, if not in love with, then at least married to, Terry? What's sauce for the goose, and so on. Anyway, it was a one-off and he was on the road, and he'd had a really bad day.

By the time he'd finished making a list of reasons why last night had been not only excusable, but fine, Todd was exhausted. He was about to lie back and take a nap when the phone rang.

"This is reception, Mr. Milstead. Checkout is at eleven."

Todd looked at the clock radio. It was ten forty-five. Fifteen minutes to shower, dress, pack, and eat two breakfasts.

"Okay," he said, rolled off the bed and got in the shower.

Half an hour later, Todd was back in the Volvo, pulling over into a Tower Records parking lot to consult his itinerary. CHARLENE, INDIANA, it said, PUBLIC LIBRARY. Two o'clock was a weird time for a reading. Todd unfolded his map, found a list of place names, and discovered that Charlene wasn't there.

An hour later, having purchased a large hardback road atlas, Todd found Charlene. It wasn't even in the middle of nowhere. *It's on the outskirts of nowhere,* thought Todd as he planned his route with a forefinger. He wondered why his publishers had thought it worth sending him here. Maybe it was an important hub for something. Maybe it was a college town. Maybe it was a secret fucking underground city with a population of avid readers. Todd had no idea, but he had a strong feeling that Charlene, Indiana, was one of the universe's completely insignificant towns.

He even wondered for a moment if he could skip it. Todd looked at the itinerary again and saw that it was exactly the midpoint between Chicago and his next destination, which was Cleveland, Ohio. Not good enough for Columbus, Todd thought to himself, only semi-humorously, and started the Volvo's engine again.

It was a featureless drive to Charlene, and Todd was bored before he got to the Indiana border. His mood wasn't helped by the fact that the highway seemed determined to hook up with every railroad crossing in America, making him stop frequently to let absurdly long freight trains pass by. He was also, despite consuming his own and Leah's breakfasts, getting hungry again, but a fear of being late *and seeing Janis and her girlfriend again* prevented him from pulling into a truck stop to get something to eat.

Eventually Todd made it to Charlene. There was, he suddenly registered, no motel or hotel mentioned on the sheet. He wasn't staying the night here—thank God, he thought, looking around at the windswept streets and the dull gray, box-like stores scattered around Main Street—but was expected to get back in the car and drive to Cleveland, where there was a bed waiting for him.

He sighed, located the public library after a few minutes' driving around, parked up, and went in.

There was nobody there. Literally nobody. Todd wandered

around for a few minutes, and even knocked on some doors. Nothing. He grew bolder, and went into the office. It was deserted. *This place is the Mary Celeste of libraries*, he thought.

He stood in the middle of the main library room, surrounded by mute books.

"Hello!" he called. There was a slight echo and Todd, never one to shy away from the sound of his own voice, called, "I said hello!"

"Will you be quiet, please?" said a voice, and Todd nearly jumped out of his shirt. A small bald man was jogging angrily toward him.

"This is a library," he said.

"I did spot that," Todd replied. "My name is Todd Milstead."

"Oh," said the small man. "Oh."

"Oh?"

"We thought you weren't coming," said the man.

"Did someone tell you I wasn't coming?" Todd said.

"Not as such," the man said. "But we didn't get a call confirming, or a letter, and when I saw the papers, I said to Mrs. Franco—that's my wife, I'm Reggie Franco—I said, he's too famous for us, Frannie."

Resisting the urge to ask, *Your wife is called Frannie Franco?*, Todd was torn between playing the aggrieved, drove-all-the-way-from-wherever card and the magnanimous, well-I'm-here-now card. He remembered the old adage about being nice to people on the way up, and said:

"Well, I'm here now. I'm sure you can rustle up a few souls for the reading."

"Rustle up?" said Franco. "The whole town's at work."

190

Now it was Todd's turn to say, "Oh."

"Charlene is home to America's largest whistle factory," explained Franco. "Pretty much everyone works there."

"Maybe I should give my reading there," said Todd.

"Oh no," said Franco. "It's much too loud. Wait here," he added, and walked off, leaving Todd in limbo.

A few minutes later, Franco returned with an elderly woman whose spectacles were bigger than her head, and a teenage boy who could have been used by the concept of reluctance as a mascot.

"This is Mrs. Maxton and Eddie," he said. Neither Mrs. Maxton nor Eddie spoke or even looked at Todd. "They're the library staff. They can be your audience."

Todd thought of his triumph in Chicago, but said nothing. At least this mess had the makings of a decent story, he thought. *Then there was the time I played to two people and a dog*, he imagined himself saying. *Wait: there was no dog!*

"Okay, where shall we do it?" he asked.

"My office will be fine," Franco said.

An hour later, Todd was done. It was hard to say who was less appreciative, Mrs. Maxton, who hadn't reacted to anything Todd had said or read out loud, or Eddie, who'd spent the entire time comparing things he'd found in his nose with things he'd found in his ear. Mr. Franco, meanwhile, had, in his own words, "used the opportunity to get on with some work," which meant he'd sat at his desk, going through card indexes and occasionally *mm-hm-*ing at vaguely appropriate moments.

The nightmare finally over, Todd closed his book and

said, "Well, thank you. Normally at this stage I like to open the floor to questions, but—"

"There's no point," said Franco. "Eddie only cares about arcade games and Mrs. Maxton is completely deaf."

"How about you?" said Todd. "Anything you'd like to ask?"

"Not really," said Franco. "But thanks for coming."

Todd said his goodbyes as quickly as possible and walked out to the car. He was just putting his bag in the trunk when there was a shout and Franco came running out of the library.

"Mr. Milstead!" he was yelling. "There's a phone call for you!"

Todd walked into Franco's office. Franco looked about ready to cry.

"This is my personal telephone," he said. "I don't like to give this number out. They told me they'd only call you if it was really important."

"Must be really important then," said Todd, and took the receiver from him like a cop might take a revolver from a man who'd lost the nerve to shoot himself.

"Todd?" said Nora's voice.

"Hi, Nora."

"How's it going? Wowing the crowds?"

"Something like that," said Todd, looking at a large wall calendar with a picture of the whistle factory on it.

"Tell them to hurry up," said Franco. "My wife might want to call. Or my mother."

"What's up?" said Todd, casually. "I saw the reviews."

"Never mind the reviews," Nora said. "You're number three."

"Number three what?" asked Todd.

"In the *New York Times* bestseller list," said Nora.

"Fuck my old boots," said Todd.

"Mr. Milstead!" said Franco.

"They don't release the list until tomorrow," Nora said, when Todd had finally asked Franco to give him some privacy, "but it's official. *All My Colors* is the number three best-selling book in the country."

"How did it happen so quickly?" asked Todd. "It doesn't seem possible."

"Our sources say it's just been flying out the stores," Nora said. "The presses are working overtime. People read about it, Todd, they hear about it, they want it."

"But number three!" Todd said.

"Do you want to know who's above you?" Nora teased.

"No," said Todd, after a moment. "I want to see it in print," he decided. "I want to see it written down, otherwise I won't believe it."

"Very well," said Nora. "Which reminds me, when the list is out, we're pretty sure that Hogan will want you."

"Hogan? You mean *Tom* Hogan? *The Tom Hogan Show*?"

"I don't know any other Tom Hogans. Yes, Todd. Tom likes the occasional author. Makes for a more intellectual show."

"I guess that would be okay," said Todd. He was deliberately understating his case. Just as a coward dies a thousand deaths before his real death, so Todd Milstead had been interviewed a thousand times by Tom Hogan in his imagination. *Well, Tom, that's a very interesting question… Tom, you've hit the nail on the head… I think "genius" is a word bandied about too often these days, Tom…*

"Todd?"

Todd returned to reality.

"Sorry."

"If Tom does want you, it won't be for a week or two. His people book well in advance," said Nora. "So just forge on with the tour for now."

"Will do," said Todd. Then he remembered.

"I've got another reading tonight," he said. "Cleveland, Ohio. I'd better get going."

"Okay, Todd," said Nora. "Drive safely. Remember you're more than an author now, you're a star."

Yeah, thought Todd, *a star investment*. He put the phone down and walked into the corridor. Mr. Franco was waiting there, a coy look on his face and a book in his hand.

"I have to run," said Todd.

"I understand," said Franco. "I wondered if you might just—"

He proffered the book.

"It's not for me," he said. "I prefer the classics. My wife, though—" He made a gesture as if to imply that Mrs. Franco read the cheapest shit imaginable.

Todd took the book. A cold shock ran through him.

"This isn't—" he began.

It wasn't his *All My Colors*. It was Jake Turner's *All My Colors*, same as in the bookstore in Chicago. The only difference was that the Chicago book had the latest edition, a brand new copy, whereas this *All My Colors* was, as Todd might have expected from a library book, old, shop-soiled, with a cloudy cellophane cover and much-thumbed pages.

"Strictly speaking, it's the library's copy," said Franco.

"But it's so old, I thought I could justify taking it out of circulation and ordering—"

"Is this a joke?" said Todd.

"Excuse me?" Franco said.

"I said, is this a fucking joke?" Todd was angry now. "Who put you up to this?"

"I don't understand, Mr. Milstead," Franco stuttered. "Would you rather I asked you to sign a new copy?" He was backing away from Todd and Todd understood that this was because Todd was advancing on him.

"I really didn't mean to offend you!" Franco said. He stepped back, tripped, and fell over.

Todd stood over him, holding the battered book.

"This," he shouted, "is not mine!"

"Get a grip, man!" shouted Franco from the floor.

He was about to *bring it down on Franco's face* throw the book away when he stopped. Eddie had appeared in a doorway, looking a lot bigger than Todd remembered.

"You okay, Mr. Franco?" he said.

"I think so," said Franco, scrambling up again. He looked Todd in the eye.

"Mr. Milstead is just leaving," he said.

Todd said nothing. He brushed past them both and headed through the door to the street.

It was only when he was buckling himself up in the Volvo that he realized he still had the library book with him.

SIX

At about the time Todd was storming out of the public library in Charlene, Timothy was considering closing up Legolas Books early so he could go home and make what he liked to call his famous chili con carne. He had it all planned: a bottle of Chianti, his famous chili con carne, and an old movie (Timothy had already checked the TV Guide, and was delighted to see that he had a choice between *All About Eve* or *The Rocky Horror Picture Show*: for such a crashing bore, he had great taste in movies).

Timothy looked at the store clock, then his wristwatch. They both confirmed what he knew already: no fucker was coming by his store this afternoon. He flipped the WELCOME STRANGER TO OUR BOX OF DELIGHTS sign over to CLOSED and was about to pull down the blinds when he heard a loud noise that soon became an ear-thumping roar. A motorbike engine.

Timothy despised motorbikes and their riders. Noisy,

polluting assholes who lurked around corners just waiting to charge out and scare the living bejasus out of people. The engine was so loud he could barely think.

"Shut UP!" he shouted, and looked around in case anyone had heard him. Timothy had no desire to be pummeled to crap by an angry biker.

And then it stopped, so abruptly that the sound echoed for a moment before it vanished. Timothy sighed with relief.

The shop bell dinged.

"We're closed!" said Timothy. *You'd think a person who wanted to visit a bookstore would at least be able to read*, he thought to himself, and went to bolt the door to make clear his point. He stopped at the door: it was already bolted and latched too. *Don't recall doing that*, he thought.

There was movement behind him. He turned, to see a woman standing at the counter. She had blonde hair and she was wearing a blue print dress.

"How did you—" he began, more irritated than angry.

There was something in the way the woman was looking—not at him, but almost through him—that made Timothy change his tone.

"Can I help you?" he asked the woman. The words seemed to float from his mouth like balloons. He felt like he was up to his waist in molasses.

The woman looked him in the eye now.

"Yes," she said. "I'm looking for a hacksaw."

Timothy knew this was a strange thing for the woman to say, but he couldn't for the life of him remember why.

"What kind of hacksaw?" he asked, knowing deep down that this was a strange thing for him to say, too.

"It doesn't matter," said the woman. "I just said that to get your attention."

And before Timothy could say another word, she had reached into his mouth and pulled out his tongue.

That's my fucking tongue, was Timothy's unhelpful thought as he watched her grab the red, fat object and drop it onto the counter like a piece of sushi. He put a hand to his face and it came away bloody. The odd thing was, Timothy thought as he tried to feel for his absent tongue in his mouth but he couldn't, ha fucking ha, because he *hadn't got a tongue*, that it didn't hurt. He felt fine, apart from the weird sensation caused by there being nothing in the middle of his mouth anymore.

He looked at the woman, and for a moment it seemed that she must have been moved by Timothy's puzzled expression because she said, "You can't be trusted, you see. You're a talker."

Timothy wanted to explain to the woman that he could be trusted, that whatever it was she didn't want him to talk about, he wouldn't. But how could he tell her? He reached for his pen and grabbed a postcard.

"Oh, that's right," she said. "You can *write*." And she slashed his throat open.

Timothy's last thought, as he stumbled to the floor, choking and gushing, was: *she had a hacksaw all the time*.

Todd ran into his motel room. He threw the library book on the desk and, without stopping to take his coat off, sat down with his reading copy. Now there were two *All My Colors* in front of him: his copy, brand new, slightly used,

printed by Franklyn and Sullivan and with the words BY
TODD MILSTEAD prominently displayed on the cover and
spine; and the library copy, at least a decade old, battered
if not well-thumbed, printed by The Whitney Press, and
credited to JAKE TURNER.

Todd looked at the Jake Turner version of *All My
Colors*. It was an unsettling experience, like seeing Spock
from *Star Trek* with a beard, or one of those British Beatles
albums with the wrong name. There was nothing wrong
with the actual book; if it was a forgery, it was an amazing
one (*but what's to forge*, Todd's mind asked, *there's only me
thinks it exists*).

Maybe, Todd thought desperately, this *isn't* my book.
Maybe it just has the same title. Like when two movies come
out with the same title (Todd couldn't actually think of two
movies that had come out with the same title, but he was
sure it happened). He remembered, from a long-ago seminar
on the English comic novel, that when P.G. Wodehouse
had written a book called *French Leave*, he had jokingly
said that he hoped it would be the best book written called
French Leave. Todd had never seen *French Leave* by P.G.
Wodehouse or anyone else but he did have both versions of
All My Colors. He opened them at the same time.

Chapter One, page one.

Todd's *All My Colors* began:

The hardware store was empty. Jimmy the store clerk
was clearing away some boxes when he noticed the

woman standing at the counter. She was in her early thirties, good-looking with blonde hair and wearing a blue print dress.

Jake Turner's *All My Colors* began:

The hardware store was empty. Jimmy the store clerk was clearing up boxes when he noticed the woman standing at the counter. She was in her early '30s, blonde and good-looking in a blue print dress.

Todd picked a page at random—106—and compared again. Todd's page 106 began:

and, when Helen asked, Harry just said no.

"Why not?" she asked.

"Honey, there's no why not," said Harry. "Because there's no why."

Jake's page 106 began:

and, when Helen raised her head to ask, Harry said no.

"Why not?" she asked.

"Honey," said Harry. "There's no why not. Because there's no why."

Todd was about to go for best of five when he saw how pointless it was. The two books were, to all but the most pedantic, identical. Any differences could be put down to a copier's bad memory. *Because that's all I am*, Todd said to himself, *a bad copier*. It felt irrational—it was irrational—but in all the time Todd had been stuck at that typewriter, letting the book flow out of him, even though he'd been nothing more than a faucet gushing words and pages, some part of him had hoped, had even believed, that he, Todd Milstead, was adding to the book in some way, some extra layer or some new ingredient.

But now, looking at the two books side by side, Todd realized he was no more than a stenographer taking dictation. *And not a very good one either*, he realized.

Todd sat there looking at the two books for quite some time. Then he picked up the older book (he refused to call it the original) and opened it at the back flap. There was no author photo, which Todd found suspicious, but there was a brief biography.

"Jake Turner," Todd read out loud, "was born in Pontiac, Michigan and held down a variety of jobs before finally realizing that he was a writer. *All My Colors* is his first novel."

That was it. Todd didn't know what he'd been expecting—"Jake Turner is a fucking ghost who is going to get you for this," perhaps—but something more than this flat, disingenuously not-really-humble piece of nothing. Todd noted also that the blurb contained exactly one piece of information.

Still, one was better than nothing. Todd went over to his grip, rummaged around for his telephone address book and went back to the desk and picked up the phone.

It was answered by a coughing fit. Todd briefly recoiled

from the mouthpiece and said, "Behm? This is Milstead."

"Milstead," said Behm when he was finished coughing. "I thought we were done."

"I'm not calling about Janis," said Todd.

"Well, that's good, I guess. How can I help you?"

"I want you to track someone else down for me."

Was that a sigh at the other end of the phone? Todd wasn't sure.

"Got a name?" asked Behm.

"Jake Turner."

"Someone you know?"

"No. And that's all I know about him."

"Just the name? That's not ideal, Mr. Milstead."

"And his place of birth. Pontiac, Michigan."

This time there was a definite sigh at the other end of the line.

"That narrows it down, a little. Okay. Is there a time limit on this?"

"Soon as possible."

"Great. Nice and vague. Is there *anything* else, Mr. Milstead? Like what the guy does for a living?"

Todd took a deep breath.

"He's a writer," he said.

Behm rang off, and Todd decided to get some fresh air. The night was surprisingly chilly, and he was about to go back inside when he saw the bike parked across the road.

It was a Harley. The same kind of bike Janis and her (*lover*) partner were riding. Whether it was also the actual same *bike* Todd couldn't be sure. The Harley was picked out plain as day under a streetlight, like it was in an Edward

Hopper painting. Todd forgot all about going back inside and crossed the road stealthily, or as stealthily as a man can cross a major road at night with cars flashing past.

The bike was cold to the touch. Whoever it belonged to had left it here for at least a couple of hours. Todd looked around to see if there were any (*lesbian bars*) bars in the vicinity, but there was nothing, just a few random stores which had all shut up for the night. Todd had no idea what to do next—he was hardly going to leave a note on the windshield—so he just turned around and crossed the road again, feeling far from intrepid, and went back to his room.

Todd went to bed, but he couldn't sleep. He kept thinking about the book. He turned on the light and went back to the desk.

The book was gone. Todd's was still there, but the other *All My Colors* wasn't where he'd left it. Cursing, Todd looked on the floor by the desk. Nothing. He stuck his head under the desk and got nothing for his troubles but a banged head. He widened his search. The book wasn't under the bed, and he hadn't kicked it into the bathroom or the closet.

Todd spent a half hour investigating every nook and cranny in the room before finally giving up. He turned on the TV and went over to close the drapes. The bike was still there. He watched TV for a few minutes—a local news station whose stories would have been interesting to only the very local—and then gave up the day as a bad job. He got ready for bed. One last trip to the window showed him what he knew already. The bike was still there. *Goddammit*, Todd thought. He didn't take kindly to being intimidated.

The book, he thought. *She took it. While I was out looking at* the Harley, *the Dyke on the Bike must have come in here and taken the book.* It was the only logical explanation. Todd turned off the room light and went over to the window again, a lone figure in pajamas glaring out into the night. The bike hadn't moved. Todd didn't know what he was expecting to see but he felt disappointed. *Is that it?* he thought. *Well, screw you, I'm not leaving it here.*

For the second time, Todd got out his old address book. He looked at his watch. *Not too late for a call.*

"Todd?" Janis's voice said.

"Hi, Janis."

"Todd, do you know what time it is?"

"I know what you've been doing."

"Are you drunk, Todd?"

"I said, I know what you've been doing."

"You don't answer my calls. You don't answer my lawyer's calls. And then you decide to pick up the phone in the middle of the night and—"

"I saw you."

"What?"

Todd thought he could detect fear in Janis's voice. *Yeah, I got you now.*

"You looked happy, Janis, I'll say that for you."

"Todd." Janis's tone changed, less harsh. "Todd, I am happy. Okay? Shall we just leave it there?"

"You have the nerve to come down on me and Sara when all the time you were—"

"What, Todd? All the time I was what?"

"Seeing someone else."

"You're pathetic, Todd."

"One rule for you, is that it, Janis? One rule for you and another for me?"

"I'm not even going to begin to discuss this with you."

"I want to speak to her."

A pause.

"Excuse me?"

"I want to talk to her. I know she's there. Put her on."

"Todd," said Janis. "I literally have no idea what you're talking about."

"I saw you, Janis. With her."

"I'm going to hang up now."

She rang off. Todd had the feeling that the conversation hadn't entirely gone his way. He went to bed.

At around about four o'clock in the morning, Todd got up to use the bathroom. He studiously ignored the curtained window. He finished peeing, turned out the bathroom light, and was about to get back into bed when (*fuck it, one look won't hurt*) he went over to the window and pulled back the curtain.

She was there.

The bike hadn't moved but now she was sitting on it, like she was posing for a magazine cover. She was holding something. Todd was not surprised to see that it was the book, *All My Colors* by Jake Turner. She stuck the book in her jacket, looked Todd straight in the eye and gave him the finger. Then—finger still vertical—she started up the Harley and roared off into the night.

After a few minutes had passed, Todd put on his coat and

went outside. He crossed the road to where the bike had been. There was no sign that anything had been there. He went back to his room, where he didn't sleep at all.

The next day, after a breakfast of chips and soda from the candy bar dispenser in the lobby, Todd called Sara.

"Hey," she said, someone actually pleased to hear his voice.

"It's good to hear your voice," Todd said, and he meant it.

"When are you coming back?" she asked.

"I have one more date on this leg," Todd said. "Cleveland, Ohio, then I'm coming home."

"I can't wait," Sara said. "I hate to admit it but I miss you."

An image of Leah came into Todd's mind. She was naked and she had his cock in her hand. It was so sudden and startling that he forgot what he was doing for a moment.

"I said I miss you," said Sara.

"No, I heard you," Todd said, and the moment the words left his mouth he knew they were the wrong thing to say.

"Okay then," said Sara tightly. "Well, let me know when you're coming back and we'll speak."

Looks like everyone's hanging up on me, thought Todd.

He got back in the Volvo and consulted his itinerary. The sheet was crumpled now, and torn, and his map was no longer the neatly folded rectangle that it had once been. The car, he noted, looked more like a garbage dump on wheels, being half-full of empty cartons, paper bags, and cups with straws in them.

Todd hit the road, and reached Cleveland in less than three hours.

He found the bookstore easily, and wondered if he was getting better at this. He had an hour or so before he had to check into whatever they had booked for him this time (*hotel, motel, Holiday Inn* as some novelty song on the radio had it) and he was just thinking about dumping all the junk from the car into a trashcan when he saw Nora.

"Hello!" she said breezily, Agnes Moorehead in a good mood.

"This is unexpected," said Todd, which was an understatement. Nora in Cleveland, Ohio was like Jackie Onassis in Cleveland, Ohio.

"I know," said Nora. "Let's get a coffee."

The coffee shop was dark and slightly pungent, and the staff seemed resigned to a fate beyond their comprehension. The coffee was good, though. Nora and Todd sat at the back, by a bathroom that enjoyed a constant stream of human traffic, most of whom seemed to have no interest in staying to buy coffee.

"Quite the hub," said Nora, as another customer budged past them into the can.

"It's great to see you," said Todd. "Although I am a little surprised. Also," he added, looking at his watch, "I'm on in ten minutes."

"No you're not," Nora said.

"What?" said Todd.

"The event is off," said Nora. "I had to cancel it. Not," she said, sternly, "because of what happened in Charlene—and yes, of course I heard about it, the poor man was on the phone to the publisher immediately. And not because of Chicago, either."

"I feel like I'm being tailed," said Todd, sulkily.

"And I feel like my client is ever so slightly out of control," Nora said. "Todd, you can't go around chewing the carpets and punching people on your first book tour. When you're established, maybe, but not before anyone knows who you are."

"You flew all the way out here to tell me that?" said Todd.

"Don't be rude," said Nora, sharply. "And no, I didn't. I came all the way out here to tell you that *All My Colors* is no longer number three in the *New York Times* bestseller list."

"Oh well," said Todd. "I guess it was fun while it lasted."

"Todd," said Nora. "*All My Colors* is number one."

Todd stared at Nora.

"What?" he said. "How?"

"I told you it was a good book," Nora said, smiling.

"But it's only been out about a day."

"Advance sales," Nora said. "And it's had rave reviews in every paper in the country. People love it, Todd. It speaks to them."

"Wow," said Todd. "Fucking wow. I'm sorry to swear."

"Not at all," Nora said. "Fucking wow is absolutely the right thing to say in the circumstances."

Todd sat there for a bit.

"So why is tonight canceled?" he asked. "I would have thought me being number one would be a crowd-puller."

"Oh, it would," Nora said. "And the bookstore were furious when I canceled."

"*You* canceled?" Todd said.

"I had to," Nora said. "You're on *The Tom Hogan Show*. Tonight."

"But isn't that taped in New York?"

"I'm not sure 'taped' is the right word, because it's live. But yes, New York. And our flight leaves in an hour."

Nora stood up.

"This really is very good coffee," she said. "We should have got it to go."

The flight to New York passed without incident, bar Todd spilling his Coke on the floor when they hit some turbulence.

"Guess I'm nervous," he admitted to Nora.

"I'm relieved," Nora said. "It would be peculiar if you felt complacent and relaxed at this point."

"I've never been on TV before," said Todd, sounding as much like a hick as humanly possible.

"There's nothing to it. You just look interested when the other person is talking, and then, no matter what question they ask you, say whatever you want the audience to hear."

"But I don't know what I want the audience to hear."

"Oh, Todd." Nora put an elegant hand on his arm. "You wrote *All My Colors*. You'll have *lots* to say."

At the TV studio they were met by a young, nervous man with a clipboard and the skinniest tie Todd had ever seen. The man gave Todd and Nora large orange stickers with their names on.

"Is that what you'll be wearing tonight?" he asked, looking at Todd's brown sport coat.

"Todd Milstead is a writer," she said. "If you wanted

someone who dresses like a fashion plate, you should have booked Halston."

"We had him last week," said the young man. "This way, please."

Todd was taken to makeup, where he was sat between a cheery-looking young man he vaguely recognized from a sitcom set in the 1950s that he hated, and a middle-aged woman with frizzy hair who was having a dispute with the makeup woman.

"I can do my own makeup," the frizzy-haired woman was saying. "I'm forty-two, I've done it before."

"But this is television, honey," said the makeup woman. "Those lights are going to bear down on your face like the desert sun."

"She's right," said the cheery young man. "You're going to look sallow."

He said this as though looking sallow was the worst thing that could happen to any human being.

"All right," said the frizzy-haired woman. "Just don't make me look like a clown."

"Shoot," said the makeup woman, "there goes my whole plan for you."

After makeup, Todd and the others were taken to the green room. Todd found himself at the drinks table with the frizzy-haired woman.

"Todd Milstead," he said.

"Jane Collins," said the woman. "And don't worry, you haven't heard of me. I think someone dropped out at the last minute."

"I thought that was why I was here," said Todd.

"You're the author, right?" said Jane. "*All My Colors*?"

"You've read it?"

"Everyone's read it," said Jane, dryly. "It's the book of the year."

Todd couldn't tell if she was mocking him. He decided not to ask her if she'd liked it. Instead he said, "So what's your thing?"

"My thing?" she said, as though she'd never heard the word before. "Well, my thing is documentaries."

"Oh," said Todd, instantly bored. "Right. That sounds cool."

"I made this film," Jane said, "about what's happening in Central America right now. Got into trouble with some people there, and here, but we got the film made and now it's up for some damn award. So here I am."

"That's great," said Todd, who couldn't think of anything less great. "I wish you every success."

"You're too kind," said Jane, and now Todd was sure she was mocking him. Todd felt uneasy, as he always did with women who had taken against him. He excused himself and went over to Nora.

"Still nervous?" she asked.

"Much more nervous now," Todd said.

"That's my boy," she said.

"When do we get to meet Tom?" Todd asked.

"You don't," said Nora. "Not before the show, anyhow. He doesn't like to meet his guests in advance."

"Right," said Todd, "I think I need a drink." He moved over to the drinks table.

"You'll be fine," Nora said, standing between him and

the wine. "Just keep your wits about you."

The young man with the skinny tie reappeared, and turned on a large television set in the corner of the room.

"Quiet, please," he said. "We are—on."

The credits for *The Tom Hogan Show* rolled. Todd turned to Nora.

"Shouldn't I be in the, you know, the studio?" he asked.

"They'll take you in," said Nora. "He's got the opening monologue to do first."

"Also you're the final guest," said the pale young man.

"He is?" said the cheery actor, looking slightly less cheery.

"Number one!" said Nora, giving Todd an encouraging look. Todd smiled back weakly.

The show revealed its treasures rapidly. Tom Hogan delivered a long but snappy monologue about the President, about Japanese cars, about the latest misadventures of the Rolling Stones, and cut to a commercial. Then he introduced his first guest—the cheery young actor—and talked to him at some length, pausing only to show a clip from the cheery young actor's movie, which seemed to take place entirely on a golf course. After another ad break, Tom brought on Jane Collins.

This was clearly a serious moment in the show, and while he was bored by the idea of Jane's documentary, Todd admired the way Tom steered the interview away from the political points that Jane seemed to want to make and into the more acceptable area of Jane as David to the Goliath of unnamed forces of oppression: how she'd secretly entered several of the countries she'd filmed in, how one of her cameramen had almost lost his life, how she'd smuggled the film out, and how, after just one screening in Los Angeles, the documentary had been instantly purchased by a major movie company and nominated for every award going.

A short clip from the documentary was shown. Todd had no idea what was happening in the clip, but it was dramatic, people were screaming and there was a lot of mud on the lens. He joined in the applause in the studio and the green room.

"Follow that," someone said as the show went to a break. Todd felt a tap on his shoulder.

"You're on," said the pale young man.

Todd stood at the edge of the studio set during the ad break. He watched as Tom Hogan held up a copy of the book, recited a couple of statistics, quoted a review and then said, "Ladies and gentlemen, the author of *All My Colors*—Todd Milstead!" The pale young man propelled Todd out onto the set. He heard applause and even cheering as the cheery young actor and Jane Collins made room for him on the sofa.

"Welcome, Todd," said Hogan.

Todd beamed. His nerves were gone. He fixed Hogan with a grin.

"Wow," he said. "It really is a pleasure to be on the show."

"You know," said Hogan. "I think you're the first cheerful writer we've ever had on the show."

Laughter.

"Yeah, we're kind of a miserable bunch," Todd said. "I guess it goes with the territory."

"But here you are," said Hogan. "The happy author. It's a first for us, it really is."

"I think that secretly all writers want to be on TV," Todd said. "If Charles Dickens were alive today, he'd be on every show going. You'd be asking him, so how did you come up with the idea for Scrooge?"

"Can we get Charles Dickens?" said Hogan, turning to an imaginary aide. "I hear he's the best."

There was more laughter. Hogan turned serious.

"A lot of people love your book," he said. "And I have to say—and I do mean *have*, because my wife made me promise to—I have to say that one of the things which surprised me about this book, and there's a lot of surprises in it, is that—well, I guess I should just say it—"

"Say it!" said Todd, almost laughing now.

"The surprise for many readers is that this is a book by a guy," said Hogan. He turned to the audience. "If you haven't read this book, and you should, it's—I don't know how to put this—it's a woman's book."

"Do you think so?" said Todd.

"I know it's an odd thing to say," said Hogan, as the cameras turned to catch women in the audience nodding in agreement. "And it's not to put down women, or say that this is, you know, a silly book, quite the opposite. But if your name wasn't on the cover, I'd say, and many people would say, that this was a book by a woman."

"I'm flattered by that," Todd decided to say. "Because it's a book about a woman, and it's a book set in the world of a woman's thoughts, and to hear that you, and others, particularly women, not that you're a woman, Tom—"

"Not that I'm a woman," said Tom, to laughter. "I'm glad we've established that."

"—to hear people say that is a sign, to me, that the book has succeeded." Todd sat back, feeling like a man who has just successfully dug himself out of a hole.

"Jane, you're a woman," said Tom, to more laughter. Jane didn't join in, Todd noticed. Todd had a feeling that Jane wasn't much fun.

"Yes, Tom, I am," she said in what Todd thought sounded like a patronizing tone.

"Did you read *All My Colors*?" asked Tom.

"I did," Jane said. "I had a spare couple of hours this afternoon."

There was an *oooh* from some of the audience.

"Sounds like you didn't like it!" said Todd. Dammit, now he was nervous again.

"Oh, no, don't misunderstand me," Jane said. "I did like it. And yes, I can see, reluctantly I admit, how a *man* might think that this was a book written by a woman."

"I haven't read it," said the cheery young actor, "I don't have a lot of time for reading." Everyone ignored him.

"I think I did an okay job," said Todd. "You know, I'm not blowing my own trumpet here, but people seem to like this book."

"People like hamburgers," said Jane. "People like soap operas and they like bad movies and they like all kinds of things."

"It's a good book," said Todd, sounding petulant even to himself.

"You know what this book feels like to me?" said Jane.

"I'm all ears," said Todd.

"This book feels like it was, I don't know, ghostwritten," said Jane. "It feels like eavesdropping, like someone heard scraps of conversation and stories, and just copied them down. Like there's no understanding of what the book is about."

"I don't agree," said Todd. "I think it's very clear what the book is about."

"Okay then," said Jane. "You wrote it. You're the man. You tell me what it's about."

Todd flailed mentally. He was aware that people were looking at him. He tried not to think how many people.

"I don't need to," said Todd finally. "The book speaks for itself."

"Humor me," said Jane. "I want to know what a man who thinks he can write like a woman has to say to a woman like me."

I know what I'd like to fucking say to you, Todd thought.

"I'm not here to lecture anyone," he said. "Least of all women. If you feel that, as a man, I have nothing to say to you, that's fine. I'm a guy, I accept that. Centuries of male oppression have given me deep-rooted attitudes that can't be changed overnight. But maybe—" and here Todd made a face that Janis, had she been watching, would have thought of as Todd's Hopeful Spaniel Look, "—maybe we can see this as one man's first step in the right direction."

Todd thought Jane was about to actually say the word "bullshit" on live TV (he wouldn't have blamed her), but whatever was on the tip of her tongue was drowned out by audience applause.

They bought it, Todd thought, *they actually bought it.*

After the show, Jane Collins left in something of a hurry. Tom Hogan came into the green room—"He never does that," said the pale young man—to shake Todd's hand. "You're a new breed," he said to Todd.

"I feel bad," Todd said to Nora. "I kind of demolished that woman."

"You kind of did," said Nora. "But she was asking for it. It's a chat show, not a Harvard debate. Listen, Todd, I need you to go home for a couple of days."

"Home?" said Todd, who had been hoping that Nora was going to take him out to dinner, someplace where there were lots of celebrities and people to take photographs of Todd with said celebrities.

"You're in the eye of the storm right now," Nora said. "But tomorrow morning, when America wakes up and digests what happened tonight, you're going to be right in that storm. You need to rest and charge your batteries."

Todd, who hadn't himself digested what had happened on the show, said nothing.

"Don't be sad, Todd," Nora said. "This is the last time you are ever going to be ordinary. Go home, wake up in your own bed, have breakfast and sit around in your pajamas. Make the most of it, Todd."

Todd was able to get the last flight out of New York. As a kind of reward to himself, he got as drunk as the airline staff would let him on the flight, and passed out in the cab back to his house. The driver had to help him open his own front door.

Todd woke up on the couch the next morning. The sun was not so much streaming in through the window as deliberately throwing up in Todd's face.

"*He could never wake up on a sunny day without thinking of that first day*," Todd said out loud. "*That first day which, he later told her, had almost been his last day.*"

Todd sat up. *What the fuck was that?* Not something he remembered reading (*or writing*), that was for sure. He dismissed it as a product of his hangover and went to get some water. After nearly passing out in the kitchen, he decided that maybe he needed more sleep, and went to bed.

The earth continued to spin without Todd, and when he finally woke up, it was the early afternoon, and someone was banging on his door. Todd put on a robe and made his way downstairs. He opened the door and Sara all but fell into his arms.

"Thank God," she said. "It's not you."

Todd led Sara inside and sat down beside her.

"You look rough," she said.

"You look wonderful," said Todd. Sara smiled, wryly. Her eyes were red from tiredness and worry.

"I thought it might be you," she said. "I don't know why, you were out of town, but I called the motel, the one in Cleveland, and they said you'd checked out and—"

"I was in New York," said Todd. "I was on TV."

Sara shook her head, as though what he was saying was absurd. Todd was slightly ashamed to realize that, whatever was distressing Sara, he was upset that she had clearly not even heard about his television appearance. *I guess being a last minute replacement I wouldn't have been in the* TV Guide, he thought, but couldn't help wondering what Sara had been doing instead. Reading a book, probably.

"They found a body," Sara said, breaking Todd's reverie.

"What? Who did?"

"The police. Somebody was walking their dog past the bookstore, and the lights were on. The door was open too, so they went in, and there was—the officer said—this bloody mess. The face, all slashed up. Like ribbons."

Todd's mind was racing to follow this.

"The bookstore—Legolas? You mean it was Timothy? Someone killed Timothy?"

"That's what the police said but when they couldn't identify the body, because of the face being all... I thought it must be you, Todd."

"But why? Why would you think it was me?"

Sara wiped her eyes.

"Because where his—they'd stuck..."

She straightened up. "They put your book in his mouth. Where his mouth used to be, anyway. They stuck your book in his face."

Todd remembered his dream, Timothy saying he'd devoured Todd's book.

I never thought he meant it literally, Todd thought.

The cops came around soon after. A predictable round of *do you know anyone who might want to harm you* and *where were you when the incident took place* (which was an enormously stupid question because both the cops had seen Todd on TV that night). Todd answered all their questions and the police went away unsatisfied. *Come back*, he wanted to shout, *I'm the killer! I just love to slice up bookstore owners and use their mouths as mailboxes! And I always leave my own book behind as a clue!*

220

Todd went to the store where, he was gratified to see, one or two customers actually started at him, and the girl behind the counter said, "Are you famous?"

"If you have to ask, then I guess the answer's no," said Todd, which he thought was both snappy and modest. The girl just looked disappointed and rang Todd's purchases up in silence.

Todd returned home, taking care not to wake Sara, who was asleep in his bed. He made a ham sandwich, poured some milk into a glass and went into the kitchen, where a huge pile of mail awaited him. Most of it was junk. There was Behm's bill, which he set to one side, and there was a letter from Janis's lawyer, telling him that as he had failed to respond to any of their attempts to communicate with him they had no choice but to *blah*. Todd crumpled up the letter and threw it in the corner, where in his mind's eye he saw it explode in a puff of dust.

Then he bent down and picked it up, read off the phone number at the top and called it.

"This is Todd Milstead."

"Oh hi, Mr. Milstead, Coughlan speaking. Been trying to get hold of you."

"I've been away. Listen, I don't want to spend my day talking to a lawyer. Janis can have what she wants, so long as it all happens right away."

"What does that mean?"

"It means if she wants a divorce, if she wants me out of the house, all that, it has to be... before the end of this month. Otherwise I contest."

"This wouldn't be anything to do with your recent television appearance, would it? Or your book?"

Shit, rumbled, thought Todd.

"Janis can have what she originally asked for. If she wants to turn this into a fight, it'll be long and drawn out."

"Meaning you're happy to give her the house and whatever piddling alimony she asked for three months ago, so long as she can't get her hands on the money you hope to make from this book?"

"Meaning we all want a clean break, don't we?"

Coughlan sighed. "Okay, Mr. Milstead, I'll speak to Mrs. Milstead. Goodbye. In the meantime—"

"Yes?" said Todd.

"As a gesture of goodwill, and because it's going to happen whatever Mrs. Milstead decides, are you prepared to move out of the marital home right away?"

For some reason Todd felt breezy. A tune came into his head. *Carry on, my wayward son*. He looked around the old homestead. It was pokey, brown, and smelled like defeat and the past. "You mean move out now?" he said.

"End of the week would be fine," said Coughlan.

Why not give them what they want, thought Todd. *I'll be rolling in the green stuff soon. Buy me a mansion, maybe*. The tune rose up in his ears.

"Sure," he said. "I'll get onto it right away."

"Okay," said Coughlan, sounding surprised. Todd put the phone down and wandered back into the living room, humming. "*Masquerading as a man with a reason*," he sang to himself and turned on the TV.

222

"I'm not sure," Sara said. They were in Todd's bed, which Todd figured was the best place for this conversation.

"It would only be for a few weeks while I found a new apartment," Todd said. *And while I waited for a royalty check*, he added to himself. *So maybe a few months.*

As if reading his mind, Sara said, "Can't the publishers advance you some money on sales? Isn't that what an advance is?"

"They already did," said Todd. "And the whole amount of that will be swallowed up by legal fees."

"I know this is going to sound odd," said Sara. "But when we live together—and yes, that is what I want—when that happens, I want it to be a fresh start. For both of us."

"I want that too," said Todd. "But—"

"You do?"

"I do," said Todd. "I really do. But—"

"No buts then, Todd. When we're under the same roof, it's got to be a new roof. I'm tired of sleeping in the bed you and Janis shared, and then the bed me and Terry shared. Fresh start means fresh start."

Todd forced a smile.

"Okay," he said.

"You do understand, don't you?" Sara said. She looked worried.

"Of course I do," said Todd.

I understand that I'm going to be living in a motel for six months.

"You moving out?" said the cop, looking at the piles of boxes in the drive.

"I am," said Todd, wondering where the cop's Detective of the Year badge was.

"Amicable split," he explained. "Books going into storage, the rest belongs to the wife."

"Okay," said the cop, slowly. His name was Officer Benedict and he said everything slowly.

"I mention it because on the TV you guys are always telling people not to skip town and to tell you when we're going somewhere," Todd explained.

"You're not leaving town, are you?" asked Officer Benedict.

"No," said Todd. "I'll be staying at the Sunset Motel."

He gave Benedict a card. Benedict looked at it like he'd been asked to memorize it.

"Not staying with friends?" he said.

No, it's kind of difficult because they've all been horribly murdered, thought Todd.

'What did you want to see me about?" he asked, and Officer Benedict's brow furrowed, as though he had genuinely forgotten.

"Well, it's kind of weird," he said. "It's about the book."

"My book?" asked Todd.

"That's what's weird about it," said Benedict. "When we got the book out of the guy's—when we removed the book, it was, like I said, covered in blood. I mean, it looked like it had been dipped in tomato soup. Just—"

"I get it," said Todd.

"Sorry. Anyway, we cleaned it up and there it was. *All My Colors*. Your book. And the place was full of it. I mean, other copies. Piled up. The whole window. It wasn't like the killer had to bring his own copy. The place was—"

"I'm with you," said Todd.

"Sorry. So we didn't look too closely."

A pause.

"Now I'm not with you," Todd said.

"At the book. We made an assumption, Mr. Milstead. Because of it being your book stuck in the guy's gullet—sorry again—we thought maybe there was a connection to you."

"Reasonable enough."

"Yeah, but the thing is, it wasn't your book."

"Excuse me?"

Officer Benedict pulled out from inside his jacket a transparent evidence bag that contained a stiff, crumpled, brown rectangle. Despite its battered, bloodstained condition, Todd recognized it at once.

"The lab guy cleaned it up some more and then he saw," said Benedict. "It's called *All My Colors*, all right, but it's not your book. It's by some guy called—"

Officer Benedict peered at the cover.

"Jake Turner."

Todd frowned.

"That is odd," he said. "I never heard of him."

"Really?" said Benedict. "We were kind of hoping that you might, on account of it's such a weird coincidence."

"You think it is a coincidence?" asked Todd, as casually as he could.

"Well, frankly, no, that was the wrong word," said Benedict. "But we can't think of any other explanation. Nobody we asked ever heard of this guy—" Internally, Todd sighed with relief. "—and we can't figure out why somebody would want to write a book with the same title as another book, that would be confusing for people, so the sergeant thought he'd just send me up here to ask you in person. If you had any ideas, that is."

"Can't help you," said Todd. "I mean, you're right, why would I give my book the same name as someone else's book? That would be absurd, it would be—" Todd searched for a word that Benedict might be more familiar with. "—crazy."

"That's what I thought," said Benedict. "So just to confirm, for the record. You never heard of this book, or Jake Turner?"

"No to both," said Todd.

"Okay," said Benedict, "Sorry to bother you."

He got up to leave.

"Can I ask you something?" said Todd, trying to sound disinterested.

"Fire away," said Benedict, putting the book back in his jacket.

"The lab guys… did they, were they able to look inside the book at all?"

"For clues, you mean?" said Benedict.

No, for spare change. "Yes," said Todd.

"That did occur to them," said Benedict. "But the pages were so stiff with blood, they'd all kind of fused together. Like a brick."

"I see," said Todd. "Thanks, officer."

"No problem," said Benedict. "If anything does occur to you, get in touch. And thanks for this," he added, putting the motel card in his pocket.

Todd closed the door behind Benedict. He sat down on the nearest chair and found that he was shaking uncontrollably.

The phone rang and Todd nearly jumped into the air. He reached out a trembling hand.

"Mr. Milstead? Behm here."

"Oh, hi," said Todd. He felt dizzy.

"You okay? This a bad time?"

"No, of course not. Where are you? It sounds loud."

"I'm in a call box, outside a liquor store. There's a lot of really drunk guys here and they're having a party in the parking lot."

"It sounds like fun."

"Oh yeah, it's a riot. Mr. Milstead, I'm in Pontiac."

For a moment the name meant nothing to Todd. Then it clicked.

"Pontiac, Michigan?"

"Where your guy comes from."

Todd's heart all but leapt out of his mouth.

"Jake Turner? You found Jake Turner?"

"Not exactly," said Behm. "Mr. Milstead, I think I need to see you."

"Today?" said Todd. "Because I'm moving out of my house."

"Divorce come through?"

"Not exactly," Todd said. "Goodwill gesture."

"You're a lovely guy."

"I know," said Todd. "So when will you be coming to see me?"

"I got a few things to tie up. Give me your new address and I'll come by in a week or so."

"You can find me at the Sunset Motel."

"Classy," said Behm, and rang off.

A couple of hours later, just as it started raining, Todd took the Volvo out of town to the Sunset. He parked in the lot, looked around—it was getting darker as well as wetter—and put the big lock on the steering wheel. Then he removed all his stuff from the car, locked it, checked he'd locked it, and went inside. There was nobody on reception, or in the office, which smelled of all the stale tobacco in history, but there was a note on the desk.

MILSTEAD, it read. ROOM 5. KEY ON HOOK.

Todd found the hook, took down the key, and trundled his cases to the room. Room 5 was on the end of a row. The window was open and a curtain was flapping wetly in the rain. Todd unlocked the door and went in. The room was everything a junkie could want from a motel room. A thin bed with thinner bedding, an armchair that looked like someone's uncle had died in it during the war, a closet apparently made of old popsicle sticks, and the kind of carpet that was so greasy it looked like it had been poured onto the floor from a frying pan.

Todd turned on a bedside lamp, which fizzed at him, flickered on and off a few times, and eventually settled down to a dull yellow glow. He turned on the TV, checked the phone was working, and lay on the bed.

Half an hour later, the phone rang. It was Coughlan and he sounded pretty clenched.

"You found me then," said Todd.

Coughlan got straight down to it.

"You have a deal," he said. "Sign the papers this week and Mrs. Milstead will grant you a divorce on her original terms."

"Thanks," said Todd.

"I have to say, I am not happy with this arrangement," said Coughlan. "I strongly advised her to go for new terms based on your new potential financial situation. But she said, and I quote, 'let him have what he wants.'"

"I knew she would," said Todd, who had known nothing of the sort. "Goodbye, Mr. Coughlan."

"I'll send the documents—" Coughlan began.

"No," said Todd. "I'll swing by in the morning and sign them in your office."

"Okay then," said Coughlan. It was the first time Todd had ever heard him sound surprised.

There was a bar across the street from the motel. It wasn't very nice, but it was warm and there were people in it. Todd went in, sat down, ordered a beer and a whiskey, and stayed there until he was warm enough, and drunk enough, to go back to his room, where he fell asleep on the counterpane, woke up in the early hours, went to the bathroom, and—unable to find the bed again—stumbled into the armchair and fell asleep in that instead.

Todd woke up with a hangover and a renewed sense of resolve. He showered, if that was the right word for standing under a kind of spitting metal tube with a sprinkler attached to it, pulled a clean shirt from his grip, and drove down to Coughlan's office.

"He's expecting me," Todd told Coughlan's secretary Gillian.

"Are you sure?" she said.

"I spoke to him late last night," said Todd.

Gillian looked as though she were about to say something about that, but didn't. Instead she said, "Well, there's nothing in the diary."

Just then Coughlan came in.

"I beat you to the office," said Todd.

"Milstead?" said Coughlan. "What brings you here?"

Todd looked around for a witness to this new-minted madness.

"Is there an epidemic of amnesia around here?" he asked. "I told you on the phone last night that I was coming over."

Coughlan exchanged a look with Gillian.

"Hold my calls," he said.

Todd followed Coughlan into his office.

"Hold his calls," he said, and winked at her. Todd felt good to be alive.

Once the door was shut, Coughlan said, "What the hell are you playing at, Milstead?"

Now Todd was confused. "I told you," he said. "We spoke on the phone last night."

Coughlan looked blank.

"Never mind," said Todd. "Now shall we get to it?"

"I'm sorry, Milstead, I'm really not with you. Get to what?"

Todd sighed deeply.

"The settlement," he said. "Or whatever you lawyers call it."

"Your divorce papers, you mean?" said Coughlan.

"Yes," said Todd. "Finally. I'm here to sign the papers. Like we discussed."

Coughlan looked genuinely puzzled now.

"You want to sign the papers?" he said.

"Yes," said Todd. "Like I said on the phone last night. Janis agrees, I agree, so let's sign and I will move out like I said last night. On the phone."

Coughlan was about to say something, when his expression changed. He affected a businesslike face.

"Normally in a situation like this, I'd ask if you'd been drinking," he said. "But it's too early even for you."

"Nice," said Todd. "Now please can I sign the damn papers?"

Ten minutes later, Todd had signed everything.

"Don't you want to read it first?" Coughlan had asked.

"No need," said Todd.

Coughlan handed Todd his copy of the documents.

"And you'll move out of the house?"

"Ahead of you," said Todd. "Already did."

Coughlan looked shocked. *Call me Speedy*, thought Todd.

"Okay," he said, and held out his hand for Todd to shake. Todd thought about thumbing his nose, but went for the polite option and shook.

"See you 'round," he said, and breezed out of the office.

"He signed it?" said Gillian.

"Like a lamb," said Coughlan.

"Why did he keep saying you called him last night?"

Coughlan grimaced. "Who cares? Maybe he's lost his fucking mind as well as everything else."

Todd drove back to the motel, the divorce papers on the seat beside him. For a moment he considered pitching the envelope out the window, but then thought, *Nah. Call 'em a souvenir of unhappier times.* Besides, you never knew with lawyers. Coughlan might try and trip him up on some fine detail of law, and it would be good to have the facts at his fingertips.

Nobody gets to push Todd Milstead around, he thought as he pulled into the motel parking lot.

The bedside light had given up the ghost completely, and the toilet apparently needed to take the morning off to refill its cistern, but other than that, the motel room was a home away from home. Todd dropped the divorce papers on the floor and flopped onto the bed.

The phone rang.

"Todd?"

"Janis?"

"I just wanted to thank you," said Janis, hesitantly.

"Hey, there's no need," said Todd.

"No, really. You didn't have to agree to everything."

"I— excuse me?" Todd could feel a knot beginning in his guts. "I didn't agree to everything."

"Coughlan called me," Janis said, not listening. "He said you came in, signed the papers, didn't even want to read them."

Todd leaned over to grab the envelope from the floor and fumbled it open.

"I just wanted—" he said, trying to turn the papers with his free hand, "—to, you know..."

"It's so generous," said Janis. "We thought you'd fight the alimony, what with your, you know, success, but—"

Now it was Todd's turn not to listen. *Whereas the aforesaid Todd Milstead agrees to pay the agreed portion of his income to the aforesaid Janis Milstead... said portion not to exceed... for the period of...*

Todd let the papers fall.

"Oh God," he said out loud.

"Are you okay?" said Janis.

"Yeah," said Todd. "Never better."

A thought occurred to him.

"Janis," he said. "When you said 'we' just then..."

"Yes?" said Janis, for the first time wary.

"Who did you mean?"

Janis exhaled. "I suppose there's no harm in telling you now," she said. "I kind of think you guessed anyway."

Todd, thought Todd, *I'm shacking up with the Dyke with the Bike.*

"Todd," said Janis, "Joe asked me to marry him."

Todd felt like he'd been hit in the head with a brick.

"Joe?" he said.

"Joe Hines," said Janis.

"Joe Hines? Joe my old pal Hines?"

"The very same," said Janis, and laughed. "God, he was so nervous about asking me out. He kept saying, I hope Todd doesn't find out, and what do you think Todd is going to say?"

"Joe," said Todd. He was all out of anything now.

"So, Todd," said Janis, a note of playfulness in her voice. "What *do* you say?"

A thousand replies went through Todd's mind. Most of them had the word *fuck* in them. Todd knew when he was beaten.

"I hope you'll both be very happy together," he said.

After a fretful hour going through the divorce papers with a fine-toothed comb, Todd gave up on looking for loopholes and instead turned his attention to wondering *what the fucking fuck is happening to my fucking brain*, which seemed to be a more pressing matter.

He'd *seen* Janis at that truck stop. He'd seen the bike, and he'd seen the woman give him the finger. Then there were Behm's photographs. All right, there was something wrong with the damn pictures, but Behm had seen something, hadn't he? *Just like I saw something*, thought Todd.

And the call from Coughlan last night. Todd was now pretty sure that hadn't happened. *Maybe it was the booze*, he thought. But he doubted it.

He made a call.

"Todd!" said Nora. She sounded ecstatic to hear from him. "How's it going?"

"Great," said Todd. "Can't wait to get back on the road."

"And we are in the process of scheduling those dates for you," said Nora, perhaps a little too quickly. "Although I must say, the book is doing so well, it seems to be quite happy without—"

Without me, thought Todd. *Join the club, book.*

"I'm glad," he said. "Nora, I was kind of wondering—my situation has changed somewhat lately, and I was thinking—is there any chance I could get an advance? You know, on sales?"

"Todd," said Nora brightly. "You've had your advance. Now all you need to do is sit back and wait for the royalties to flow in."

"Yes, I know that," said Todd, perhaps a little too tersely. "But I have certain, as I say, fresh financial issues, and…"

"Relax," said Nora. "You'll get your first check in April."

"That's months away!" cried Todd.

"Yes it is," agreed Nora. "I'm sorry, Todd, that's how publishing works."

"Okay, okay," said Todd. "There must be other ways to get money. How about movie rights?"

"We could look into that," said Nora. "In fact, yes, that's a good idea. That might net you a few hundred dollars."

"A few hundred?" Todd said.

"Rights don't really go for that much," Nora said. "But listen, Todd, and this is something I was going to broach later…"

"What's that?"

"How ready are you to write another book?" said Nora.

Todd was silent.

About as ready as I am to swim the fucking Pacific Ocean, he thought.

"Would that entail a larger advance?" he asked, slowly.

"As your publisher, I can say that we are in a good position regarding an advance on a sequel."

"A sequel?"

"It doesn't literally have to be a sequel," said Nora. "Although people would love to know what happens to the characters."

Me too, said Todd. He thought of a piece he'd once read about the late Elvis Presley. Asked about his new movie, Presley had apparently said, "Yeah, it's a good script. I'd like to read it some time."

"That ending," said Nora, mistaking his silence for encouragement. "It's ambiguous. And people hate loose ends."

"A sequel," said Todd. He was thinking fast now. *I wrote the first one, didn't I? How hard can it be?* "And if I say yes, you can guarantee me some decent... a proper advance?"

"Yes," said Nora. "You come up with the goods—and I know you can, in fact I shouldn't be surprised if you haven't been working away at something already—and I will negotiate an advance as big as the Ritz for you. Not that this is all about the money of course," she added.

The hell it isn't, Todd thought.

"Okay," he said. "I better get to it."

Nora rang off, and Todd leaned back in his seat.

Todd reached for his copy of *All My Colors*. He had it in his head, or so he thought, but every time he tried to focus on it, on the characters, or the story, it slipped away from him. Holding the book down like it was an animal that might otherwise escape his grasp, Todd tried to read it. Passages came back to him, familiar scenes, but he was damned if he could retain anything. In the end, he got out a pencil and started making notes. By early afternoon, Todd had written out—slowly, and with tremendous effort—an outline of most of the story. Now he was on the final stretch (*thank God*, he thought).

The last mile was, indeed, the hardest mile. Todd struggled to recall characters he'd been following for chapters, and he kept going back to earlier scenes to refresh his memory of major plot developments, but somehow, with a tremendous effort of will, he made it to the final page.

He drank some water, picked up his pencil and began to copy out the last paragraph of *All My Colors*.

"Helen knew then," Todd copied down, *"that if life were made up of a series of colors, then it was not, as she had believed, a spectrum of feelings ranging from empty, mindless white through bland gray to the darkest, deepest black, but something else entirely. Life, she had learned, was—and she could almost laugh at the simplicity of the idea—a kind of bright rainbow, made of colors that a child would love. Bright blues and garish yellows and furious purples. Greens and browns and, yes, blacks and whites, but all mixed in with magentas and scarlets and golds.*

'This is my life,' she told herself as she walked out the door, into a new world. 'And these are all my colors.'

The End."

Todd put his pencil down. *Is that it?* he thought. *Is that what the critics are going crazy for?* It seemed pretty hokey, but then he'd always been what he considered a manly kind of writer. Still, it sold, and he was the guy who'd— well, it had come out of him, hadn't it? Todd was always reading about writers and painters and musicians who'd said that they were just the conduit for great art, that it just flowed through them. Todd remembered the diaper days.

He looked at *All My Colors* like an adversary.

"I wrote you once," he told the book. "I can write you again."

CHAPTER ONE, Todd spelled out, in large penciled capitals. He missed his typewriter but it was in storage and if he went to the storage place to get it, the storage guys might ask him about the money he owed them. He underlined the words. *CHAPTER ONE*.

Helen walked into the bar, he wrote. *Why*? he thought to himself, and realized that he had no idea why Helen walked into the bar. In *All My Colors* she didn't even drink. He crossed the line out. *Helen walked into the diner*, he wrote. But writing the word *diner* just made him think about Janis, and how she'd tricked him by making him think she was seeing the Dyke with the Bike and not Joe Hines, good old best buddy pal Joe who, not content with drinking Todd's liquor, was now screwing Todd's wife...

Todd sat up with a jolt. The piece of paper he'd been writing on was now balled up in his hands. He tossed it into a waste paper basket and started again.

By five o'clock, Todd had written precisely two words. One was *CHAPTER* and one was *ONE*.

"Fuck this," he told both words. "I need to find a bar."

By nine o'clock, Todd was awesomely drunk. He was trying to drink his whiskey from the shot glass without using his hands. As Todd's head was resting on the bar at this point, and the bartender pretty much didn't care if his clientele were alive or dead, Todd might have gotten away with it if he hadn't become ambitious and tried to do the same with his bottle of beer. The bottle failed to connect with Todd's mouth and spun across the bar where it frothed into the lap of a big bearded man.

"I'm very sorry," slurred Todd.

"You're gonna be," said the big man, and hit Todd in the eye with his fist. Todd rolled on the floor and, after a while, climbed to his feet again, which was when the bartender asked him to leave.

It must have taken Todd a half hour to cross the road from the bar to the motel. Twice he got turned around and found himself heading back toward the bar. Two or three times the sudden presence of a truck honking down on him caused Todd to scurry back to his starting point. And once he set off too fast, tripped and saw the sidewalk coming up at him like a drawbridge being raised.

Eventually he made it to his room where, after dropping his key several times, he got himself onto the bed and passed out with the door open and his shoes still on.

The next day, Todd wrote six pages in a hungover frenzy.

The day after that, he tore them up, went to the bar, learned he was no longer welcome there, and went to the liquor store.

The day after *that*, Todd spent in bed. When the maid came, he hid under the blanket until she left.

This pattern repeated itself for a few more days until one morning Todd got out of bed, took all the empty bottles to a dumpster, showered, sat down at the desk and began to work.

SEVEN

It was a sunny morning in a crappy part of town as Sara walked up to the Sunset Motel's reception desk. There was a grimy bell on the counter. She pressed it and it rang faintly.

"Help you?" said the clerk, appearing from the office.

"I'm looking for Todd Milstead," said Sara.

"Room five," said the clerk, and headed back into the office.

"Room five it is then," said Sara to herself.

Sara walked around the side of the motel. The door to Room 5 was closed and she could hear the sound of the TV blaring out from behind it. She knocked hard and, a few seconds later, harder.

"Go away!" she heard Todd shout.

"It's Sara."

The TV sound cut out and the door opened.

"Sara?" said Todd.

Sara stepped back in surprise. Todd was unshaven. His hair was uncombed and he was wearing nothing but his underpants.

"You'd better come in," he said.

Todd closed the door behind Sara and instantly she wished he hadn't. It wasn't that she didn't feel safe—Todd looked so ill and thin that she doubted he could have harmed himself, let alone her—but that the room was awful. There was a fug of unwashed *everything*—unwashed clothes, unwashed dishes, unwashed Todd—and while someone had hoovered the greasy carpet, they hadn't opened any windows or removed any pizza boxes.

But that wasn't the worst thing. True, Sara would have been hard-pressed to pick the worst thing—it could have been that Todd seemed neither pleased nor annoyed to see her, just kind of accepting, like she was now part of the furniture, or it could have been the whole muggy gray-green atmosphere of drawn curtains and lamps with towels over them, giving the whole place an underwater look.

The worst thing was the writing.

It was everywhere. Pieces of paper, torn and crumpled and balled-up, on the floor and on the desk and on the bed. Paper, scrawled on and scribbled on, in the armchair and the closet and even the bath. Writing everywhere, on pads, on leaflets, even on the walls.

Todd looked at Sara.

"They come like that," he said. "The words. They just come like that, in no particular order. And I can't put them together again."

Sara backed away a little.

"What do you mean, 'put them together again'?"

"Like Humpty Dumpty," said Todd. "The words. Jumbled up and messy. No use to me. I mean, look at them."

Sara looked at the walls. They were randomly covered in words and phrases. Sometimes there was a whole sentence— SHE CLIMBED INTO THE CAR AND SAID DRIVE, JUST DRIVE—and sometimes it was just one word—HELEN or NIGHT. But it was everywhere, from floor to ceiling.

"Todd," said Sara slowly. "What is this?"

"What does it look like?" said Todd. "No. Okay. You can't see it."

He scratched his armpit thoughtfully.

"Can you get me a typewriter?"

Sara looked at the walls again. *I don't think a typewriter would help*, she thought.

"I just need to get everything corraled," said Todd. "The old roundup."

"Todd, you need to get some rest," said Sara. "You've been under a lot of pressure, I know, what with the divorce and the book doing so well…"

"I don't have time," Todd said. "I have to write the new book. It shouldn't take too long. The first one came out like a river."

"I don't know anything about writing," Sara tried again. "But you look— Todd, you look terrible."

Suddenly Todd's head jerked, like someone had slapped him.

"He looked like anyone would look if they'd been him," he said, his voice mushy like he was talking in his sleep. *"He looked like his face was a diary and the diary was full of bad things."*

243

Todd's expression changed. He was alert, and worried, now.

"What did I just say?" he said.

"You— I don't know," said Sara.

"You heard it, didn't you," said Todd anxiously. "What did I say?"

He turned around and scrabbled on the table for a pen.

"Todd," said Sara. "Come with me."

"It's gone." Todd was angry now. "It's gone, it won't come back."

"Todd—"

"None of it comes back. Do you understand me, Sara? It comes in pieces and it goes and it doesn't come back. *None of it comes back!*"

He was staring at her now, rage in his eyes.

"I'd better go," said Sara.

"Yeah," said Todd. "Thanks for coming."

Sara made it to her car without crying. She drove two blocks, then wept at a red light. When the light changed, she was still crying. Cars honked at her. She closed her eyes as they swerved around her, and drove off into the evening traffic.

She never saw Todd again.

Todd sat in his armchair, looking into the darkness. The curtains were drawn, as they always were, and he hadn't turned the lights on, because he needed the darkness.

The darkness was the only time when Todd could see.

Todd didn't like what he saw. There were shapes but

they had soft edges. Todd knew the shapes were the book, and he knew they would get clearer, and the book would be there.

All he needed was the book to be there.

A few days later, the phone rang. Todd had difficulty finding it under the tumbleweeds of paper.

"Is that you, Todd?" a woman's voice said.

"This is Todd," said a rasping voice that Todd took a moment to recognize as his own.

"Todd, this is Nora."

"Hello, Nora."

"Nora, your publisher."

"Hi."

"Are you okay, Todd?"

Todd thought for a moment. There were sores on his legs, and he thought one of his teeth might be loose.

"I'm fine."

"Oh good."

"I'm working on the book."

"That's great news, Todd."

"I'm working really hard."

"Todd, I have some slightly puzzling news, and I wondered if you could help shed some light on it."

The woman sounded annoyed. Todd wondered what he was doing wrong. He tried to focus.

"Todd," said the woman. "I looked into the movie rights like you asked."

"Right," said Todd. "I remember now." Someone was going around his brain, turning all the lights on.

"I spoke to your lawyers, and they were about to draw up the contract, but first they did a routine check. And Todd, you're not going to believe this. They'd been sold already."

"Oh. Does that mean—"

"I know, it's obviously a mistake. For a start, the book didn't exist a year ago so how could the rights be sold? And there's some problem with the name."

"The name?"

"The name of the writer. Todd," said Nora slowly. "Did you—have you ever come across another book of the same name as *All My Colors*?"

Todd sat up. He turned the light on.

"Todd?"

"No," he said slowly. "If I had, I wouldn't have called it that."

"That's what I said. But the lawyers are saying the only explanation is that someone already wrote a book called *All My Colors*."

"Did they say," Todd asked carefully, "did they say who the other person was? The other writer?"

"They did," said Nora. "But the name slipped my mind. I can find out for you. Maybe it'll help jog your memory."

"Is this a problem?" Todd asked. By now he was fully back in the room.

"It shouldn't be," said Nora. "Lots of books have the same name as other books. It's only a problem if what's inside is the same." She laughed. "But I guess we're okay there, right?"

"Right," said Todd.

•

Todd sat down and thought. It had to be a mistake. Nobody else knew that there was more than one *All My Colors*. Because there wasn't more than one *All My Colors*. The only book of that name was written by yours truly, Todd Milstead. *Accept no substitute*, thought Todd.

It's a mistake, he thought, turned the light off again, and waited for the shapes to form.

More time passed. The shapes came and went. Sometimes they whispered to Todd—odd phrases, names, and even entire paragraphs. Todd tried to catch what they whispered to him, but it was like trying to catch water. Still, he did what he could, and he wrote, and he listened, and he wrote.

Later there was a knock on the door.

"Go away," Todd said.

"Milstead?" It was Behm's voice.

Todd turned the light on and went to the door.

"Jesus, Milstead, you look like shit on two legs."

"Come in."

If Behm found the state of the room unusual, he didn't say anything. He just pushed a heap of paper off Todd's favorite chair and sat down without being asked. *Rude*, thought Todd.

"I'm sorry I haven't been in touch," Behm said, although he didn't look sorry at all.

"That's okay," said Todd. "I've been busy myself."

"Yeah, I can see that," said Behm.

He settled a large canvas bag at his feet.

"At first I thought you'd sent me on a wild goose chase," he said. "I mean, all I had to go on was a name and a town."

"Pontiac," said Todd. "Jake Turner."

"That's right," Behm said. "Glad you remembered. I'd hate to think I went to all this trouble and you forgot about me."

"I'm very busy," said Todd. "Can we—"

"Sorry," Behm said. "You're going to have to set aside a few minutes in your packed schedule. I got a lot to tell you."

"I'll get the whiskey," said Todd.

Behm took the smeared glass Todd offered him, drained its contents and said, "So first of all, I did the usual offices. I got the phone books, I got the street directories. I went to the library. I went to the *newspaper* library. And nothing. Nobody in Pontiac, Michigan was ever called Jake Turner. Which you'd think wouldn't be the case. Even if it wasn't our guy, there's got to be at least one Jake Turner in town."

"I guess," said Todd.

"Then I got in the car, and I went to Pontiac," said Behm. "It's not one of the great towns, believe me. Detroit up the road and there's nothing happening there anymore. And I asked around. I called up Turners in the phone book and told them I was a friend of Jake's and had they seen him lately. I asked in bars. I spoke to librarians. That kind of thing.

"Then I had an idea. I thought instead of looking for the guy, I'd look for the book."

Todd tensed. "The book?" he said.

"Yeah. You told me he was a writer. That was the third piece of information I had, and I almost forgot about it. So I went into a secondhand bookstore and I asked the guy behind the counter if he'd heard of Jake Turner."

"What did he say?"

"He said no, but I was welcome to take a look on the shelves. Said it was a big place and there could be anything back there. So I went and took a look. It was a mess. The guy had no respect for the alphabet. There were Hemingways mixed up with Chandlers, Thackerays stacked up next to Graham Greene... a mess.

"I stayed there half the morning. Guy even made me a coffee and brought me a sandwich. I went through those shelves like an auditor. I counted every single book. You okay?"

Todd looked at Behm. Behm nodded downward at Todd's hands. Todd was knitting and unknitting his fingers in a perpetual cat's cradle.

"I'm fine," said Todd. "Did you find it? The book?"

"No," said Behm, and Todd's heart almost burst with relief. Then Behm reached for the bag. He tipped it out onto the floor. There must have been ten or eleven books there. Paperbacks and hardbacks. Mint condition books and books fit only for the fire. Some were copies of *All My Colors* and some weren't, but they all had one thing in common. They were all by Jake Turner.

"I found the books. Plural," said Behm.

Todd got down on his knees among the books.

"I don't understand," he said.

"Well, if you don't, nobody does," Behm said. "You asked me to find Jake Turner, and I guess," he indicated the small heap of books, "I came pretty close."

"But I never heard of these books," said Todd, picking one up. *The Green Road*, it was called. Now he had it in his hand, it seemed somehow familiar.

"The store guy hadn't, either," said Behm. "He guessed

they must have been a job lot left by the previous owner. But you know the weird part?"

Why is there always a weird part? thought Todd. *Just for once, why can't there be a normal part?*

"No," he said. "What's the weird part?"

Behm looked at Todd, as if wondering what Todd really knew.

"The guy starts off saying, gee, I never saw these books before, and, gee, who is this guy, and all that. He's really insistent," he said. "But then he stops, and he says, gee, wait a minute, I'm remembering something. Jake Turner, Jake Turner... And he starts tapping his teeth with a pencil like it's gonna wake up his memory. Then all of a sudden he opens this drawer, and—"

"And what?" Todd said.

"I had to give him twenty dollars for it," said Behm. "He was reluctant to sell it, he said, but you could tell he hadn't looked at the fucking thing in ten years—"

"*What?*" repeated Todd.

Behm sighed. "Now we're eager," he said. He reached into the bag again, and pulled out a folder. Todd grabbed the folder off him. Inside it was a small yellowing bundle of typescript.

"I'll be charging that twenty dollars to your account," said Behm as Todd carefully unfolded the paper. There were five or six closely typed pages.

"What is this?" asked Todd.

"Guy told me he found it inside one of the books," Behm said. "Read it. I'll get some more whiskey."

Todd unfolded the first page.

THE CONFESSION OF JAKE TURNER, it said.

"Is it a story?" he asked.

"You're the writer," said Behm, returning with the whiskey. "You tell me."

Todd sat back and began to read.

THE CONFESSION OF JAKE TURNER

I, Jake Turner, writer and bum, do hereby confirm that this here is my true confession. Read it and weep, gentle reader, and excuse the clichés, because I don't have the time or the money to hire an editor.

I was born where I'll die, in Michigan, the son of a truck driver and a housewife, and I was educated in the school of hard knocks and the university of life. My ma and pa provided the hard knocks and the world showed me life. By the time I was fifteen, I'd been with a woman, I'd drunk a bottle of whiskey unaided and lived to tell the tale, and I'd punched a man so hard he lost an eye.

You could say I was born to be a writer.

I was born too late to ride the railroads. My uncle did that during the Depression, but all he ever got from it was a drinking problem and a sore butt. And I was born too early for rock'n'roll. It sounds crazy to say it, but man, I would have been the best rock'n'roller. I could play the guitar a little, I was good-looking and mean, and I knew how to keep a crowd in the palm of my hand. I was just a kid in a leather jacket, but I could stop a fight and snare a woman, sometimes in the same moment. So I was too old for Elvis, but I was just the right age for Brando. And Dean. And Jack.

I don't know when I first came across the Beats, but when

I did, it changed my life. Because it was my life. Sitting around listening to jazz and smoking tea—marijuana—and talking. God, I could talk. Sometimes I even talked women out of going to bed with me, I talked so much.

Anyway, I read On the Road and I read Ginsberg and I listened to Lenny Bruce and I was hooked. And one day, I was pushing my motorcycle past a pawnshop and there it was in the window. A Smith Corona typewriter, black as hell. All I had with me was the motorcycle. Yeah, you guessed it.

I pawned the helmet and got the typewriter. (What, you think I pawned the bike? Are you crazy?)

After that, I was a writer. First I wrote rip-offs of Kerouac, and then I found a voice. It wasn't much of a voice at first, but it was the only voice I had, and over time it got louder. It was hard to work out what to do with that voice at first, though. I wrote some science fiction stories and someone printed them. I wrote some horror stories and someone printed them, too. I was just about to try my hand at true romance when the voice said, "Jake, what is this? You have to figure out who you are before you write anything else."

So I got on the bike and I went—you guessed it—on the road. I rode from Detroit to New York. I went to smoky clubs and I saw the kids who were kicking out jazz and replacing it with protest. They were protesting about nuclear war, which seemed kind of pointless when there was so much else to protest about. I went out west and saw the Pacific. Nobody was protesting in Los Angeles, but I did meet Ginsberg in San Francisco. He told me to "keep writing." I told him he was too fat for me.

And then I came home. My pa was dead and my ma was drunk. I sold the motorbike and married a local girl and worked nights at the steel factory to support us.

During the day she worked in a movie theater and I wrote. I had a plan. I was going to write The Great American Novel. It was a simple plan, and it didn't work out. First of all I wrote The Worst American Novel, then The Shortest American Novel, and finally I wrote The Okay American Novel, and someone printed it.

After that, it was easier. The voice and me were getting on okay. The voice told me what to write, and I wrote it. The books got better, even if they didn't sell. Then one day, the publisher phoned me and said I needed to give them a hit or they were going to drop me. I said I'd see what I could do.

What I could do, it turned out, was nothing. The voice was no good. It was too quiet, too ordinary. It was like someone you were close to when you were a kid, fun to hang out with and kind of provocative, but when you're a man, when you need men around you, it's no use. I needed a different voice.

Then one night, after I'd finished my shift at the steel factory, I went to a bar, just to relax before I got home and had to listen to the wife telling me all about her day, which was always the same day, except they showed different movies. They changed the movies but she never changed her day.

The bar was quiet, and there was nobody else there. Then the jukebox came on, as if by itself. It was an old jazz tune, "Bad Penny Blues." I turned around to see who was there, and there she was. She was dancing by herself—no, she was dancing with herself—and singing, even though there were no words to the tune, just ba-ba and yeah-yeah, softly.

I couldn't see her face, but I knew it would be beautiful.

Her name was Helen.

Todd started at that.

"Something wrong?" said Behm.

Todd ignored him and went back to reading. His knuckles were white against the paper.

Her name was Helen. She told me she lived a couple of blocks away, in a cold water apartment.

"Is that why you're here?" I asked her. "For the hot water in the bathroom?"

She shrugged. "Know how big my apartment is?" she said.

"I'll bite," I said.

"I can lie on the bed and put my hands out of both windows at the same time," she said.

For a moment I had an image of her as a modern-day Alice, trapped in the doll's house. Then her face cracked into a smile. It was a great smile.

"Sucker," she said.

"Seriously," I said, when she'd finished laughing, "how big is your apartment?"

"You wanna see?" she said.

There was a moment.

"Sure," I said.

We did everything that night. Everything, that is, but screw. You recall I said I liked to talk? Turns out I was a rank amateur. Helen talked, and talked, through the night. I know that sounds like a putdown, but this wasn't ordinary woman's talk. Helen was a poem. She had no idea how wonderful she was to listen to. Her talk wasn't like a man's talk—it wasn't full of opinions and facts and lists and boasts. Helen liked all kind of things, but she didn't think she was a better person for liking them, or that the things she liked were more important than the things other people liked. She just liked. And sometimes she loved. She loved jazz, she loved books, she loved to dance.

And later, she loved me, and I loved her.

I got home in time for breakfast and bad temper. My wife wanted to know where I'd been all night. I told her. She walked out that morning.

Later that day, I put a note through Helen's door. I HAVE HOT WATER, it said. An hour later, Helen appeared on my doorstep with a cardboard valise.

"Hi," I said.

"Invite me in," she said.

It was a weird thing to say.

"Come in, beautiful," I said, and she stepped over the threshold.

We didn't talk much that day. Nor the day after. Then, one morning when we could scarcely move for aching, she came back from the bathroom with a book in her hand.

"What's this?" she said. It was The Green Road.

"Oh, that old thing," I said. "The Free Press said it had promise, but never got around to saying what that promise was."

"You never told me you were a writer," she said, sitting down on the bed.

"Nobody ever told me I was a writer, either," I said. I must have sounded a little prickly, because she kissed me then and said, "I think it's pretty good. Not bad, anyway."

Then she looked at me in a strange way. Like she'd found something to distrust.

"I want you to know," she said, "I won't be used."

"Baby," I said, and I meant it, "I would never use you."

"I mean it," she said. "I'm not on earth to be anyone's inspiration."

I didn't really know what she meant, so I just kissed her. "Relax," I said. "I got my own voice."

As it happened, though, my own voice wasn't doing much for me. Everything I wrote turned clean sheets of white paper into great balls of crap. I just couldn't get an idea worth anything or a sentence worth typing. But it didn't seem to matter. I had Helen. What we had was what the philosophers talked about. Live for today. Live in the moment. Be here now. That was us. We just lived a life together. If the words weren't coming for me, that was okay. I had my job, I had Helen. We were happy.

Then I started to hear stories at the factory. They were laying men off, men who'd been there for years. Men with families. And one day the supervisor called me into his office, and gave me a check, and said he was sorry.

Helen said she'd work, but with the factory laying off, every wife and girlfriend and mother and daughter in the area was looking for work. Pretty soon, we had nothing.

My wife called. She wanted a divorce and she wanted her share of the house. The house was sold, and with my share of the money—minus her alimony—Helen and I moved into a new apartment. It had hot water, but apart from that it was no palace.

Still, during that time we became even closer. We started to tell each other everything we knew about ourselves. Filling in the gaps, Helen called it. I told her about my pa and his fists, and my ma and her drinking. She told me about her childhood on a farm, way out in the middle of nowhere. I told her about riding across America, and she told me about going to farm college and one day, halfway through a lecture about the importance of manure, realizing that anything would be better than farming.

We told each other everything. We were like two people assembling jigsaws of ourselves. Then one day, after I'd cooked a meal (I could do that now), Helen said, "Do you know what today is?" I thought about saying something flip and then thought about not saying it. "Today is my tenth wedding anniversary," she said.

I nearly dropped the pan I was holding. I thought we knew everything about each other.

"You were married?" I asked as casually as I could.

"Still am, I guess," she said. "I never got around to signing a piece of paper. Not that it matters. I'm never going to see the bastard again."

"Do you want to talk about it?" I asked. I don't think I'd ever cared about a woman enough to ask her if she wanted to talk about it before.

"No," she said. "Yes."

We sat down. I got us two beers, and she told me everything. It was a hell of a story.

Of course, if you're reading this, and you know who I am, you know the story, so I'll confine myself to the basics. The woman, who was young and naïve, a country girl in the big city who didn't want to go back to the farm. The man, who was a bastard, and drank, and was violent. And the day she walked out on him, went straight to the hardware store and told the clerk that she wanted to buy a hacksaw to cut off her ring finger.

"Fuck," said Todd. Behm looked at him curiously, but Todd didn't elaborate.

Yeah, that story.

And when she'd told me the whole thing, she cried in my arms, and made me promise I would never, ever tell it to anyone else.

I promised. How could I hurt Helen? When she'd been hurt so much already.

After that, things were different. Helen was different. It was as if she'd revealed the most secret part of herself and without that secret part, she had nothing. She kept saying,

"I wish I'd never told you." And no matter how often I said that I'd never tell, no matter how much I crossed my heart or swore on my own life, she kept on saying it.

It drove me crazy, I guess. I stopped seeing her as this beautiful, damaged woman who had fallen in love with me, and started to view her as a kind of albatross, clinging around my neck and making us both miserable.

"I wish I'd never told you."

I wished the same thing too.

I suppose that's why I started cheating on her. I couldn't stand the reproach. I mean, I'd done nothing, right? I'd been faithful to my promise and told nobody Helen's story. But all I was getting in return was misery. Dark looks. Sideways glances.

I started staying away from home. I started seeing other women. You could say Helen and I drifted apart. Like two sailors shipwrecked on ice floes. I could see her floating away into the Arctic night. Still giving me those reproachful looks. I was getting hell for something I hadn't done. And one day I woke up and I thought I might as well get hell for something I had done.

I got up one morning, I put a piece of paper into the typewriter and I started writing. I changed the names to protect the record, and I altered a couple of facts, and I wrote it. God forgive me, I wrote her story, and I called it All My Colors, and I sent it to my publisher, and he loved it.

I wish now I'd never done it, but what good is that? I wish now I was living in that apartment still, with no money and no food, with the bones of our love to gnaw on. I wish she was still here.

The day I came back from New York, the day I signed the contract, was also the day it happened. I came in and there she was, in the bedroom. She was packing. She didn't have to tell me why.

She picked up her case—it was the same cardboard valise she'd moved in with—and she walked out onto the landing. I stood in her way.

"Please move," she said, not even looking at me.

"We need to talk," I said. "You owe me that."

"We talked," she said. "You made a promise and you broke it."

"I don't know what you're talking about," I said.

"I found your manuscript," she said, and even though I had been expecting this moment for weeks, months even, a chill ran through me like a rod of ice.

She looked me square in the eye. "I knew this would happen," she said.

"You made it happen," I said.

"I did nothing!" Helen shouted. "It was you!"

She shoved me in the chest with the case, and I staggered backward. I grabbed her, without thinking.

"Get away from me!" she shouted, and shoved me again.

This time I can't say I did what I did without thinking. I grabbed her hard. I was so angry. All I'd done or tried to do for her, and all she'd done was drive me away.

"Fuck you!" I said.

The last words I ever said to her. Fuck you.

She took a step toward me and I kicked her feet out from under her. I didn't mean to do it—did I?—but I did. Helen went backward down the stairs, hit the banister, flipped into a forward roll and crumpled at the foot of the stairs.

I ran down after her. She lay there at a crazy angle. Her neck was broken. But she was still looking at me.

After unpacking her valise, I got out of there. When I came back two hours later, I called the police and told them I'd found her at the bottom of the stairs when I came back in. They suspected me all right—they'd be crazy not to—but the autopsy was inconclusive. Because I'd unpacked the valise, they didn't know she was leaving me. Because I was clearly distraught at her death, and because people knew how much I loved her, I got away with it. I was lucky, or so I thought.

After the funeral, I went in the bedroom and I saw something under the bed. I thought it was maybe a farewell note. I was about to burn it, when I noticed that it had been typed, on my typewriter. It was the last paragraph of *All My Colors*. She must have typed it out herself. I couldn't imagine why.

For those of you who are familiar with the book, I reproduce those lines now. Maybe you can make sense of them, work out why Helen *felt they were worth typing out. I know I can't.*

"*He* ran across the road. It was after him. He didn't know what it was, but it was after him. The road was clear. No cars, nothing. He stepped out—and a wall hit him. It crushed him, it flattened him, it pulled him to the ground and it mangled and broke him.

The last thing he heard as his lifeblood seeped from his smashed body was a voice, a whiney voice, saying again and again, 'He just stepped out right in frunna me! Right in frunna me!'"

"But that's not how it ends," Todd said.

"That's all there is," said Behm.

"No," said Todd, and got up. He pulled his copy of *All My Colors* from his case.

"Look," he said, opening the book. Behm looked at the last page.

"Yeah," he said, "it's different. So what? It's a different book. Same name, different book."

Behm looked at Todd, as if realizing something.

"Is that what all this is about, Milstead? The book?"

Todd didn't hear him.

"You're right," he said, and there was a wild tone in his voice. "You're right. It's a different book."

"That's what I said."

"No, you don't get it. *It's a different book.*"

"Okay…"

"If this—" Todd jabbed at the book. "—is different to that, to what he wrote, then—then there's a chance."

"A chance of what? Mr. Milstead, you're losing me."

Todd grabbed Behm by the shoulders.

"There's a chance I can change things!"

"Let go, would you?"

"If the books are different, I can write my way out of it! I can move the shapes! Behm, I can move the shapes!"

"Milstead…"

Behm's voice seemed to be coming from far away. Todd barely noticed that his hands were no longer on Behm's shoulders.

"Behm!" he shouted, and his own voice filled the world. "Behm! I can do anything! There's a—"

Todd laughed. "There's a *spirit* inside me! It's like when I wrote the book! A spirit! Guiding me. Guiding my—"

A thought occurred to him.

"Behm, what happened to Turner?"

There was no reply save a sick groan. Todd looked at his hands. They were tight around Behm's neck. Behm's head was lolling in his grip *like a fucking cauliflower* thought Todd wildly. He let go, and Behm's lifeless body thumped to the floor.

Shit, Todd thought. *Fucking shit.*

He sat on the floor next to the corpse. Behm's body had fallen onto the yellowing pages. Todd looked down. One of the pages was different to the rest. It had a handwritten scrawl in red pen at the bottom, maybe written by the bookstore guy or whoever had found the confession. Todd picked it up.

Jake Turner died two days after writing this, said the note. *He walked onto the highway and was killed immediately by a speeding truck.*

Todd made a pile of the books, heaping them at Behm's feet like a sacrificial offering. He found a book of motel matches, lit one, and dropped it onto the books. It went out. Todd ripped up some newspapers. He tore up Turner's confession and scattered it over Behm.

He went out to Behm's car. In the trunk he found, as he knew he would, a can of gasoline (Behm was, or had been, a prepared kind of guy). He brought it inside and sloshed it all over the carpet. Then he put everything he needed inside a pillowcase and threw that outside.

Todd lit another match and dropped it onto the carpet, which caught alight with a *woomph*. Then, before the flames got too high, he dropped his own copy of *All My Colors* into the fire and walked out, closing the door behind him.

The Volvo pulled out of the parking lot, just as smoke started to pour from the motel room's windows. In the distance he could hear the sirens of fire trucks.

After a few miles, he turned off at a White Castle and got something to eat. He hadn't felt hungry for days and, judging by the horrified look on the face of the girl behind the counter, he hadn't eaten for days either.

"Give me a box of sliders," he said. "And a Coke, and fries." Damn, he was hungry.

Todd barely made it back to the car before finishing the box of tiny burgers. He crammed a fistful of fries into his mouth, gulped some Coke down, and was about to start the car when he saw it in the rearview mirror.

A black Harley-Davidson, headlight on, pulling into the parking lot.

Todd adjusted the mirror so he could see better, but he didn't really need to confirm what he was looking at. *It was her.* Of course it was. Who else would it be?

Todd peeled out of the lot as fast as the Volvo would let him. He ran a red light in his haste, and decided to slow down in case a cop pulled him over. *I am,* he thought, *technically a murderer on the run.* For some reason the word "technically" made him giggle, and he almost had to pull over in case he choked from laughing.

Calm down, he advised himself, stealing a look in the mirror again. A few yards behind, he could see the bright white circle of the Harley's headlamp.

Todd kept driving, he wasn't sure where to, but even in his current state, he knew that a Volvo estate was no match for a Harley-Davidson. He kept looking for exits where he could lose her or side roads where a sudden turn might throw her, but there were none.

So he just kept going.

He didn't feel like a guy being pursued by a maniac on a motorcycle. He felt lightheaded, if truth be told. He opened a window and took a sip of Coke. He turned on the radio. Music filled the car. The radio told him that he was a wayward son, but not to give up. Not that Todd felt like giving up. He felt alive, and energized Let the bitch try and catch him. He was ready for her. After all, wasn't he Todd Milstead, best-selling author of *All My Colors*?

He turned the radio to another station, which told him not to look back.

"Darn straight," said Todd, and turned it up.

It was night but Todd had no sense of being part of time anymore. Cars flashed past, headlights on, in a constant slipstream. Lights changed, pedestrians crossed, the night came in, and Todd scarcely noticed. He was a driving machine now, with one aim: to shake that bike and its rider.

It wasn't going to be easy. The Harley never came near enough to overtake or for Todd to get a really good look at the rider's face, but also it never fell back far enough for Todd to make a sudden swerve and lose it. Once he contemplated making a U-turn, but a truck passed and Todd remembered what had happened to Jake Turner.

Night in the Midwest could be a circular thing, Todd thought, especially when you got out of town. There would be a red barn, and a water tower, and a few miles later a church. And then farther down the road, another red barn. Then maybe a water tower, a red barn and another church. It was like God had run out of ideas for things to put into America.

Todd drove past the barns and the churches and the water towers, occasionally letting out a "Well, hey there" when he saw a roadhouse or a gas station put there by the Lord in a rare moment of inspiration.

Where the fuck am I going? he thought. Behind him, the Harley's headlamp followed like a bright persistent star.

The night went on. The song about the wayward son had long passed, to be replaced by songs about something that was more than a feeling, or cold as ice, or hot-blooded, or the spirit of radio. Todd drummed his fingers on the steering wheel and sang along when he knew the song.

Suddenly the song – it was about two kids who died or something – ended. A squall of guitars, a rumble of drums. The roar of an engine. Like a motorbike. Like a—

Like a bat out of hell.

As if on cue, the Harley revved up. Todd could hear its engine roar and flare like someone opened a furnace door. Before, it had just been *toying with him* following him, but now it was coming at him, surging up roads at Todd, falling back, surging up, almost passing, and falling back again.

Todd saw what was happening: the fucker was *shepherding* him.

He turned off the radio and looked out the window. He was on the outskirts of a small town. Todd put pedal to metal, swung a left, and headed for Main Street. The Harley did the same, but luck was with Todd, as a pickup truck nosed out from a four-way crossing and forced the bike to slow.

They were on Main Street. Todd didn't have much time until the Harley caught up with him. *New plan.* Todd slung the Volvo at the curb, braked it, killed the engine, and leapt out onto the sidewalk.

Now he was running down an unlit alley, away from the bike. And yet there it was, coming right at him, engine gunned and headlight glaring in his eyes.

Without thinking, Todd jumped into a doorway.

Silence. Nothing. Todd stepped out of the doorway. From nowhere, the bike charged at him.

Todd stumbled back into the doorway and banged on the door.

"Let me in!" he shouted.

And then, just as the Harley was on him, the door opened and Todd fell inside.

The darkness was total, cold and soft like fog. Todd breathed it in. The door clicked shut, but he didn't notice. He moved farther inside, looking for a light switch. He ran his fingers along the wall, found something, and flicked it.

Instantly globes of yellow light snapped into existence across the ceiling, waking one by one with an irritable clicking sound. Todd was momentarily blinded. He looked up. The ceiling was pretty high. Below it were shelves. Hundreds of shelves. And on those shelves were books, thousands of them.

What is this, some kind of warehouse? thought Todd. And then he realized. He was in a library.

The library was massive. The ceilings were high enough to need ladders (Todd imagined a store clerk wobbling at the top of one of them, as if in a silent movie), and the walls were huge. The entire stock of Legolas Books would have fitted against one of these walls.

He wandered through the shelves, the Harley forgotten. There were famous books here, classics of English literature—and French literature, and Russian and German literature, and even Chinese and Arabic literature. There were science books and art books and children's books. But mostly there were novels. Some he knew well, and some he'd never heard of. Some were new, and some were so old the gilt had worn off the spines. Todd had a feeling that if you had time, you could find any book you wanted in here.

Todd stopped by a shelf and pulled a book out at random. *The Poor Man and the Lady* by Thomas Hardy. Not one he'd heard of. He pulled out another. *A Brilliant Career: A Play* by James Joyce. *Joyce wrote plays?* he thought. Another one, much older. *Adam Unparadised* by John Milton. *Love's Labours Won* by William Shakespeare.

Todd was starting to feel pretty ignorant now, and a little bit annoyed. It was like the books were conspiring to make him look stupid. He slammed one more back into place— Gibbon's *History of the Liberty of the Swiss*—and decided that he'd had his fun, and now it was time to find the exit and get out of here.

The library was a maze. *Yeah, I get that one*, thought Todd, as he tried to make his way out through the towering shelves. But the farther he went, the deeper into the library he seemed to go. It was as if the paper in the books had remembered its origins and was trying to become trees again. Todd was seriously thinking of looking for some thread to mark his path when he found himself in what he couldn't help but think of as a *glade*.

The shelves had parted to make a kind of square. Empty shelves loomed above him. He *knew* he was in the middle of the library. He listened for a moment.

No motorbikes. Todd had been walking for—minutes? hours?—and decided it was time for a break. He sat down on the floor.

Then he noticed that he'd been wrong about the shelves being empty. There was something on the bottom shelf. Unsurprisingly, it was a book. Todd went over and picked it up.

All My Colors. By Jake Turner.

"Typical," said a voice, so suddenly that Todd nearly dropped the book. "They never have the book you want, right?"

Todd turned around. A man about his own age was standing there. He was wearing a longshoreman's jacket and blue jeans.

"Evening," said the man. He stuck out his hand. "The name's Jake Turner."

EIGHT

Todd couldn't speak for a moment. Then he said, "I thought you were dead."

"You read the confession, right?" said Jake. "Yeah, I'm dead. Happens to all of us in the end, right?"

"You were hit by a truck," Todd said, almost accusingly.

"Is that right?" said Jake. He didn't seem too concerned about it. "I guess that's what they call 'dramatic irony.'"

Jake looked at Todd quizzically. "I guess you know what that is, being a writer."

"How'd you know that?" said Todd.

"Why else would you be here?" said Jake. "Jesus, look at this."

He took the copy of *All My Colors* from Todd's hand.

"This was gonna be it, you know," he said. "Reviews, sales, everything. I poured my fucking life into it."

"You poured her life into it," said Todd.

"Thanks," said Jake. "Nice to be reminded. At least I

fucking *wrote* it, know what I mean? Yeah, I took someone else's life—literally, as it turned out—but I did the writing, pal. Helen told me her story and I used it as the raw material. I shaped it, I gave it a structure and you know what? I gave her a *voice*. They should have given me an award for what I did. Instead—truck."

He slammed his hands together.

"Todd Milstead," he said. "I just realized. You're Todd Milstead."

Todd didn't know what to say to that. He'd never been recognized by a dead person before.

"That's why you're here," said Jake. He laughed. It was a pretty nasty laugh. It was a laugh that actually smelled bad. *Good trick*, thought Todd.

"Fuck me, Todd Milstead. You know, you're kind of a legend in here."

"I am?" said Todd, almost pleased despite himself.

"Yeah," said Jake. "You know why? Because you're the *copyist*. Come on," he added before Todd could ask him what he meant. "There's a lot of people want to meet you."

As Jake spoke, two figures stepped out of the shadows. Todd almost screamed. One of them was Timothy, or used to be him. Where Timothy's mouth should have been, there was a red hole like a ragged fleshy bomb crater. And the other was Billy Cairns. Billy didn't even have a face. The front of his head looked like someone had been using it as a skating rink.

"I guess you already know these guys," said Jake. "Come on, let's go."

And before Todd could move, the things that used to be

Billy and Timothy took one of his arms each and propelled him gently back into the shadows.

They kept walking, and they kept walking. Todd didn't know if it was miles, or hundreds of miles.

"Where are we going?" he asked, even though he knew it was a ridiculous question.

"Oh, you'll see," said Jake. "Say, Todd," he added, "there's something I wanted to ask you."

"What?" said Todd.

"Where do you get your ideas from?"

Jake laughed. Billy laughed. Timothy laughed.

Todd screamed.

"Here we are," said Jake. Timothy and Billy fell back into the shadows, and Todd rubbed his arms. For dead and mangled corpses they sure had a strong grip.

"You see, Todd," said Jake. "There's a special place for the likes of you and me, and it ain't posterity. It's not the shelves of fancy bookstores and it's not the bestseller lists. It's this. You want to know what *this* is?"

He gestured around him, at the miles and miles of empty shelves.

"Is it... Hell?" asked Todd.

"Oh no," said Jake. "It's much worse than that."

There was a sound behind Todd. And above him, and around him. It was a rustling sound, like leaves or tiny wings. Todd was reminded of one of Sara's favorite movies, *The Birds*, the part where the woman is in the children's playground. Only these weren't birds. They were books, suddenly appearing on the shelves.

271

"Hell is for people," said Jake. "People come and go. If they didn't, we'd be knee deep in our ancestors. People are just flesh and bone, and then they're dust and ashes. But books go on."

He gestured around him. The shelves were full. Book after book lined the walls.

"Books are our memories," Jake said. "They're like babies, in a way, in that they contain something of us when we're gone. Books outlive us, right? Books get passed on from generation to generation, and books are kind of unforgettable."

"But this place—" he said, and pulled out another book: *All My Colors* by Todd Milstead, "—is where books come to die."

Todd almost laughed at that.

"Come on," he said.

"You think you'll be remembered, Milstead?" said Jake. "You think future generations will fall in love with your work? Kids will study you in school? Movies will be made of your book? Ain't gonna happen. Your book is going to be forgotten, just like mine was. Your little head's gonna slip beneath the surface of history and drown."

"Bullshit," said Todd. Suddenly he was angry, and why not? He was having a fucking *terrible* day. "I'm going to write a new book. A sequel. Maybe. Maybe not. But it's going to be the real deal, this time. It's going to be *massive*."

"Oh right," said Jake. "Of course. You fucking idiot, what do you think I was doing when the truck hit me? I was *working on the follow-up*, Milstead. I was writing the sequel to *All My Colors*. And I tell you, it would have been a damn sight better than whatever jumbled atrocity you were bashing out. And I wasn't a fucking photocopier like you, I could *write*."

Todd pushed Jake. He was surprisingly solid.

"Fuck you!" he said. "I'm a writer! Fuck you!"

Jake stepped back, laughing.

"Okay, have it your own way," he said. "You're a writer. You wrote *All My Colors*, you're a writer. I wrote *All My Colors*, I'm a writer."

He smiled at Todd, and it was a horrible smile, with too much knowledge in it.

"You don't get it, do you?" he said. "This isn't about the book. This isn't even about writing."

"What is it about then?" said Todd.

"It's about her," Jake said.

They were in an old part of the library now. Todd hadn't really noticed, on account of the two animated corpses, but the shelves had gone from modern metal to Victorian polished wood, and there was a smell of age in the air. The motes of dust caught in a shaft of sunlight (and where was *that* coming from? There were no windows) seemed heavier here.

"Welcome to the stacks," said Jake. "You know what stacks are, right, Todd?"

Todd knew what stacks were. They were the backstage part of libraries, the storage areas.

"I told you this is where books come to die," said Jake. "And these books are scheduled for the furnace."

He gestured, and Todd saw that the shelves were

stuffed with old books, a careless jumble of hardbacks and paperbacks, parchments and manuscripts, books without spines and books with illuminated covers.

"All trash," said Jake.

"Is that why you brought me here?" said Todd. "So I can see my book being burned?" He laughed. "My *New York Times* best-selling book?"

"Todd," said Jake, "you don't think my book was a bestseller? Jesus, you heard of it, didn't you? And if you heard of it, it must have been a bestseller. *All My Colors* by Jake Turner was huge, pal. Just like you thought *All My Colors* by Todd Milstead was going to be huge."

"It *is* huge," protested Todd.

"Size Matters For Todd Milstead," laughed Jake. "Todd baby, your book—my book—came out of nowhere and it went straight back there. You think people remember stuff? They forget their friends, Todd, they forget their parents. They're not going to remember some stupid *book*."

"Why not?" Todd said, stubborn now.

"Because is why," Jake replied. "Because she makes people forget."

Todd was about to ask Jake what he meant when he saw it.

The shelf.

"What the fuck?" said Todd.

"Oh, you noticed," said Jake. "Take a proper look, why don't you?"

Jake pulled out a book, a worn paperback.

"*All My Colors*," he read out. "By Henry Mortimer, 1946. Nice guy, Henry, cheated on his wife and strangled her when she found out. Stole the story from a girl he met in a bar."

He grabbed another, a distinguished-looking hardback.

"*All My Colors*," he said. "Frederick Schwimmer, 1924. Freddy killed his mother for the insurance, but not before he wrote down the story she told him had happened to her cousin."

Jake began tossing books at Todd.

"*All My Colors*, Edward Graham, 1907. Killed his sister after she threatened to tell on him. The story came to Eddie when his sister visited him in a dream...

"*All My Colors,* Martin Portland. Chemist, poisoned his wife, got the story from a lady customer..."

Jake looked Todd in the eye.

"You beginning to get the picture here, Todd old boy? You beginning to join the dots?"

Todd didn't answer. He was looking inside the books.

"They're the same book," he said disbelieving.

"Of course they're the same," Jake said. "They're *All My Colors*. By you, by me, by Tom, Dick and Harry, John Doe, and everyone bar, of course, Jane Doe."

"That's impossible," Todd said.

"Right," said Jake. "You're in a library with a dead guy and you're telling me that *that's* the impossible thing?"

"But I thought—"

"You thought we were the only ones," said Jake. "Like the sailors shipwrecked on the Rhine thought they were the only ones."

"I don't understand," Todd said. "Why are there so many books?"

"Buddy," said Jake. "I told you. It's not about the books."

He scratched his head. Something came off in his hand.

"Whoops," he said. "Looks like I'm running out of time."

He dropped the something onto the floor.

"You think you remembered the book—my book—because you got a good memory, don't you?" he said. "You think an entire fucking novel—a best-selling novel—just floated into your head one day like a fairy godmother at a time of need? Just when you could use a few dollars, there it was, the answer to an asshole's prayer?"

Todd nodded. There was no point denying it. Besides, this guy *knew*.

"And that's what I thought. When I worked out I could write down Helen's story. Oh sure, I was devastated by her death. But I knew I'd get over it. And there would be the money, and the success."

Jake paused, then laughed.

"Even when she died, part of me thought, *now I won't have to split the writing credit*. Because men like you and me, Todd, we're kinda cold."

"I'm not," said Todd. "I'm one of the good—" But he thought of Janis, and Sara, and Leah in a hotel room, and he shut up.

"You ask me, that story came to us for a reason," said Jake. "Sure, I got it from Helen herself, and you got it from me, but truth be told, that story's been around for a long time. Maybe *this guy*—" Jake threw a book at Todd. "—heard the story at a cocktail party. Maybe *this other guy*—" Jake threw another book. "—read it in a magazine but never could find the magazine again. And maybe *this guy* and *these guys* heard it out bear-hunting, or saw it in a movie, or it happened to a friend of a fucking *friend*—"

Jake was almost crying now.

"It doesn't matter. Don't you get it? It doesn't matter. You steal the story, you die. Doesn't matter how you got the story. *You steal the story, you die.*"

"I didn't steal it!" Todd heard himself shout. "It just came to me!"

"Buddy, it came to all of us," said Jake. "And all for the same fucking reason. We did someone wrong. We did *her* wrong. Ain't that right, boys?"

At first Todd had no idea who Jake was addressing. Then he saw them. There were dozens of them—no, hundreds. Every one was carrying a book. *The* book. And the books were old, and they were mildewed, or they were fresh, or they had never been opened, but they were all the same book. His book. Jake's book.

They were all men. Men dressed like him. Men dressed like his father. Like his grandfather. Victorians, and further back. Now they weren't even Americans, but men whose sons would settle America. They came from every place, and every time, and they had all told the same story.

"Jesus," whispered Todd. "How many of them are there?"

"How many of *us*, you mean," said Jake. "As many as there are years, old man. As many as there are years, and as many as there are men. They all wrote the book, Todd, just like we did. They all stole the idea and wrote the book. So they had to die."

"But I didn't steal it," Todd said in a *not-fair* kind of voice. "It was in my head."

"Jesus, Todd, you are slow," said Jake. "There was nothing in your head until she put it there."

"Why?" said Todd. "I never killed anyone. I never harmed—"

He stopped.

"Yeah," said Jake. "See, Todd, you're an asshole. An asshole who treats people like shit. I say people, I mean women. And I guess she just wanted some fun. So she dropped an idea in your head to see if you'd steal it."

"I didn't steal *anything*!" Todd almost wailed.

"You wrote the book. You took the credit." Jake shrugged. "Also, you're an asshole. I guess that's enough for her."

"But who *is* she?" asked Todd. He felt wronged. Dammit, he was wronged.

"I told you. She's Helen. At least that's the name she uses," said Jake. "The Helen I knew, that was her, and the Helen who killed your friends on account of they were witnesses, that was her too."

How did you know about that, Todd wanted to ask. But he didn't, because Jake was just getting warmed up.

"Oh, yeah, Helen can do a lot of things," Jake said. "That conversation you never had with Janis's lawyer? The time you saw Janis at the truck stop? All those people who read the fucking book and bought the fucking book and forgot all about the fucking book and then fucking remembered the fucking book? She did all that."

"But how—"

"That's what she *does*." Jake almost spat. "Todd, she put a fucking *book* in your head, how hard would it be to make you see someone who wasn't there? She made you think

Janis was seeing the Dyke with the Bike, she made Behm think it too…"

Jake leaned into Todd's face.

"And that's not all she wrote," he said.

The room was suddenly empty again. Todd and Jake stood alone amongst the shelves.

"You're an educated man," said Jake. "You've heard of the Muses. The Greeks, they had a fucking Muse for everything. A Muse of Dance, a Muse of Poetry, Theater…. they even had a Muse of Tragedy, did you know that?"

Todd didn't know that, but he wasn't going to admit it. He still had some pride left.

"But Helen is something different," said Jake. "She's the Muse of Death."

Todd looked at Jake.

"Okay, fine," he said. "She's getting revenge on men, I can understand that. None of us is perfect. But I just screwed around. I never killed anyone."

"You killed your private eye buddy," said Jake. "You killed Timothy when you opened your mouth about the story. Oh, and Billy. Poor old boozehound never harmed a fly. But someone had to tell you about their trip to the hardware store else how would you remember the book, Todd? So that's why he died."

Todd was barely listening now. In amongst the terror and the disbelief an old familiar emotion rose up: self-pity. All he could think was *how dare someone do this to me*.

"I still don't see how any of this is my fault," said Todd.

"Okay," said Jake, and this time his teeth were blades. "Don't take my word for it."

In the distance, Todd could hear a familiar roar.

"Ask *her*," said Jake.

And there she was, in leather and black, straddling that damn motorbike. She was smiling at him, as if to say *Do you get it? Do you get it now?*

She had a knife in her hand. It was sharp, and it dripped.

She gunned the engine.

"Run," said Jake.

Todd ran. He ran through the stacks and past the shelves. He ran like he'd never run before, like he never thought he *could* run before. Behind him, the Harley's engine roared. *Silence in the library!* Todd thought mirthlessly. He could hear the bike getting nearer by the second. Desperately, he tore through the building, looking for a doorway.

And then, miracle of miracles, there was a doorway. Todd grabbed the handle. It was stuck. The bike was rounding a corner now. Todd tore at the handle, and it turned. He looked behind him. The bike was bearing down on him now like a missile.

She grinned.

Her teeth were white.

Her teeth were red.

Todd yanked the door open, leapt through, and slammed it behind him.

The truck was only doing fifty when it hit him but it splashed him across the sidewalk like paint.

A small crowd gathered. A man who said he was a doctor bent down.

"There's nothing we can do," he said.

"Ambulance is on its way," said a store owner.

The driver of the truck jumped down from his cab.

"I saw it all," said a woman. "It wasn't your fault."

They looked down at the body on the ground. It was still moving.

"He just jumped out," said the truck driver. "He just jumped out right in frunna me."

The Harley and its rider waited in an alley until the paramedics came. They put Todd's body on a gurney, and placed a sheet over his face.

The Harley roared away into the night.

EPILOGUE

It was a Saturday night in June, 1986, in Madison, Wisconsin. "Live To Tell" by Madonna was number one and a group of college students were talking in a bar.

"No," said one of them. He was wearing a greatcoat with the cuffs rolled up and his Ray-Bans were brand new. "Women aren't like that."

"Kevin," said a girl. She was called Zoe and had just discovered Marlboro Lights. "I am a woman. You need to defer to me on this."

"She's got you there," said another guy. He was called Lewis and he was uncomfortable in his tight Depeche Mode T-shirt.

Kevin shrugged. He wasn't going to defer to someone because of mere facts. Facts were tools, and when tools didn't work, you discarded them. Like his girlfriend back in Wisconsin.

Kevin adopted a conciliatory expression.

"It's like the guy said…"

"What guy?" said Lewis.

Kevin ignored him and took a deep breath.

"*Men were men, her father always said, and women were women. But looking at the flabby old fool now, sitting there in his vest like a soft queen of some race of grubs, she saw that some men were not men.*"

Even Zoe was impressed when Kevin quoted stuff. When he was done, she said, "Wow. What was *that* from?"

Kevin looked at her over the top of his Ray-Bans. *You are mine*, he thought. He didn't voice that, though. Instead he said, "Whoah! You're kidding."

"No, I'm not," she said, reddening delightfully. "Maybe I'm just not as well read as you is all."

Inferiority complex! thought Kevin. *Fucking bingo!*

"Okay. But are you seriously telling me you never heard of *All My Colors*?"

"The Bunnymen song?" said Lewis.

Kevin ignored him again.

"*All My Colors*, the novel," he said, turning his full attention on Zoe. "*All My Colors*, by Todd Milstead."

"No," said Zoe. "I haven't heard of it. Should I?"

Kevin smiled. It wasn't a nice smile.

"Oh boy," he said. "Have I got a surprise in store for you…"

I'd like to thank David Haviland at the Andrew Lownie Agency, all the team at Titan Books, and Gary Budden for his superb editing. Special thanks for advice and encouragement to Antonia Hodgson, Mark Billingham, Martyn Waites, and Stav Sherez.

www.davidquantick.com

David Quantick is an Emmy-winning television writer for such shows as *Veep*, *The Thick of It* and *The Day Today*. He is the author of *Sparks*, *The Mule*, and two writing manuals, *How To Write Everything* and *How To Be A Writer*.

For more fantastic fiction, author events, competitions,
limited editions and more

VISIT OUR WEBSITE
titanbooks.com

LIKE US ON FACEBOOK
facebook.com/titanbooks

FOLLOW US ON TWITTER
@TitanBooks

EMAIL US
readerfeedback@@titanemail.com